THE DIARY OF A MURDER

Proudly Published by Snowbooks in 2011

Copyright © 2011 Lee Jackson

Snowbooks Ltd.
email: info@snowbooks.com
www.snowbooks.com

British Library Cataloguing in Publication Data
A catalogue record for this book is available from the British Library.

Paperback ISBN 978-1-9067277-932

The Diary of a Murder

Lee Jackson

CHAPTER ONE

The sergeant, dressed in plain clothes, stood upon the front step and rang the bell. Behind him, the young constable remained on the pavement, removed his glazed hat, and stared up at the tall sash windows.

'All shuttered up, sir. I haven't seen them open these last few days. I thought they'd gone and took an holiday.'

'Perhaps they have,' said the sergeant. He tugged the bell-pull a second time.

'What's the fellow's name, again?'

'Jones, sir.'

'Occupation?'

'Clerk. The Crystal Palace Company.'

'And they haven't seen him at his office?'

'Not since Friday,' said the constable.

Sergeant Preston, a seasoned member of the Detective department, pursed his lips, and glanced through the gated railings that protected the house's sunken basement from the street. Two bottles of milk stood by the kitchen door, their delivery ignored.

'And it's the wife's family that's been making a fuss?'

'They say she's gone missing. Her mother was expecting her to visit her at Chelsea, Friday evening. She never turned up.'

'What do you think, constable?'

'Could be they were behind with the rent,' suggested the constable. 'They could have bolted.'

'They could have,' replied Preston, unconvinced.

'What should we do next, then, sir?'

Preston pondered the question, stepping back onto the pavement.

'You say the wife's father has called here, too?'

'Twice, sir. No answer.'

'Is he anyone in particular?'

'Depends what you mean, sir. His name's Willis. I heard that he owns a draper's warehouse: a big establishment, near the Regent's Circus.'

'Has a few pennies, then,' muttered the sergeant. 'Right, I suppose we better have a look. Follow me, son.'

Sergeant Preston swung open the iron gate and walked briskly down the steps to the basement.

Moments later came the sound of breaking glass.

§

'We ain't got a warrant, sir,' protested the constable.

'I thought I heard someone cry out for help,' said Preston, without any hint of conviction. 'Didn't you?'

He did not wait for a reply but made a swift and methodical examination of the kitchen. Pots, pans and skillets were in good order, hanging from hooks on the wall; every utensil and plate was neatly stored in cupboards and drawers. The modest pantry and scullery were well-stocked, neat and orderly. He placed his hand on the range.

'Stone cold. Well, come on then, up we go.'

They ascended the stairs to the hall. The walls were papered, in a pattern of intertwining roses; a recent adornment, the colours, red and green, still bright and vibrant. The plain drugget, which covered the polished floorboards, likewise bore few tell-tale traces of wear and tear.

'Anyone at home?'

Preston's rich baritone echoed through the house. There was no reply.

'Very well,' said the sergeant, with a sigh of resignation. 'You start at the top of the house. I'll have a look down here.'

'What are we looking for, sir?'

'I wish I knew. Just be a good lad and have a look about the place. That way, we can tell my inspector that we've made a thorough job of it, eh?'

The constable nodded, and made his way up the steep, narrow stairs at the rear of the hall. Preston, in turn, wandered into the dining-room at the front of the house and, finding nothing of particular interest, tried the door to the morning-room.

The second room had been left in a very different condition to its neighbour: the windows were not shuttered and daylight fell upon a chaotic scene. The gilt-framed mirror atop the mantelpiece was cracked; bookcases lay open, their contents strewn here and there; an overturned chair sat beside a leather-topped writing desk. The most striking feature, however, was a disordered pile of foolscap, promiscuously scattered across the surface of the desk, pages spilling over onto the floor. The sheets themselves appeared to be filled with prose in a neat hand, with a solitary exception. It sat atop the heap on the desk, as if placed there with deliberate intent, and bore only a few lines of hasty scribble.

Sergeant Preston, puzzled, read its contents.

I know in my heart I am the man to blame. I have valued at nought all I should have held dear and pursued a sinful illusion of happiness at the cost of my own soul. When I am gone, this testimony will remain. If you care to read these wretched pages, then you will know how it came to this ...

'Sir!'

Rapid footsteps on the stairs.

It was the voice of the young policeman. He stood at the threshold of the room, his face terribly pale, his voice quaking with excitement.

'What is it?'

'I've found her, sir. In her room, on the second floor.'

Preston looked up from the paper, grim-faced.

'Mrs. Jones?'

The young man nodded, breathless, unable to speak.

'Now then, pull yourself together, son. Is she alive or dead?'

'She's dead, sir.'

'How?'

'Bashed her head against the mantelpiece, far as I could see, sir.'

'Her head? Did she fall?'

'I mean it's been bashed good and proper,' said the policeman. 'I don't know how many times it must have been —'

The young man fell silent.

'Right, you stay here, son,' said Preston. 'Let me have a look, then we'll send to the Yard.'

The constable gratefully agreed to the plan. When the sergeant had left, he grasped the jamb of the door, fearful that his legs might not support him a step further. Yet, he could not resist surveying the scene before him; and, once he had recovered his self-possession, it was not long before his curiosity drew him to the writing desk and the mess of paper.

A diary.

He began to look at the dates. It would be a simple task, he concluded, to put the sheets in order.

DIARY

Monday, 9th December

Success!

I have met with the house agent a second time — Mr. Phillips, the affable old gentleman, with a liking for port wine — and signed the lease. We are bound for Amwell Street. It is merely a modest Islington terrace, but the terms are commensurate and the six rooms are light and airy. Dora in raptures. I fear, however, we must hope for an increment in my salary, if my little wifey has her way. She says it must be 'painted prettily and nicely furnished', which is as much to say 'at the greatest trouble and expense'. There is only one nuisance: our leasehold commences not on the quarter-day, but New Year's Eve.

Mary-Anne, meanwhile, 'hopes the stairs will suit her knees' (an unlikely contingency, I fear) and raises complaints at every opportunity, reciting a litany of the endless trials which await her in Islington. One might think the wretched creature received no recompense for her trouble.

Friday, 13th December

More preparations for the 'move'.

I quit the office an hour early (Mr. Hibbert's dispensation) and visited *Bedford's Pantechnicon*. It is a large furniture warehouse and carriers on Tottenham Court Road with stables at the rear. Inspected the covered vans — which were most satisfactory — and queried their estimate, which was promptly reduced by two shillings. Made arrangements for 'wrappers, mats, boxes & waterproofs' to be delivered; also took insurance against damage *en route*.

I could not bear the dreadful huddle of the omnibus and so walked home, even though it was cold and inclement. The London trader is very much 'alive' to the season: more gas-lit signs than ever; shop-windows universally wreathed in holly. In short succession, walking down to the river, I saw Christmas books; Christmas hats; Christmas 'diamonds' (Brummagem work, doubtless). Toys are much advertised this year. On hoardings by Hungerford Market, there was pasted a monster line of posters, with the imprecation, 'Papa, do buy me Dugwell & Son's Mechanical Spiders'. We did not possess such things in my youth, I think – *I* certainly did not – nor did the likes of Messrs. Dugwell & Son heap such importunate puffs upon the public.

Then the question struck me.

Whatever shall I buy my dear Dora?

Saturday, 14ᵗʰ December

Returned from work and found that Dora had gone to Chelsea to visit her mother (who wrote yesterday complaining of ill-health). Alone in the house with Mary-Anne. The girl has a genius for turning the simplest task into a cause of vexation! I had her light a fire in the dining-room. Within seconds – though I was closeted in the room above – I could hear her cursing the coal-bucket (for what failings, I could not hazard a guess), and attacking the fire with such loud and vigorous prods of the poker that I feared she might demolish the chimney. I descended to ask the cause of her rage – a polite inquiry – and she informed me, with the utmost gravity, that the cat had 'gotten at' her herring during breakfast, and put her 'quite out of sorts'. I found it quite impossible to answer her.

A brief vain attempt at writing. I could not muster my thoughts; perhaps it is the 'move' preying on my mind. Still, the MS. goes well, I think; it needs but a little time devoted to its completion.

I wonder whether it will ever be published?

D. returned at seven. Mama Willis not so sickly as she had feared.

Sunday, 15ᵗʰ December

A black day.

A little before noon, a nervous-looking boy, no more than fourteen years of age, called at the house. He informed me that he had 'come directly from Mr. Willis'. I suddenly had a presentiment that Mama Willis had unexpectedly died during the night – that she *had* been ill. And if Papa Willis lay prostrate with grief –

I was wrong. It *was* news of a tragedy – the boy put in a cab and instructed to travel to sundry friends and relations with the dreadful information – but it came from another quarter entirely.

Dear me! It is an evil thing to write it, but I suppose I must.

Prince Albert has passed away.

What news! Of course, the man was but flesh and blood; and we had heard all the reports concerning his health. Nonetheless, I felt a sense of profound amazement and great sorrow. A bulwark of our great Nation lost to us forever.

I gave the boy a penny for his trouble and spent the afternoon in solitary reflection. D. suggested we close the shutters; I concurred.

We went to evensong – though it is not our custom – and found the little church quite full. It would be uncharitable to suggest that the ladies wished to display their best black silk; but there was a good deal of that material in evidence. Dora, too, most fetching in her *moirée*.

Dull service, awful choir. A dreadful intake of breath, from all present, when the customary prayers were said for the Queen and her family, and *his* name left absent.

It is a salutary lesson that we all live on quicksand; nothing is sound or certain.

Tuesday, 17th December

Pervasive gloom in the City; the funeral will be Monday 23rd at Windsor. One must respect Her Majesty's wishes, but it is a shame for London that it cannot be in the Abbey.

The conundrum of a gift for D. is preoccupying me. We are not long since married and yet possess – as far as I can establish – every possible item of household utility. It must be some small token of esteem and affection, such as a man might give to his wife, without – I wish it were not so – incurring undue expense. But what? Last night, I inquired, off hand, whether her work box might not be replaced in due course. The wood is chipped in several places; the painting on the lid, a mother and child in bucolic setting, quite faded. D. replied that it was her grandmother's; that it meant a good deal to her and that she would sooner replace me (!).

A fine sentiment in a wife!

Luncheon at Lakes, Cheapside, in company of Fortesque. Chops; much foolish ambitious talk from F., 'starting out on his own account' &c.

Played one game of billiards; lost.

Saturday, 21st December

Went up Regent Street in the afternoon; an opportunity to visit the shops. All in mourning; even the crossing-boys at the Circus with black armbands; shops once wreathed in holly now decked out in crape, thin black borders painted on their plate-glass. Finished my expedition at Medici's, the photographer's. Crowds all around the place, looking at the few portraits of the Prince which remained. Went inside and inquired, but none to be had. Even articles in window were 'reserved for particular patrons' – 'I can put your name down for the next batch, sir, but I can't make no promises.'

Found another photograph, of the Queen and Prince and children, in smaller shop off the principal thoroughfare. Last one which remained (or so I was assured!); paid four shillings for what might have cost me eighteen pence the week before.

I have never known public feeling at such a pitch. One feels enormous sympathy for the Queen and her loss, but it is also a noble thing to see a nation so united in sorrow.

Monday, 23rd December

The Prince's funeral. Our poor Sovereign!

Also, a letter from Mama Willis in the first post – an invitation to 'A Christmas gathering of family and friends'. I remarked to D. that it was ill-timed, to arrive upon a day of national mourning. She replied that her mother 'was too practical to think of such things'. I suggested this showed a remarkable want of feeling; D. obliged to agree.

In truth, I cannot muster much enthusiasm for Christmas in Chelsea. I have attended on two previous occasions, and, in both instances found myself addressed with such arrogant condescension *by certain parties* that I vowed never to return. It is only out of fondness for D. that I shall go this year. Now we are married, at least, I hope that I may be treated with due respect and a degree of consideration.

A hour or two after I returned home, a boy appeared in the street selling 'a memorial sheet of the funereals'. No commercial opportunity is missed in our great metropolis.

Purchased two copies.

Tuesday, 24ᵗʰ December

Went to Bond Street, in search of *the gift*. What blessings must the sellers of fancy goods and bookshops heap upon our Lord, on the eve of His birth! Never have I seen the streets so crowded. It was a challenge simply to cross the threshold of many an establishment, and I soon lost heart. In the end, I found a set of *Mendelssohn's Piano Forte Compositions*, in four volumes, all elegantly bound with gilt edge.

I hope D. will be satisfied with my efforts. I have no idea what she might prefer. I suppose it is a rare husband that knows the secrets of his wife's heart!

After dinner, D. warned me – dear little wifey, so strict and stern! – that I must not be 'too particular' in Chelsea; that her father 'will speak his mind, without thought for others' and that I must forbear 'for her sake.'

The very thought of it put me in a bad humour. I spoke to Mary-Anne about the state of the dining-room. I asked if she possessed a duster – 'yes' – and if she was familiar with dust – 'yes' – and if she understood how the one might stand in relation to the other. Met with mute insolence.

I should not care over much if the stairs at Amwell Street *are* too much for her; with luck, she may fall and break her neck!

Wednesday, 25ᵗʰ December

Exchanged our gifts after church. Dora gave me a writing-box in rosewood and maple, which *is* very fine, and a new pipe. For her part, D. said that she had already determined to practice more often, once we are removed to Amwell Street; and that the Mendelssohn would suit her nicely.

She is such a sensible creature!

12 noon. D. making lunch in kitchen (!) as she has given Mary-Anne leave to visit her sister ('we cannot forbid it, if she is to forego the New Year with her'). No Cook – she broke the news last week that she 'cannot come in during the festive season'. I did not press for a reason but the woman is decidedly not of the temperance persuasion; I suspect she is quite determined to be thoroughly incapacitated throughout.

If only we had a better class of servant!

Will we find a cab to take us to Chelsea, I wonder?

10pm. Returned from Chelsea; will write to-morrow.

Thursday, 26ᵗʰ December

The Christmas-box nuisance is greater than ever this year; my change in matrimonial circumstances is noted amongst the tradesmen, and they double their demands accordingly. In truth, I do not grudge them a few pennies; but they have been admixed with every sort of street-scavenger and itinerant musician, who believes they should be recompensed for their 'constancy'. In such cases, if I recognise them at all, it is only as a recurring source of irritation. I said as much to one stout fellow with a cornopean, who has a habit of interrupting my Sunday afternoons, strolling down from the Common, playing (if that be the word) 'Gone to the Crusades' and other dismal ditties. He appeared at the door, cap in hand, and was most affronted by my refusal. He said that 'he would wish me an 'appy New Year, but was sure an ounce of 'appiness would stick in my miserable throat and choke me'. I told him I would *happily* stick his wretched instrument down *his* throat; and we left it at that.

Now, I should, I suppose – if I am to be 'constant' to my diary – write something of Chelsea. I must mix the good with the bad, after all, if I am to bequeath to my future self a truthful account.

We took a hansom, as I had planned, at one o'clock, though it was quite hard to come by, due to the weather. The day had begun quite clear, but a thick fog had come down along the river, noxious and burnt brown in colour. It sent D. – poor thing! – into choking fits and made the cabman go wrong on at least two occasions. We did not arrive, therefore, much before two. The house inside had been done up gaily enough; mistletoe, holly, ivy in abundance and a Christmas Tree in royal fashion, heavy with pendent *bonbons* and gilt gingerbread. I remarked to Mama Willis that it was a 'fine display'; she replied that 'it was not done for ostentation, but to mark the season'. She seemed quite determined to misconstrue me, so I held my tongue.

Some twenty or so had arrived for dinner; family for the most part, but also a pair of spinster sisters

– Misses Harris – whom, I later learnt, lived in the neighbouring cottage. It was, I concede, an excellent meal, though I found the goose a little too rich for my liking. Nonetheless, I determined to eat all my portion, lest D. chide me for my ingratitude. In consequence, left feeling dyspeptic throughout the afternoon and evening. With the sole intention of calming the stomach, I fear I indulged too freely in brandy.

Much post-prandial conversation amongst the men concerning the Prince; and a toast to his memory. Then Papa Willis held forth on the American War, summoning up a good deal of the popular prejudice, railing against the Yankees for their seizure of the *Trent* &c. Asked me if I thought it was a cause for war? I said not; that the Royal Navy had been known to exercise its rights with equal belligerence; that the Southern negroes were the victims of a gross evil, long since banished from these shores; and that, if he were to appear in the room, I would heartily shake the hand of Mr. Lincoln. It was a fine piece of mischief; I could see he was much provoked, though he strove to conceal it – he flushed bright red about the gills! For, like any decent draper (he is no *more* than that, however much he puffs himself up) he is obliged to bow before *King Cotton*, and declare the Southerners the most benevolent, peace-loving capitalists as ever lived.

We were reunited with the ladies for music. I call it 'music', but was very much the drawing-room variety, principally the work of a young lady of 'accomplishment' and an elderly uncle, who regaled us with such outlandish gestures and grimaces – even during the most plain ballad – that I half expected the man to reveal a banjo at any moment, and adopt the pose of an Ethiopian serenader. I remarked as much to D. but her father overheard and commented, much to *his own* amusement, that I 'thought a good deal too much on the subject of negroes'.

Tea was served, then we proceeded to 'games'. I cannot see the need for 'games' in a gathering composed mostly of persons above the age of majority. The first was acting *charades*, a French amusement for which I have little enthusiasm. I suppose it *may* be done in a lively and entertaining fashion, in respectable company. In my experience, however, it leads to all manner of vulgarity and all manner of tiresome dispute. I need only say that yesterday was no exception to this rule (fortunately I was not called on to play the fool). I was, however, not long afterwards the victim of a juvenile prank. The assembled company had embarked on a game called 'Prussian Exercises' which required us to form a line, in regimental fashion, and to 'follow the leader', obeying whatever order our 'captain' commanded (Papa Willis taking this role; enjoying it greatly). The commands were of a military nature, 'eyes right', 'show arms' &c. but interspersed with unlikely freaks, such as 'tweak noses' or 'slap cheeks', that were designed to elicit laughter and produce a forfeit. I need hardly record that I did not find these manoeuvres amusing but, for D.'s sake, obliged with as much good grace as I could muster.

At the last, however, we were told to 'ground right knee' and 'present arms'. I cannot say if it was planned, or merely childish mischief; but a younger cousin of D.'s, a whey-faced boy of thirteen years or so, took the opportunity to nudge me in the ribs. He did this so forcefully, in fact, that I fell over, directly into one of the Misses Harris, who fell into the Uncle, who then sent most of the company tumbling, like a row of dominoes. I concede that most of the party took this in good spirits; but I do not see how any self-respecting gentleman can relish being the butt of such 'practical jokes'.

The evening drew to a close with demands for a 'ghost story'. The gas was turned down, and Papa Willis obliged with a tale about a haunted railway carriage (could there be anything so unlikely?) and ended with the revelation (I use the word loosely) that our protagonist was himself, too, some form of ghastly revenant. I fear my scepticism must have been betrayed by my countenance, for he then said (and I can recall *verbatim*):-

'Of course, my dears, I can lay no claim to poetical or literary distinction in my simple story; I aim only to please. Now, tell me, Jacob, my boy, do you still harbour literary ambitions? Shall we see your name in print, this year?'

I could take *my boy* but it was the *this year* which galled me; I could not contain myself.

'If you do, sir,' I replied, 'it will not be appended to some old nurse's tale, best suited to credulous children.'

Perhaps it was the brandy; for it was not *simply* the words themselves; I spoke too freely, with too much passion. There was an awkward silence; then the Uncle remarked 'these literary men and their spats!' in jovial fashion, which restored some semblance of good humour. D. looked quite miserable.

We left the house not long afterwards, D. pleading a 'head'. At the door, Papa Willis took me aside, and said he 'hoped there was no unnatural ill-feeling between us,' on account of his views on the American War. I replied, truthfully, that there was not, *on that cause*. I knew he had not done with me. He went on to say that he was glad on Dora's account that I had found a *decent house* in time for the New Year (do we live in a sty, at present?), *one more akin to what she is accustomed* (!); that he hoped I thrived *in that little office* and that if *I ever wanted something with decent remuneration, there was always a good place for me in the business.*

And what a prize 'place,' that would be! A draper's clerk!

D. silent in the cab home. I asked if she thought it proper that I should be subjected to such insults, on every occasion I met her father. She said he 'meant no insult at all' and that I should 'be more charitable in disposition'.

My little wifey is such a sweet innocent.

Friday, 27th December

Alone in the office with Fortesque, Mr. Hibbert having removed himself to the country until the

New Year. I asked him how he had spent Christmas Day, and he regaled me with an account of his acquaintance with a young milliner, whom he met dancing at the Holborn Casino. Asked − merely in fun − if he intended to marry her and he replied that he 'might well, at that; she's a fine-looking bit of muslin'.

I represented to him that no woman who frequents the Holborn Casino, however interesting in appearance, can possess the morals and character one expects in a wife; indeed, even if her morals have miraculously remained intact, she cannot possess the *ignorance of vice* which is desirable in one's mate. F., however, considers himself something of a 'swell', professes a profound liking for 'fast' women, and affects a youthful disdain for conventional *mores*.

He asked where I had met D. − I told him we met whilst attending a lecture at the Polytechnic. He replied that *that was a guarantee of ignorance, in any female.* He thought himself very droll and amusing; but, if he has any hopes of rising in society, attaching himself to this milliner will be the end of them.

In any case, I believe I have returned to D.'s good graces: she greeted me this evening with a kiss on the cheek, and Cook had done a fine side of beef for dinner.

This business with her father has but one moral: 'family' is a curse.

Saturday, 28th December

The house now quite over-run by boxes &c. supplied by Bedford's. Moreover, our worldly goods seem to have expanded and enlarged themselves in the process of marshalling them for packing. I now cannot believe they ever fitted into the house in the first place.

I wrote yesterday of 'family'. I wonder sometimes if I possess the 'second sight'. It has been five months since I last heard from my father, and, this very evening, a letter arrived in the post. I knew the hand instantly; as spindly as a spider's web. I opened it in secret, when Dora was occupied with her needlework.

The letter itself is full of the usual bluster: he blames *the world* for his condition; he blames his *bad luck* that he cannot raise himself up; he blames *the parish* for not coming to his aid. It all has the usual import: a heavy debt (three pounds, to a boot-maker in Soho) has been accrued; and the interest upon it has swelled to such a sum that he must *swallow his pride* (!) and beg from his son.

It is worse than the last occasion; he tells me – as if it occurred by some mere chance – that I am *named as guarantor*.

He would drag me into the very pit in which he rots.

I will not be a part of it.

It is fortunate that we are moving.

Sunday, 29ᵗʰ December

A dreadful development.

The area bell rang when we had just finished dinner. It was a curious hour for a delivery, and I chaffed Mary-Anne that she had a 'follower' (a romantic possibility so unlikely that even my ever-sensible Dora could not suppress a smile). Mary-Anne assured me most earnestly (blushing, no less!) that she did not; and hurried to the kitchen. She returned, some minutes later, and said that there was a man to see 'the master'; that he would not give a name, but that it was a 'private matter'. 'A man?' said Dora. – 'A gentleman, do you mean?' – 'I couldn't rightly say, ma'am. He speaks proper enough; but he don't dress the part.' – 'Well, is he some sort of hawker?' – 'No, ma'am; least, I don't reckon he's selling anything. He ain't carrying nothing with him.'

I am sure my face must have turned quite pale; for I had a clear presentiment of who our unexpected caller might be. I did my utmost to regain my composure and went downstairs directly.

It *was* my father; and, although more than a year since I last laid eyes upon him, I found him quite unchanged.

He remains the finest example of the 'shabby genteel' type that you might care to meet: – *viz.* his coat is a decent woollen affair, but the buttons hang loosely, as if attached (or, rather, re-attached) by the slenderest thread; his trousers are peg-tops, after the latest fashion, but shiny as beeswax at the knees, where they have worn thin; his 'white' gloves, meanwhile, have long since turned an admixture of yellow and grey.

I noticed one 'improvement' to his appearance: a weary-looking pair of Dundreary whiskers (ridiculous on a man of his age) which served to partly hide the gouty, bloodshot condition of his countenance. There was no concealing, however, the sharp aroma of liquor, the same degrading stench that has clung to him for the last twenty years.

He looked at me, his hat clasped against his chest, and broke into a smile. 'My boy!' he exclaimed, in a false tone of lachrymose affection that quite turned my stomach. – 'You are not welcome here,' I replied, bluntly. – 'I know, my boy, I know. I deserve every rebuke you may heap on my old grey head. But did you get my note, my boy? I'm being imposed upon terribly …' – 'And you thought you might impose upon me.' – 'Now, now,' he cried, 'that isn't it. Not at all. I just thought you wouldn't want to see your poor papa persecuted by a scoundrel …'

And so it went on, the solemn, well-rehearsed tale of woe which I have heard a dozen times before. The truth of the matter was, however, easy to discern amidst all the flummery: the money owed to the boot-maker is not, of course, for a pair of boots; it is a 'debt of honour between gentlemen' (gentlemen!) acquired at a gaming table. The boot-maker, moreover, is an insalubrious character, who runs his own gaming-house above his shop, and is given to 'bashing the life out of' anyone who crosses him.

'If this boot-maker threatens or harms you,' I said, 'you may go to the police' − a likely eventuality! − 'And if he comes to me, he will find your "guarantee" is worthless.'

Then came the prayer I anticipated.

'Can't you oblige me at all, my boy? For your mother's sake?'

In truth, I could have struck him down upon the spot. I checked myself and told him that I would give him nothing and that if he had any doubt as to how I could be so cold-hearted, he should look to his own history − that I well recalled how my mother worked herself to death, while he had drank himself into oblivion − that it was the bitterest pill to think of her lying in a parish plot, while he still drew breath − that he might one day repent and find forgiveness in Our Lord, but that I could never be so saintly. I spoke so violently that I grew fearful that D. or Mary-Anne might have heard me.

He hesitated, then spoke once more, abandoning his previous tack.

'I got talking to your girl,' he said, at last. 'I gather you're moving up in the world, my boy. Islington, isn't it?' − I cursed Mary-Anne under my breath. − He looked back at me, as conniving and artful as a fox − 'Well, I'm sure I won't trouble you there, dear boy. I wouldn't wish to disturb a respectable house, nor distress your dear lady wife; but, of course, if my creditors make inquiries −'

And there it was − blackmail. His meaning was plain: if I did not supply the three pounds (plus interest!) then, upon moving to Amwell Street, I could expect to be dunned by every importunate ruffian that ever made my father's acquaintance!

What could I do? I would have paid him the money, there and then, just to be rid of him. As it happened, I did not have more than a few shillings in my pocket; nor could I return to my study and write a cheque, without incurring suspicion. Then I heard the sound of Mary-Anne descending the stairs to the kitchen.

My father immediately understood my embarrassment and pressed a piece of paper into my hand, with which he had plainly come prepared.

'It need not be this very moment; but it must be soon, my boy. I won't trouble you at home again; you have my word. Come to my lodgings to-morrow evening; we'll make the place decent for you, on my oath.'

He was gone in an instant. When Mary-Anne appeared, I reprimanded her for being so free with her gossip.

Dora, quite naturally, asked me to whom I had been talking. I told her it was simply a well-spoken beggar. I said that he had told me a long tale, in the hope of pecuniary reward – that much *was* true – and that I had given the man nothing for his pains.

If only *that* were the whole truth! If only I could confide in her!

In fact, I am now obliged to visit 'Pear-tree-court, Goswell-street, Clerkenwell' and give three pounds (plus interest!) – which, in fact, I can ill afford – to one of the most worthless creatures in God's creation. I even wonder if this bullying boot-maker exists; or if he is a profitable figment of my father's imagination.

I cannot think I shall sleep much tonight. It is a dreadful thing to have raised oneself up so far, by dint of toil and perseverance, and then to be obliged to look back into the abyss.

CHAPTER TWO

The Detective Inspector arrived in a hansom, one hour and a half after the discovery of the body. He was a man of modest stature, dressed in tweed, with dark brown hair and neatly clipped whiskers, but possessing an air of authority that more than compensated for any deficiency in his height. He strode briskly up the steps, greeting the constable stationed at the front door. He then entered the house with as much confidence as if it were his own.

He was met by Sergeant Preston, whom he addressed in familiar tones. The latter, after a few brief words of explanation, led him upstairs, to the upper floor. A final precipitous set of steps continued to the attic above, but Preston came to a halt on the landing.

'This is it, sir. Two bedrooms. The gentleman's at the front with a little dressing-room, the wife's at the back. That's where we found her. Well, you only have to follow your nose, eh?'

Inspector Delby nodded, his manner quiet and business-like. He pushed open the door.

Like the rest of the house, the bedroom was tastefully furnished. The bed, wardrobe, chairs and chiffonier were polished mahogany; the curtains, partly concealing the sash, were of thick crimson rep, beneath which was placed a low couch, upholstered in a matching colour.

The woman's body lay beside the cast-iron fire. She was dressed in a pale cornflower crinoline. At first glance, judging by appearances, she seemed to have simply fainted, collapsed across the black hearth-stone. But it was plain from her ashen-white face, which lay flat against the floor, mouth agape, that she was long dead. Moreover, there could be no doubt she had been murdered. For her hair, though it was still pinned into a delicate chenille net upon one side, had fallen loose upon the other. The long brown tresses were matted into thick bloody strands; the cracked and crushed bone beneath cruelly exposed, visible in jagged fragments.

'How long has she been here, do you think?'

Preston frowned. 'Judging from the odour, sir, it must be a day or two.'

'Quite right,' murmured Delby, stepping gingerly around the hearth. 'It is quite chastening, is it not, how, bereft of animation, we begin to rot so quickly?'

He glanced from the woman's clothes, up to the mantelpiece. The back of her dress was flecked with carmine drops of dried blood; the mantelpiece and mirror were painted in the same fashion.

'From the blood on the mirror,' he continued, 'I should say there were at least two or three blows. It goes off in all directions, you see?'

'I drew the same conclusion, sir.'

'If it was a mere fracture, of course, one might consider the possibility of an accident. She is a small woman – perhaps there was a heated argument – she might stumble backwards – her head would be at the right height …'

'You only have to look at the state of her, sir,' interjected Preston.

'Quite. The fellow must have shook her like a rag-doll, until he'd cracked her head open. What manner of man could do such a thing?'

'I shouldn't like to say, sir.'

'Now, she *is* the lady of the house, I assume. We can be certain of that?'

'Oh, it's Mrs. Jones, all right, sir. A local lad – local constable, begging your pardon – recognised her.'

'And what of the husband?' said Delby, turning away and peering through the window, down into the narrow back-garden below.

'Scarpered. He's left a confession, mind – well, if that's the right word for it. Here, see what you make of it, sir.'

The sergeant produced the piece of paper which had rested on the desk downstairs. Delby, in turn, perused its contents.

I know in my heart I am the man to blame. I have valued at nought all I should have held dear and pursued a sinful illusion of happiness at the cost of my own soul. When I am gone, this testimony will remain. If you care to read these wretched pages, then you will know how it came to this dreadful conclusion.

My only recourse is to throw myself on the mercy of my Maker. I do not have the stomach to wield a blade; and I do not possess a gun. It must be the water; I pray I may find the strength..

I expect no forgiveness; I deserve none.

J.J.

The inspector raised his eyebrows.

'It's a queer sort of note, sir, isn't it?' said Preston.

'What are these "pages" he talks about?'

'Sorry, sir, I should have said – our Mr. Jones seems to have kept a diary. There's three or four years' worth in a little locked cabinet, nicely bound. But we found the pages from the last few months all loose, scattered about on his desk; and this was left on top of them. I've had that lad I mentioned putting them in the right order. I thought you might want to read through them.'

'I'm sure the fellow's account of his domestic tribulations are of great interest, sergeant, but I'd prefer to lay my hands on the man himself, as soon as possible. Now, for a start, do we know if he kept to his stated intention? Have you made inquiries with the Marine Police?'

'Not ten minutes ago, sir. I've telegraphed to Wapping. But I haven't heard of any suicides in the route papers at the Yard; not in the last week.'

'Nor I. Still, the river does not always give them up so quickly, if at all. Well, suppose he did not kill himself, where has he gone to ground? Does he have family in London? Friends?'

'Wish I knew, sir. I've found nothing in the house. No correspondence whatsoever, except with tradesmen and his wife's people; no photographs, nothing. It seems they've only been in Amwell Street since January. Now, the dead woman's family are from Chelsea; the father's a draper, one of the grand sort. Big premises off the Regent's Circus.'

'Well, it seems unlikely Mr. Jones has gone there, eh? But they must be informed; we had better make the draper's our first stop. What's become of the servants?'

'I've had a couple of words with the maidservant next door, sir. I didn't tell her anything in particular, apart from how we wanted to find Mr. and Mrs. Jones. It seems they just had a cook who came in for breakfast and dinner, and a skivvy who lived on the premises. This girl I spoke to hasn't seen the cook this last week; and she reckons they dismissed the skivvy on Thursday night – saw her leave – exchanged a couple of words with her.'

'They must both be found. Do we have a name? An address?'

'Mary-Anne Bright was the skivvy, sir. We think she was heading for lodgings near King's Cross; that's all I know. I've got a man looking for her now. Likewise for the cook, a Mrs. Galton.'

'Very good, sergeant, you've been very efficient. Well, let us go down and have a look at Mr. Jones's diary. I suppose we had better give it a quick glance, if the fellow was so determined that we should read it.'

Preston nodded and the two men descended the stairs. They found the local constable – the same young man who had first discovered Mrs. Jones's body – having completed his task, quietly reading through the assembled papers.

On seeing Delby, the constable jumped nervously to his feet.

'Sorry, sir, I was only …'

'I can see what you were doing,' said the inspector, walking over to the desk. 'I take it you've put all this in order, since you appear to have time on your hands. Well, I suppose you are the man to tell me: do the dull minutiae of Mr. Jones's life explain why he should do away with his wife?'

'Dull? It ain't that, sir – what he's writing about – I mean, well, you had better read it for yourself – all of it –'

DIARY

Monday, 30ᵗʰ December

Fretful night; no better than I had expected. Headache. Arrived at the office later than is my custom.

Fortesque remarked, 'Saint Monday, is it?'

I told him I would be obliged if he were to spare me his witticisms.

Tiresome day. Several needless errors whilst draughting certificates; I was obliged to start anew on three separate occasions.

I quit my desk at five o'clock; walked directly to Goswell Street on my unfortunate errand. There was a persistent mizzling rain in the air, which only served to make my task the more difficult. Having given up any idea that I might simply chance upon the place – too gloomy for that – I inquired at a coffee-house. The man there knew the district well and provided directions.

Pear Tree Court! The quaint name, of course, quite belied by the reality: a small plot of ground, littered with animal and vegetable refuse. It sits behind an old public house, upon the eastern side of the road, at the heart of a maze of alleys and passages, bordering upon the grey outbuildings of a small, foul-smelling gas-works. The houses surrounding it mostly of ancient wood, black and rotten, topped with tar. I saw two examples which were made of brick and they seemed even less substantial: patchworks of rags had replaced glass in half the windows; cracked tiles abounded; roofs had all but collapsed.

Not one building was numbered or marked (not even the customary promise of 'dry lodgings') and I could not fathom which, if any, might contain my father. I met, by chance, with a rough-looking fellow in corduroys. The man was, it transpired, a hawker of old china, and promptly offered me 'half a dozen cups, good as would grace Her Majesty's table, hardly chipped but here and there,' … for a shilling! I politely demurred. I asked after my father but he did not know 'any old parties hereabouts'. Knocked at several doors – to be met with blank incomprehension by a family of Irish; several rebuffs of 't'aint convenient, mister'; and, in one instance, the foulest abuse. At the last, contemplating abandoning the attempt altogether, I heard a familiar voice.

'My boy! Come up, come up!'

I looked up, peering into the gloom. The only light was the dim glow of the lamps in the neighbouring works. Nonetheless, it was my father. I made no reply but followed his calls, walking up a flight of rickety steps.

The interior of his room was a miserable sight, though I had expected nothing better. The floor was bare boards – not even the cheapest rug or drugget – and all upon a peculiar incline. The hearth in the corner was little more than a hole knocked into the chimney, surrounded by cracked plaster and surmounted by a makeshift wooden mantelpiece, constructed from three struts of flaking timber. A piece of cord was strung from one wall to another, on which hung a pair of damp shirts.

He rose to greet me, 'I ain't been in a condition to spruce it up, like I planned, my boy,' he said, gesturing to the scene before him, 'but don't think worse of me for it.'

I did not catch his meaning at first. The only light in the room – excepting the fire – was a pair of tallow candles on a small deal table. As he stepped forward, however, I realised that he cradled one arm with the other, and that he sported the most dreadful black eye.

I asked him if it was the boot-maker's doing.

'Him? He's a brute, my boy. Don't think of him; don't speak his name!' – 'I would rather have never heard anything of the man, rest assured.' – 'Well then, let's not spoil our reunion! Come now, won't you shake your father's hand?'

Reunion!

I let his outstretched palm hang in mid-air, until it wilted away like a flower. He pretended to look downcast.

'Just business, is it? Ah, well, you're a practical man, I know that, my boy. That's how you've got on in life. Your mother was the same. It's a credit to you; I never had the head to be practical.' – 'You were generally too inebriated.' – 'Just so! I was a weak vessel, my boy. Dreadful weak. You're right to castigate me, quite right. But let's talk of finer things … now, tell me about your missus. I bet she's a fine beauty, eh?' – 'I did not come here to talk about Dora.' – 'Dora, eh? A pretty name! Wait, now, talking of which, here comes my little Ellie – '

The sound of footsteps upon the stairs provided the interruption, though I found his words quite mystifying; the name itself meant nothing to me. To my surprise, a mere girl, no more than fifteen or sixteen years of age, knocked, then entered the room. She was dressed in the plainest frock, perfectly neat, though the cream-coloured cloth was frayed about the wrists and betrayed various rents where it had been carefully sewn together. A long shawl hung around her shoulders. She possessed a youthful, quick expression, though her face was quite pale and her eyes refused to meet my own. Neither interesting nor even pretty, there was something fascinatingly lively about her features, even as she looked shyly down at the floor.

'Ah, Ellie dear,' exclaimed my father, making no introduction, 'there you are! This is my dear boy, just as I was telling you.'

The girl looked at me, hesitantly, and spoke some common pleasantry. I replied in kind. She then produced two bottles of porter, which she had kept concealed in the folds of her shawl.

'Won't you sit and take a drop with me, son?' said my father – 'I would rather not.' – 'No? I sent dear Ellie out especially. Still, I suppose it's more for your old man …'

I refused. My father, in turn, took a swig of porter and continued to gabble. It was 'a fine thing to be reunited with family'; and how he 'often thought of me' &c. &c.

This was too much for my stomach. I told him plainly that I would only discuss *the business in hand*

and it must be strictly in private. The girl, conscious of my embarrassment, quietly took her leave with no further prompting.

This was the moment. I had had ample opportunity to prepare my thoughts, and so I laid out my terms. Namely that, however uncongenial it might prove, I would visit the boot-maker myself – though it could not be until the New Year – and pay the money into *his* hands; that it would be on strict condition that my father never trouble me at Amwell Street; that, if there need be any future communication between us, it should be in writing.

This speech of mine produced a revolting display of gratitude. Tears and blessings and prayers mingled in an unconvincing torrent of words. In truth, I would rather he had said nothing.

To stem this flood, I asked him about the girl. He informed me she was an orphan; the child of the landlord of his former lodgings. That her mother and father had both died of a fever two years since, and that she was good with the needle and supported herself by taking piece-work from a slop-seller of trousers and coats. That she had 'grown fond of him, on account of a few small kindnesses when she was but a child' and 'ran an errand or two' on his behalf.

I observed that the generosity of the fairer sex towards even the most wretched specimens of manhood was nothing short of a marvel. I did not mention my mother's name; but he understood me well enough.

'I am undeserving of even such small attentions, yes, I confess it,' he replied.

Never was a truer word spoken! Poor, foolish girl!

Our business concluded, I left with all expedition. Outside in the alley, a man lumbered past me and I was obliged to step aside. He was the burly bullying sort who set their course straight ahead and will not deviate left or right, however much space is left open to them. He wore a rough gray coat, possessed wild uncombed hair, a low brow, and the restless, roving, eyes which are the hallmark of the Hibernian in London. Behind him scuttled a woman in scant garb, with one babe at her breast, and another slung over her back, wrapped in a dirty sheet, like a sack of coal.

I said nothing to the Irishman; I let him have his petty triumph. I merely whispered a silent prayer, thanking the Lord that I had risen above such filth, then walked briskly back to Moorgate and caught the Clapham 'bus.

How sweet is a decent home and hearth!

And how bitter is everything connected to my father.

Tuesday, 31st December

Our 'move'!

I was obliged to attend the office in the morning – Mr. Hibbert having granted only a half-day's leave. Went early to Moorgate, toiled at the accounts for the requisite period, quit my desk at twelve and promptly caught the 'bus home.

I knew that the van was expected at 3 o'clock, and I felt sure that everything would be in order. The scene that met my eyes, therefore, was quite unexpected: numerous empty crates filling the hall; and a remarkable amount of stuff, scattered higgledy-piggledy, all about the house. I am by nature the most uxorious of men but I must confess to feeling a degree of disappointment in my little wifey. Praise where praise is due: Dora is a fine manager of the house; she commands, to a degree, the respect of Mary-Anne; she even possesses a natural preference for neatness and cleanliness. But – alas! – she has no genius for organisation. I searched the rooms and found her upstairs. She admitted herself that she was 'in a muddle'. She was, at least, able to particularise the domestic casualties accrued during the morning's many struggles: *viz.* five cups, plates, saucers all smashed; eight glasses cracked or broken; a scratch on the piano stool, requiring a fresh coat of varnish; three missing crinolines (how is such a thing possible?) and, the gravest loss, *one missing feline.*

She also informed me that Mary-Anne – as soft-hearted as she is soft-headed – was quite distraught that her nemesis in the kitchen should have chosen this moment to absent himself. I replied that, in this instance, the cat had probably shown acute discernment.

I took instant charge of the packing. D. was most relieved. Mary-Anne, upon the other hand, seemed to resent my intrusion (into my own affairs!) and proved more hindrance than help. To take but one example, I reprimanded the girl for retaining a battered hat-box, when D. had ordered its destruction only yesterday. She thereon insisted – with typical perversity – on bringing every item to my attention.

'Will the master want this vase in the new house?'
– 'Will the master want this cup in the new house?'
&c. &c. If only she might be persuaded to pay such
fine attention to my every whim in the general run
of things!

It is otiose to record every skirmish: the war was
won – every box and crate sealed and labelled – with
moments to spare. Bedford's van arrived promptly;
and the men proved most efficient, orderly and
obliging.

I then ordered a hackney. We sped towards
Islington, leaving all our worldly possessions
creaking along in the giant waggon, pulled by two
cart-horses. It was a strange, affecting sight; D.
herself even shed a few tears. We reached Amwell
Street at five o'clock. The van, meanwhile, arrived
at seven and was unpacked by nine. I gave each man
something for his trouble and we ate a gypsy's supper
on an upturned crate.

It *is* a fine house – even though, as yet, one feels
something of an intruder. I have inspected every
room and found nothing amiss. I have, moreover,
already recovered my desk and I am writing in the
morning-room, overlooking the garden upon the
ground floor; it will serve as an excellent 'study';
much superior to my little closet in Clapham. I
believe we shall be quite content here.

D. and Mary-Anne busying themselves with
the bed-linen and mattresses; no more can be
accomplished until daylight.

Wednesday, 1st January

A fine start to the New Year!

Woken at six o'clock — the new house still in darkness and disarray — by a piercing shriek. A fire? A burglar? I lit a candle; ascertained that Dora was quite safe; then grabbed the poker from the hearth. I met Mary-Anne on the stairs. She had a lamp in her hand and looked up at me with fearful eyes.

'Is that you, sir?' — 'Of course. What was that noise?' — 'Me, sir! Beg your pardon! There's something in the ottoman! Something unnatural! I can hear it moving about. I ain't going near it!'

I descended and opened the ottoman, which had been left in the hall. The 'something unnatural' was none other than *the cat!* It had plainly secreted itself therein the previous day, and sprung out as soon as the lid was raised. I sent a spirited kick in its direction, but the beast was far too fast. It occurred to me later — my senses perhaps having been dulled by sleep — that I would have done better by aiming at the creature who had woken me from my tranquil slumber. Mary-Anne, meanwhile, having recovered from her fright, assured me, most conscientiously, that she would now 'butter its paws' to prevent the animal from straying (a remarkable treatment, which, she informed me, was the wisdom of her ancestors). I enjoined her to refrain from such an unlikely experiment until I had left the house; and to hurry up with some hot water.

I had expected some semblance of domestic order to be restored by the time I had finished with my shave. I was quite mistaken; matters only worsened. I arrived downstairs to discover there was no sign of Cook. I reassured Dora that she had been given the correct address. No breakfast to be had, regardless; only a collation of cold meats, which had travelled with us from Clapham.

A fine start, indeed!

I quit the house at eight, somewhat vexed, and walked to the office down the City Road. This buoyed my spirits a little: the entire journey did not take more than half an hour, a great improvement. Fortesque himself was late in arriving, on account of 'it being dreadful icy' (more likely a night spent at the Argyll Rooms). Mr. Hibbert, meanwhile, appeared at eleven o'clock or thereabouts, having come direct from the station. He professed himself much revived by his holiday. I gave him all the accounts, transfers &c; very pleased with my work.

At noon, I lunched with Fortesque at Gilroy's. We spoke a good deal about the new house; I had a glass of claret and became so enthused that I rashly promised him an invitation to dinner: a dreadful idea, occasioned by temporary intoxication. He is decidedly *not* the man to introduce into one's home.

We walked back from the chop-house along Cheapside, as is our custom. A curious incident then occurred, on the far side of the road, which is worth recounting in full:–

A young girl, poorly but neatly dressed, sat crouched upon the pavement, not far from St. Mary's church, her skirt trailing in the dirt, clutching at numerous boxes of matches which lay scattered about. She was attempting to return them to a wooden tray balanced on her lap, though a good number had already been crushed underfoot by the pedestrian traffic. Although we had not seen the cause of the upset, it seemed likely that, whilst hawking these pathetic articles along the street, she had come into collision with a certain elderly gentlemen. The man in question now stood over her, much embarrassed, and was pressing her to take a shilling as reparation for her loss.

'What a pert little piece, eh?' said Fortesque, as I casually scrutinised the girl's features.

I reprimanded him for his vulgarity; which only occasioned him to laugh out loud.

'You think not?' he said. 'Come here. I'll show you something.'

Fortesque then drew me to one side, in conspiratorial fashion. Much to my consternation, he had us skulk behind a large dray which had stopped at the nearby public. He directed my gaze back to the girl. She had, at last, tearfully accepted the man's shilling and begun to walk away in the direction of the Mansion House. F. took my arm and indicated — despite my protests — that we should follow her. I had no conception of what he was about, but reluctantly yielded to his persuasion.

It was not long — alas! — before I understood. For, near the Bank of England, the self-same girl 'collided' with a second elderly banker; and acquired a limp in the process. It was a remarkable performance, worthy of Mrs. Kean.

'Nothing wrong with *her* legs,' said Fortesque. 'Third time I've seen her at it round Cheapside. She knows how to pick out the old gents, eh? Anything for a pretty face. I suppose it's always good for a shilling or two, until the Peelers nab you.'

Wretched girl!

And – though I did not trouble to utter a word of reproof – wretched Fortesque for showing her to me! It is base thing to revel in the misery of others; and a measure of F.'s conceit that he considers himself a young 'Corinthian,' introducing me to the wicked ways of the town.

For my part, upon sober reflection, I can only feel pity for her. To practice such imposture requires a woman to have lost every feminine virtue – modesty, honesty, &c. What chance for her of a decent life? She has already lost everything of value; it cannot easily be regained.

I returned home at six. No improvement in domestic felicity; Dora much put out. She gave me a letter she had just received from Cook:

'*Dear Master and Missus,*

I have been thinking on it, and Islington not suited to me, on account on the altitudes.
I give my notice and I will not be coming no more.

Mrs. Gertrude Sutherland'

One might hardly call it 'notice', I think!

She is too old, I suppose, to want another place and does not require a character. Still, it is no great loss. Dora has promised that she will post an advertisement at the nearest registry. We shall find someone easily enough; with luck, they may be better at performing their duties.

11pm. I cannot sleep. The blackguard business with *the three pounds*. I have endeavoured to put it from my mind; but I cannot struggle against it any longer.

I must visit the boot-maker to-morrow.

Midnight. Still no sleep. I will take some brandy.

I think of my father, then – for some unaccountable reason – I keep recalling the face of the poor Cheapside 'match-girl'. What will be her fate? If she is caught, then the inevitability of imprisonment will, most likely, only slow her progress towards final ruin.

If she is not, then what hope of salvation?

Thursday, 2nd January

A gloomy day. Dreadful cold. Determined to resolve the matter of *the three pounds*, I caught the 'Paddington' to Oxford Street, on leaving the office.

It was a troublesome journey. Within minutes, as the 'bus drew to a halt on Cheapside, my legs were crushed by several crinolines; then an elderly woman came inside, swaying with the movement of the vehicle, wielding an umbrella like a life-preserver, inflicting considerable punishment on myself and another passenger. I fervently hoped that I might be asked by the conductor to 'oblige a lady' and weather the remainder on top. Unfortunately, no such party was forthcoming and I had no excuse.

I found the boot-maker's premises easily enough. His name is Halifax and his shop is in Greek Street, Soho, near to the square. Several young 'hands,' male and female were busy at their work in the front, surrounded by bluchers and ankle-jacks in various stages of their creation. I made inquiries of a young woman, who directed me to the 'master's office'. It was a pleasantly appointed room – a roaring fire and substantial pedestal desk – but still retained the tannery smell of glue and leather that suffused the nearby work-rooms. The man himself, though dressed in a respectable black suit, was a large, barrel-chested individual with the face of a true 'rough', quite worthy of Hogarth. He might easily have passed for a professional pugilist, with skin as rugged and lined as the untreated strips of hide in his work-room.

'Mr. Halifax?' – 'Who are you, sir?' he said, barely raising his head. – 'I have come to pay a debt.' – 'Is that so? I don't believe you owe me anything.' – 'A debt of honour. On behalf of George Jones.'

At the mention of my father, the boot-maker looked up from behind his desk and cast an appraising glance in my direction.

'"George Jones"? Why didn't you say so, straight off? He told me you'd come and I didn't believe none of it. Well, well!'

Without any preamble, I told him that I would pay him his money quite readily. I would impose but one condition: that he could never expect me to pay another debt, whatever my father had to say on the subject.

The boot-maker shrugged.

'It is all the same to me, my good friend. I always take back what I'm owed, one way or another.'

I told him that I had already seen his handiwork.

'Oh,' he said, with a laugh, 'that was just a lover's kiss, to jog your old man's memory. You don't seem too cut up about it, anyhow.'

I did not reply. I gave him the envelope, which I had prepared, containing the money. I could not help but feel a sharp pang of anger that such a vulgar rogue should reap a profit from my father's weakness. He took it out and counted it; then, satisfied, he smiled.

'You can tell old Georgie he's square with Halifax. And if he wants to come back, he's good for a couple of quid at the table. He can bring that little woman of his again, too.'

I said that I would do nothing of the sort; that I did not know, nor did I care to know, any female with whom my father associated. I was on the point of quitting the room, when his reply brought me up short.

"That mot of his, I mean – ain't you met her? Ellie, isn't it? Ah, I can see you have; I can tell from your face. Queer little thing, she dotes on him. Not a beauty, but – well, all the same. Very sweet on him – lucky dog. I know a few highly respectable gents who'd pay good money – well, we're both men of the world I'm sure – I'll say no more. Your pa's a lucky fellow.'

The man's imputation was plain enough; but I could not let it pass. A girl who, in years, could be his daughter – his grand-daughter! I asked him what he meant by it.

'You mean is he tupping her? Well, I suppose it's not my affair. I couldn't say for certain, my friend. I know that I would, given half a chance, eh? Young and fresh like that. And, do you know what, I fancy she's the sort who'd like it.'

Confronted with such ignorance, I turned on my heels and left. What else should I have done? Had I the strength to deal with such a villain – for I *did* possess the inclination – I would have knocked the wretched man down flat.

Instead, I merely sought out the 'bus to the Angel.

It is a queer thing. I had thought paying the despicable debt would serve to relieve me of my troubles; unburden me of my association with my father, at least for a few months.

Instead, as I ascended Pentonville Hill, I felt strangely disconsolate.

Perhaps the cold weather is to blame; it leaves one in a bad humour.

Saturday, 4th January

A brighter day.

Dora most pleased with herself on three counts:-

First, to 'decorate the house nicely' is her dearest wish. Yesterday, therefore, she despatched Mary-

Anne to the nearest oil-and-colour shop, to obtain the names of tradesmen. Two local men came today and gave estimates. I have agreed to employ one of them – a man named Saunders – to *paper* the hall and downstairs rooms. This will be, of course, a dreadful expense – more than paint. Yet, there is something so pure and unaffected in D.'s simple enthusiasm, that it is difficult to temper it. If we 'must' have paper – and paper of the choicest variety – then we must!

Dora's second achievement – one which she recounted to me with much pride – is to have made the acquaintance of a neighbour. For we have no intimates in Islington and must begin anew. D. had proposed, at first, that we leave our cards, in promiscuous fashion, at all the neighbouring houses; but I pointed out that this would resemble the actions of a commercial traveller. I must confess, however, having discounted this plan, I was somewhat unsure myself how we might proceed.

I need not have been concerned. This very morning D. fell into conversation with a 'delightful, sensible, busy woman', in the hosier's on Islington High Street. Such a thing would not occur in masculine company. But a shared enthusiasm for those trifles of feminine dress, which are so dear to the sex, will serve as an introduction between any pair of females. Thus the two ladies 'got to talking'. The lady in question is one Mrs. Antrobus; her husband is a doctor; her house is on the southern side of Claremont square, and most respectable. She has, moreover, already called and left her card.

Dora's third triumph is to have resolved the matter of a cook. She has interviewed two women and settled on 'a rounded, pleasant creature, with strong arms and a ruddy complexion, neither too old nor too young' by the name of Galton. The woman comes with an excellent character from her last employer. D. has made a written inquiry to the household in question, and it is likely she will come for a trial on Monday.

At last, we may eat something more than cold ham!

Midnight. Again, I cannot sleep. Dora will wonder why I keep returning downstairs. She can surely hear me traipsing about on the landing from her room.

Ridiculous! I can hardly account for it. 'All goes merry as a marriage bell' in the house; and the business with my father is done.

And yet –

I must be true to myself; I must confess all. If I do not, what is the value of this journal?

It is my wretched father that keeps me from sleep. Damn him! I cannot help but think of his words – '*my* little Ellie,' – and the boot-maker's insinuation. It has plagued my mind for these last two days; it nags at my conscience. She seemed such a quiet, good little thing.

The very idea – that at a mere girl – whatever her character – should be *his* 'wife'!

Why would any woman subjugate herself to such a man? She cannot know his true nature; she cannot have seen his brutal drunken rages; the piteous, tearful recriminations that follow.

And then one thought comes foremost –

Perchance the boot-maker is wrong? What if she has not fallen; if she *is* still honest and virtuous?

Then what *will* become of her in *his* company?

Of course, it is 'not my affair' either.

I shall take another brandy; then back to bed.

Sunday, 5th January

Headache. Too much brandy.

We attended church at St. Mark's in Myddelton Square. It is undoubtedly the grandest in the district – a lofty Gothic building with a high tower – and was full to the very rafters. Many respectable people. I found a warden at the end of the service (not without difficulty) and quizzed him regarding sittings. The price is five shillings a quarter, *each*. It is not an negligible expense; but to sit indefinitely in the open pews is intolerable. I gave the old man sixpence, and he swore we should be notified 'as soon as there's a place'. I expressed a preference for the gallery.

The sermon rather fine – *How Saints May Help the Devil* – decrying both worldliness and self-regarding piety.

On the way home, we chanced upon Dora's new acquaintance, Mrs. Antrobus. She introduced us to her husband: a plump fellow in his early fifties; polite and amiable in his manner, though rather taciturn. His wife, upon the other hand, some fifteen years younger and a busy, bustling, garrulous creature. She proceeded to supply all manner of advice regarding places of local recreation and fashionable resort on the Sabbath. I later remarked to Dora that she is one of those amiable women who could start a conversation in an empty room; which is not to say I did not find her charming or agreeable (D. will do well to cultivate her acquaintance).

The front door opened to the announcement that the new house 'infiltrated by rats' (another example of Mary-Anne's idiot regurgitation of our mother tongue). The truth of the matter: a *single* rodent caught by the cat and deposited in the kitchen, 'frightening her half to death'.

I buried the rat in the garden; made sure the cat received a double portion of horse-meat.

Monday, 6ᵗʰ January

The reply regarding Mrs. Galton, our new cook, arrived in the first post this morning. Very good; nothing to her detriment.

The woman herself, meanwhile, had already come for her trial, an hour beforehand. We put her to the test – with the instruction to produce a plain breakfast. A great success:– poached eggs (perfection) and haddock (nicely smoked). I then had Dora call her up and we discussed her salary. Settled on twenty pounds p.a. and the firm understanding that there will be no 'perquisites'. Made it quite clear that dripping, bones &c. all have their uses and have been bought and paid for. Indeed, to permit anything else would be to sanction a species of theft. Gratified to find that she agreed wholeheartedly and without hesitation.

Much work waiting to be done in the office; in consequence, I returned home quite late. I noticed that a letter from Chelsea lay on the mantel. Dora, however, said nothing of it's import until I had had my supper and a piece of her Twelfth Night cake. She then remarked, with casual aplomb, how Mama Willis was most desirous of seeing our new home; how she herself would welcome her mother's advice, in 'arranging things nicely'; how 'I know you, Jacob, would not want me to burden you with such things'; and, finally, how Islington is such a inconvenient distance from Chelsea &c. &c.

It is impossible to describe in words how *winning* is my wifey's expression, when she looks at one in a certain way.

The result: my mother-in-law will shortly pay us a week's visit; a week of quibbling and sniping and awkward silences. I shall endeavour, I think, to spend a good deal of time, in the evenings, on my MS.; and if that proves to be yet another cause of reproach, so be it.

'Family'!

CHAPTER THREE

The hansom, carrying the two policemen, gradually slowed and then came to a halt on Oxford Street, fifty yards short of the Regent's Circus. Delby, visibly impatient, pulled at the check-string.

In response, the cabman opened the trap in the vehicle's roof and peered at his passenger with an incurious eye.

'Well?' said the policeman.

'Stoppage, sir,' replied the cabman. 'Other side of the Circus. Can't budge.'

'Is that so?'

'Just! Take a look! Not a blessed inch of ground.'

Delby sighed.

'I see. Here, take your two bob and we'll walk.'

The cabman took the coins. The two policemen, meanwhile, clambered out onto the pavement and made their way to the Circus and down Regent Street. Neither spoke a word as they passed the various shop windows, immune to the gaudy displays of millinery and fancy goods which lured their fellow pedestrians to the 'finest thoroughfare in London'.

In truth, it was only a brief walk to their destination: the 'Grand Metropolitan Warehouse' of James Willis, Draper and Haberdasher; part of a substantial Regency terrace, no more than fifty yards from Piccadilly. The terrace itself was an elaborate, elegant construction; but the building's classical purity was somewhat tempered by the shop's proprietor's name writ large, in letters two or three feet high, decorating the upper storey.

'I sent the telegram, sir,' said Preston. 'He'll be expecting us.'

'Yes, well, I suppose that is something.'

The two policemen stepped into the shop, already busy with customers, though barely open an hour. Fashionable young women predominated, seated before low wooden counters, where catalogues and samples were presented for their approval by elegantly dressed shopmen and their female assistants. Preston turned to the liveried doorman who stood close at hand and whispered a few words. In a matter of moments, they were discreetly conveyed to stairs at the rear of the store – past rooms of rolled linen and silks – up to an office situated on the topmost floor, overlooking the busy street. Its occupant was none other than the self-same Mr. James Willis whose name loomed in giant proportions just outside his window, albeit abbreviated to the more convenient and commercial *Jas.* He was a sturdy-looking, round-faced man, shorter in stature even than the inspector, dressed in a suit that could only have come from the finest Mayfair tailor, with a small diamond tie-pin adorning his neck, and a gold chain just visible in his waistcoat pocket. He was undoubtedly a man of business; a man accustomed to all sorts of dealings. But there were nerves in his voice – an unwelcome sense of anticipation – and he addressed his visitors without any politeness or preliminary.

'You have some news, I suppose?'

'We do,' said the inspector.

'Well?'

'I'm afraid it is the worst news. Perhaps you should sit down, sir.'

Mr. Willis's gaze faltered; he wiped his brow with the palm of his hand.

'Speak plainly,' he said. 'I beg you. I can't abide a man who won't speak plainly.'

'Very well. These things are never … well, to be blunt, sir, I'm afraid to tell you, sir, that your daughter is dead.'

Willis fell silent. When, finally, he spoke, he looked directly at the inspector.

'I had guessed as much from your telegram. Has there been an accident?'

'No, sir. No accident.'

'No? Then what?'

'It is not a pleasant matter, sir. You might wish to fortify yourself before we talk any further. I'd recommend brandy.'

'Damn you, man, and damn your brandy!' said the draper, as the undercurrent of agitation turned to anger. 'I said to speak plainly! What is your name?'

'Delby, sir. Inspector Delby, of the Detective department, Scotland Yard.'

'Well, Delby, speak, won't you? Do you wish to torment me? What has happened to my poor girl?'

The inspector took a deep breath. 'She has been killed, sir. We found her body this morning, in Amwell Street.'

'In Amwell Street? You mean, at the house? But I have been there –'

'We think it was a couple of days ago that she ... that she passed away.'

'She has been lying there – all that time?'

'You were not to know, sir. Do not blame yourself for that.'

'How did she die?' demanded Willis.

'As I say, sir, the details are not pleasant.'

'I will hear them.'

'I believe someone took hold of her and shook her violently ... so that they forced her head quite suddenly against the mantelpiece in her bedroom –'

'Go on.'

'That they did so with considerable force and then repeated the action, until they killed her.'

Mr. Willis strode towards the grand marble fireplace that ornamented his office, turning his back on his visitors.

'She was not ... I mean to say ... there was no other interference with her person?'

'No sir. Thankfully nothing of that nature.'

'God help her. My sweet Dora! And where was her wretched husband, during all this?'

'We should like to ask Mr. Jones that ourselves, sir. He appears to have vanished.'

Willis turned around, looking sharply at the policeman. 'Vanished?'

'Yes, sir. We can't find any trace of him, at present.'

'I see.'

'What do you see, sir?'

'I see it all. He has murdered my poor girl.'

'Mr. Jones's disappearance tells against him, sir,' said Delby, cautiously, 'but we cannot know that, not as yet.'

'I know it, inspector, and I'll bloody well see him hanged.'

§

'Do you have any children, inspector?'

Mr. Willis sat at his desk, some minutes later, sipping from a glass of brandy as he spoke; the two policeman sat opposite.

'No, sir.'

'Dora was my youngest; my darling. She was never wilful; always kind and loving. She was raised in a God-fearing home. I gave her the opportunity to acquire every female accomplishment. She had a good dowry. She was fit to marry a gentleman; a man of distinction. Do you know how my darling repaid me?'

'No, sir.'

'She married a clerk, and not even a clerk at the Bank or the Exchange, at that. A man who, although fifteen years her senior, could barely scrape together two hundred a year.'

'It was a love match, then, sir?'

'On her side,' said Willis.

'I take it that you have never thought much of your son-in-law, sir?'

'Two hundred a year! Who can support a family on that? On his marriage, I even offered him a place in the firm – not once, but half a dozen times – an opportunity for advancement. He turned me down flat.'

'Perhaps he was too proud to accept?'

'If you mean that he considered himself superior to his father-in-law – and my business – then I do not doubt *that* for an instant.'

'I see,' said Delby. 'You could have forbidden the match?'

The draper sighed. 'My daughter had just reached her majority, inspector. There are times when a girl sets her heart on a man ... well, a father may say what he likes.'

'Can I just ask a question, sir?' interjected Preston. 'You said just now, quite emphatically, that you felt certain that your son-in-law was the guilty party?'

'Who else?'

'Well, indeed, sir. It's likely enough, on the face of it. But, begging your pardon, I thought you might have had some particular reason. It rather sounded like you did.'

Mr. Willis hesitated, then spoke.

'I suppose it must out; it may help you find the brute. My daughter came to me, sergeant. It was no more than two weeks ago. I had never seen her so distraught. When she had done with crying, it turned out that she wanted my advice. She asked me to swear that I would keep a secret. I gave a solemn oath; though, in all honesty, I was most disturbed by the whole proceeding. Then she told me that she had every reason to suspect her husband – well, what can I say – that his affections were engaged elsewhere. She feared he might desert her. She wanted to know – if he did so – whether she must remain his wife, or if the family could contemplate the scandal of a divorce.'

The inspector raised his eyebrows. 'An awkward business, sir.'

'Until Dora spoke to me that day, I had believed that my son-in-law, whatever his faults, was an honest man, possessed of some morals. In truth, I had thought him something of a prig. And to hear such a thing from her lips! You can imagine my state of mind. I swore that I would have it out with him.'

'But you did not?'

'My sweet girl begged me – fell to her knees and begged me – that I should do nothing; that I should recall my promise, keep the matter a secret; that she might yet win him back! She would not even tell me the name of the woman whom she suspected. "Win him back", inspector! Such a prize! And, like a fool, I kept my word. I confided in no-one but my wife and made her swear to say nothing.'

The draper took a large swig of brandy.

'And now she is dead.'

Inspector Delby paused, then spoke up once more.

'Sir, I have no wish to intrude further on your grief, but I fear I must. Did your daughter ever speak to you concerning a young girl named Ellen Hungerford?'

§

The two policemen walked back through the shop.

'You said nothing about the diary, sir,' said the sergeant.

'I fear he would demand to read it. Besides, I think it best we hear from all parties, without prejudice. Then we can form our own conclusions.'

'It all tallies, though, don't it?'

'Perhaps. In any case, do you think Willis would think any better of his son-in-law, if he knew the whole truth?'

Preston did not hesitate.

'No sir, not for an instant.'

DIARY

Saturday, 11ᵗʰ January

This afternoon, an opportunity to observe Dora's *painter and decorator* at his work; a privilege I will happily relinquish, at the first opportunity. For Mr. Saunders is a vulgar little man who finishes every sentence with 'do y'see what I mean?' or 'understand me?' and I cannot say that I relish his presence in our home. Moreover, he brings with him three journeymen! I had thought, at first, that this was an excessive number of employés, but – to the contrary – since three quarters of their time is spent in private conversation (of a coarse and common nature) and the remainder in the going-in and going-out for beer, their numbers are quite insufficient. Observing this laxity, I quizzed Saunders as to when the work proper might commence, only to receive a lecture on the subject of 'preparation'. Nonetheless, after renewed work with pumice stones &c. he announced this very evening that the walls are now 'ready' – the papering will begin on Monday and will not take more than two days. Saunders himself seemingly much pleased with this progress, but the 'proof of the pudding' &c.

Another letter from Chelsea – the fourth in as many days. D. tells me it is further elaboration on the requirements for Mama Willis's comfort (apparently she suffers from 'a delicate disposition'; I have never seen any sign of *that*). Her ordinances cover a variety of topics, from diet (a list to be provided for Cook!) to number of pillows for her bed. She is to have D.'s room; which is no great trouble.

I spent the evening working up my MS. The story proceeds to my satisfaction and I am very near the conclusion; it may be finished before Mama W. arrives.

What a poke in the eye for dear Papa W., should it be published!

Sunday, 12ᵗʰ January

Saw Mr and Mrs. Antrobus at church. They made a point of 'noticing' us, and introducing us to several of the congregation. *Mirabile dictu*, not content with that, Mrs. A. informed us that they had orders for Charles Hallé at St. James's Hall on the 22nd inst. – a gift to the good doctor from a grateful client – and would we care to attend?

Dora wild with anticipation.

Mrs. A. proving a most useful acquaintance.

Monday, 13ᵗʰ January

Dora is unwell. The papering has commenced and Saunders's paste has a rare smell; it leaves her both nauseous and, she tells me, afflicted by colic. I do not suffer so badly. Windows left open during the day, but the cold intolerable at night; also, fear of burglars. Asked S. if he could use a different solution.

'With this paper?'

'Yes.'

'Not if you want it 'anging on the walls, I can't.'

Such impertinence is typical of the man.

Wednesday, 15ᵗʰ January

Saunders <u>still not finished</u>. What can one do? It would be 'cutting off one's nose' to dismiss him, with the job half done.

D. suffering terribly.

One of the journeymen is also making himself far too bold with Mary-Anne, in word and gesture. She is too naïve and foolish to realise that it is not a species of flattery but an insult, to herself and to her sex.

Have instructed Saunders to speak to him.

Friday, 17ᵗʰ January

At last, the papering is complete; the last sheet was applied this afternoon. Saunders already gone by the time I returned home. Much relief!

They *have* been dilatory but I cannot fault Saunders's men on the *quality* of their work, even if I might fault their *method*. Dora's choice – the 'roses and thorns' – looks very fine. The smell, however, still lingers and D. still suffers, though less so than before. Saunders apparently has assured her that it will diminish in 'only a week or two' (!).

Another letter from Chelsea, evening post. Mama Willis has now settled on a date for her regal progress – it will be the 24th. I asked D. 'where should we have Mary-Anne hang the streamers and flags?' but she was not greatly amused.

This unfortunate sickness has dampened her spirits considerably.

Saturday, 18th January

At last, a true cause for modest celebration – a burst of activity and my MS. is finished – the work of some six months.

I completed the final page in a frenzy of mental exertion at nine o'clock this very evening. Went down to D. directly and had her read the last chapter – she pronounced it 'most striking and affecting'. Took a glass of port together.

There is still much to do. I am convinced that, in the case of an author who is unknown to the public, a good deal rests upon the title. I am inclined to *An Unfortunate Advantage* but D. assures me this is 'too perplexing and promises nothing'. She says herself that she 'much prefers something more particular'. When pressed, she suggested *Mr. Avery's Progress* – which I found utterly flat and insipid, though I did not confess as much to dear D.

It is a question of *taste* and I must think on it.

Of course, the other point for consideration – a trivial matter! – is that of publication. It must be a periodical; and one that might consider the work of a mere tyro. I shall visit the City Office of Mudie's during the week and look at all the London magazines.

Curious sense of elation.

Sunday, 19th January

Crisp and bright; best day since New Year.
Still lingering smell of paste.

Church, then gave Mary-Anne her half-day's leave; took cab to Hampstead, walked the Heath – pleasant recreation and <u>fresh air</u> – we lunched at Jack Straw's Castle. D. says she is still a little out of sorts, though the walk brought roses to her cheeks.

Mary-Anne returned an hour late. Strong words from D.; a *show* of remorse from M-A, but nothing more.

It occurs to me that two weeks have now passed and I have heard nothing from my father.

The very thought of him is like a dreadful shadow that dogs my every step. For I know in my heart that it is not a question of whether he can keep his word and leave me in peace; merely, for how long I am to be spared.

Why such gloomy thoughts at this time?

Monday, 20th January

Decided to forego another lunch with F. and visit Mudie's, Cheapside.

The place very busy: a sale of old and surplus volumes; tempted by a set of *The House and Home*, beautifully bound, but cannot afford the expense. Made pencil notes of likely publications; addresses; editors &c. Also visited Reynolds, the copyist's; engaged him to copy MS., on moderate terms (7s.).

On my return to the office, Fortesque remarked that he had seen the 'match-girl' – the conniving 'actress' we observed some weeks ago – arrested near the Bank.

Poor wretch!

Tuesday, 21ˢᵗ January

Mr. Hibbert out on business all day.

Lunched with Fortesque at Lakes's. I have grown sick of the place. Chops terribly burnt and the waiter *would* argue the point. I do not like the fawning German-type of man at some City establishments, but the fellow at Lakes's – a self-regarding Cockney – is too conceited by half. I will not go again.

F. very talkative; discoursing on his prospects in the company. Nothing out of the ordinary, until I mentioned some trivial domestic circumstance, and the following escaped his lips:-

'Well, old man, I'm still walking out with Betsy and I shan't wonder if *we* shall be married soon.'

Married!

This 'Betsy' is the self-same milliner whom he met at the Casino. Their courtship has lasted a whole *month*. He is evidently quite enamoured of the girl; heaps extravagant praise on her appearance and character. She is, moreover, 'game as anything', a compliment which, to my mind, would better suit a bull-mastiff than a prospective spouse. In F.'s 'fast' set, however, unchecked high spirits are considered unequivocally admirable, whether in man, woman or canine.

I endeavoured to dissuade him. I reminded him of his position: that a junior clerk can ill-afford a wife or family, with all it entails; that I myself – yes, I confessed it to F.! – found my salary barely sufficient for my needs; moreover, that such a union, no matter how agreeable he might find it, could only damage his prospects and not enhance them.

In turn, F. asserted that the girl, though 'unpolished, I'll give you that, old man,' was 'a good sort of woman' and 'not half so bad as you paint her'.

I conceded, naturally, that it would be wrong to prejudge the girl's character.

Then – alas! I remember it too well – he spoke out once more.

'Well, old man, I shouldn't half mind hearing your opinion of her – and I should think it would be a good one – if you met her. If that dinner at yours is still going, I could bring her along, don't you think?'

The dreaded dinner!

I had thought – nay, prayed! – my New Year's invitation was quite forgotten.

What was I to do? The situation was quite impossible. I found myself praying the quarrelsome waiter might return and serve as a distraction. I even wondered if F. understood my acute embarrassment and, in typical fashion, was merely attempting to wring some humour from it – but he appeared quite serious. I did my best to prevaricate: I said that Mrs. Galton was still on trial; that there was a good deal of decorating still to be done &c. &c. but that I would not scruple to meet the girl, and discover her many good points, under better circumstances. My enthusiasm for this course of action, however false, must have carried a note of conviction. For, no sooner than I had spoke, F. set about arranging a time and place.

In consequence, myself and 'the missus' cordially invited to an evening at Astley's Amphitheatre (!) on the 28th inst.

At the time, I was too dumb-struck to refuse; and, I suppose, was somewhat surprised and flattered that F. should be so desirous of my good opinion.

Astley's! Indeed, I am half inclined to go – with Mama Willis in tow! She might enjoy a night at the 'theatre', albeit one featuring the latest scantily attired 'equestrienne' and her troop of performing horses. It might be rather entertaining, to put her in F.'s company.

Of course, it is utterly out of the question.

But how to get out of it?

To-morrow, at least, we have Hallé – *from the ridiculous to the sublime!*

Wednesday, 22nd January

Returned home to bad news. Dora had taken to her bed; much fatigued; nausea; &c. &c. It is the same complaint that has dogged her this last week or so. I offered to send for a physician but she refused.

The damnable wallpaper!

Much agonising over Hallé ensued. D. insisted that I should go by myself. I protested that my playing the part of the 'bachelor husband' might be considered somewhat ungentlemanly by our new acquaintances, under the circumstances. She replied that she had already written to Mrs. Antrobus and had settled the matter.

My dear, sweet selfless wifey! For I *did* very much want to hear Hallé; and she knew it full well. I yielded to her entreaties and, reluctantly, presented myself at Claremont Square at six thirty.

I found the Antrobus's house to be a good size; similar in design to our own, but larger in proportion, the interior furnished in excellent taste. On my arrival, there was a party of six in the drawing-room: Dr. & Mrs. Antrobus; Mr. and Mrs. Wynne-Smith (he, a barrister, some forty years of age, with chambers in the Temple); Mr. Poulford (student of medicine, nephew of Mr. A.; lively); and Mr. Taunton (acquaintance of the latter; very dull). Two Clarence cabs came at seven; and I was to travel with the young men. There followed some ghoulish talk from Poulford about the dreadful demise of the Northumberland miners – much in the papers these last few days – and the effect of gas in the disaster; he insisted that any medical man could have told them the 'rescue' was in vain. Taunton, meanwhile, informed us that he had taken rooms in Knightsbridge and planned to 'let at a fierce profit', come the International Exhibition.

Did not 'warm' to either young man. Fortunately the cab made good progress to the West End and we arrived at half past seven.

St. James's Hall itself is a marvel. We entered from the Piccadilly side: the building much grander than I had expected; remarkable panelled ceiling; two dozen star burners hanging from the intersections of the beams, giving out enough light for the whole place.

I was seated next to Mrs. Antrobus. She is a good woman − most solicitous after Dora's health − but *will* talk. She told me that she herself cannot not abide paint and paste; all such fumes fatal to the female constitution; listed many acquaintances who had fallen victim &c. She then asked her husband his medical opinion. He merely confirmed her views and returned to perusing the programme.

Dr. Antrobus is an intriguing study. His wife, in her garrulous fashion, is always referring to him in speech: 'would you not agree, my dear?' 'My dear husband always says ...' 'isn't that so, my dear?' The man himself, however, generally maintains a stolid silence. Does he merely ignore her idle chit-chat; or is he so firmly under petticoat government that he cannot put a stop to it? One suspects, in this case, that the wife has the upper hand; she may *refer* to him but I do not imagine she often *defers*. Mrs. A. doubtless has many virtues − and, indeed, has shown a good deal of consideration to D. and myself. But what must it be like to be married to such a female!

Hallé appeared at the appointed hour and took his seat at the piano. We were fortunate to be seated in the stalls, from where I could observe the great man as close quarters. He possesses a high brow and prominent nose; the eyes, of course, betray great intellect and understanding. His playing of the Beethoven sonatas − from memory − deeply moving and very fine; great mastery and delicacy in every note. Mr. Wynne-Smith − who sat on my left and followed the music from his own book (would that

I had the same facility!) – described it as 'pure and refined' and 'utterly truthful'.

A standing ovation at the conclusion; much deserved.

We returned to Islington a little after eleven; I did not accept an invitation to Claremont Square. At home, Mary-Anne met me at the door and informed me that her mistress was asleep. Nonetheless, D. woke as I passed her room. I went in and found her in the most wretched mood. She did not wish to hear a word about the concert. Furthermore, she complained that I should have 'given a thought to your wife' and 'not have made such an awful row on the landing'. I was quite taken aback. Indeed, I cannot recall ever being spoken to in such terms in my own house.

Mrs. Antrobus has promised to pay a call on her to-morrow. Perhaps that may raise her spirits; this sickness is clearly very trying.

Thursday, 23rd January

Fortesque still believes that we are to attend Astley's on Tuesday! I might have pleaded Dora's health, but for that fact that – before the unwelcome topic arose in our conversation – I had already boasted to him of my going to see Hallé, *solo*.

Must I snub him? Very awkward.

I came home to find D. much improved. I had expected to hear that she did not receive Mrs. A.; but – quite the opposite – I was told that they had had 'a long talk' and Mrs. A. 'the most useful friend a woman ever had.'

Dora smiled as she said this; she has been very girlish and gleeful all evening.

Who can fathom the female mind?

My spirits, however, are not so buoyant; our house guest arrives to-morrow.

Friday, 24th January

Paid another call on Reynolds at lunch; he had finished the copy of my MS., as promised. A good piece of work; worth every penny.

Mama Willis now installed at home *with three trunks.*

Smoked mackerel for dinner at her request; I should never have acceded to it, as I cannot abide strong fish. Barely touched a mouthful.

Saturday, 25th January

Clear day but sharp frost; pavements very icy. Saw two horses down on the City Road; no hope for either.

I left the office at 12. Returning to Amwell Street, I met a youth, no more than fourteen years, standing at the front door carrying a large rectangular object, tightly wrapped in brown paper. The problem of balancing the cumbersome item and sparing a hand to pull the bell seemed to be causing him difficulty; he was visibly relieved when I joined him on the steps.

'Might you be Mr. Jones, sir?'

Quite mystified, I informed him that I was.

'Delivery, sir. I was just goin' to ring, see? My master always says not to take 'em down the area, on account of 'em taking knocks. Hope you ain't particular how it gets in the 'ouse.'

I told him that I could not say whether or not I was 'particular', since I had not the slightest idea of what the parcel might be. The boy informed me that it was a gilt mirror, ordered from 'Berwick's on Upper Street', the previous day.

I went inside and, after some to-ing and fro-ing, I discovered that the item had been ordered *by Mama Willis,* on a shopping expedition with Dora, the previous afternoon, with a view to adorning the mantel of our morning-room. I assumed that it was a house-warming gift and reluctantly accepted the delivery, even though the thing was not to my taste.

I was surprised to learn, therefore, later in the afternoon, three significant facts: first, that Dora *did not much like it,* but was too timid to contradict her mother's taste; second, that whilst Mama Willis had chosen the item, it was *not* a gift and *we* were to pay for it; third, that it cost *four pounds!*

It is an awful extravagance which we can ill afford; and yet I can hardly let *that* be known to Mama W.

What am I to do?

It sits there even now, a silent reminder that I am not master in my own home.

I cannot help but wonder whether this is the 'help' Dora had expected. If so, it is proving rather costly!

Mary-Anne, meanwhile, already complaining of 'Missus W.'. I overheard her talking to D. that 'she can't do nothing right with her sheets' and 'keeps having me change her jug and flannel every two minutes'.

For once, myself and Mary-Anne in complete sympathy – a curious sensation!

Sunday, 26th January

To church.

Still in the open pews; Mama W. remarked that she found it 'a little draughty and tight-packed'; that perhaps she 'no doubt had grown too accustomed to her quiet little chapel in Chelsea'; but 'supposed one could worship the Lord anywhere, if one set one's mind to it.'

Would have happily sent her back to Chelsea on the spot!

Still, it *was* a crush. I spoke to the same warden with whom I conversed three weeks ago. He waxed lyrical on the difficulties of 'accommodating so many good Christians.'

Dreadful graft practised by this man!

I had half a mind to complain to the curate, except I feared that he might be no less venal. Gave the warden a further shilling; if no result within a fortnight, I shall demand it back!

After some cogitation, I have decided about the MS. The title is to be *An Unfortunate Progress* and I shall first send it to *The Gentleman's Remembrancer.* This, I think, is a good place to begin. It is neither particularly well-known nor possesses a wide circulation outside of London. Yet the editor, a Mr. Filks, frankly solicits 'lively and intelligent contributions from our readers, on any subject,' which gives me some hope they will consider my literary endeavours; it would be folly to aim too high with the first shot. Will go to their office to-morrow.

Mama Willis, meanwhile, complains of Mary-Anne's slovenliness; says grate left dirty; floor not swept.

D. reluctantly reprimanded M-A and 'atmosphere' all afternoon.

Monday, 27th January

Lunch, then took the MS. to offices of *The Gentleman's Remembrancer*; small set of dusty chambers, situated in a court, off Fleet Street, near Dr. Johnson's House.

I had hoped to speak to editor himself but 'Mr. Filks at lunch'. Pondered whether to wait and risk Mr. Hibbert's disapproval. In the end, lost my nerve and left MS. with office-boy, who gave me his solemn word that it would receive his master's full attention in due course.

It is done! I have launched myself upon the literary ocean: let us hope I do not come crashing down upon the rocks!

Returned home to find Mama Willis sitting in the morning-room, engaged in some needle-work, admiring *our* new mirror. Says she finds the room most agreeable; that it has the best light for 'dainty stuff'.

My study quite lost to me!

Midnight. Astley's— to-morrow!

What am I to do?

Tuesday, 28th January

More domestic hostilities to begin the day.

Dora − still in her night things − confronted by her mother and informed that, whilst performing her morning duties, Mary-Anne had flicked coal-dust on the floor and blacked Mama W.'s new dress.

I pleaded the office and left the house, without breakfast. Instead, I took a coffee at the City Road stall, amongst a mixture of artisans, mechanics and clerks huddling round the braziers. It is a poor state of affairs when stopping for a 'warm' on the pavement is a more pleasant prospect than one's own breakfast table!

I found Fortesque already at his desk, and in full feather regarding our coming night at Astley's. I warned him that Dora was fatigued; and − falsely − that I had a bad head. He told me that 'Betsy would be awful cut up, if you didn't show' and said that she had even bought a new hat 'for the occasion'. We were interrupted by Mr. Hibbert and I did not commit myself one way or another. On leaving the office, however, F. very insistent that we should come. I felt a dreadful sense of obligation. I said that, all being well, he might expect us outside Astley's at eight.

An out-and-out lie!

I left the office at six, but felt rather disinclined to go home. I had no particular purpose, but loitered by the turnpike at Angel, watching various grand equipages pay their toll. Took some 'Dutch courage' in the saloon bar – which is decidedly <u>not</u> my custom – then went home just before seven. My fears about Amwell Street proved quite justified: for I came back to a dreadful scene – Dora in the drawing-room, almost in tears!

I immediately gave her a small glass of port to steady her nerves; and, at length, she recounted a positive litany of disasters:-

First had been the incident with the coal-dust. Mary-Anne had remained sullen and unrepentant all morning; and her apology to Mama W. was quite unconvincing, though the fault was plainly her own.

Second, Mama Willis had made a further accusation – a little after lunch – that her new bed-linen was damp. This was denied outright by Mary-Anne. Dora – my poor sweet innocent! – told me that she herself had examined the sheets and remarked to Mama W. that they *were* cold but hardly damp; and that, even if they were, they should soon dry.

This, of course, did not satisfy her.

The worst catastrophe, however, was yet to come. Mama W. retired to her room for an afternoon nap (the sheets having been changed) only to awaken to find *the corpse of a dead rat at the foot of her bed*. She swiftly became convinced that this was not simply the work of the cat, but a token of esteem from our own housemaid. She then hunted down Mary-Anne in the kitchen, accused her of perpetrating the outrage and *gave her notice*.

Dora – my poor wifey! – begged that I 'should not be too angry' and 'Mama meant for the best'.

My little D., of course, could no more countermand her mother's orders than a captain could be insubordinate to his general.

Must I record that I myself possessed no such inhibitions?

On hearing of these proceedings, I went directly to beard the lioness in her lair. I found Mama W. sitting in the morning-room where she had set up camp for the day. I asked what she meant by giving Mary-Anne *notice* when she was employed in *my* house; whether neither my wishes nor those of my wife counted for anything; whether she did not consider her own daughter capable of managing her own domestic economy, &c. &c.

She knew that she was quite in the wrong. She meekly conceded that she had 'no *practical* right, although perhaps a *moral* one' to discipline the girl; and that it should have been left to D. or myself. But – but! – she averred that she 'could not sleep' whilst 'such a diabolical creature was in her daughter's employ' and either Mary-Anne must go or she herself would quit the house.

I replied that I could not give the girl warning with no firm evidence of wrong-doing.

She said, did I not consider a *dead rat* to be evidence?

I weighed in that assuredly I did not; that it was most likely the cat's doing. Moreover, that I considered Mary-Anne had been treated in a shabby and peremptory fashion, and that, if the girl felt inclined to remain after such treatment, I felt *morally* obliged to give her a rise in her wages.

It was a palpable hit – never had I seen her face turn so sour, so quickly!

'Very well,' she replied, 'if you place the fine feelings of *your housemaid* above any respect you might possess for *me*, then I shall leave this very night.'

A threat! But I did not relent. Rather, I went straight to Mary-Anne and told her, to her astonishment and gratitude, that she might remain.

On my return downstairs, however, I found that Mama W. had already gone to her daughter and told her all. Dora was in much distress: would I not beg her mother's forgiveness? had there not been a misunderstanding? I confess, it disconcerted me to find that my little wifey took the side of her mama so readily.

I held my ground. I said there had <u>not</u> been any misunderstanding; that I was master in my own house; and that, if I had understood Mrs. Willis correctly – *Mrs.* mind you, for I now had a full head of steam – she would be requiring a cab.

Mama W. – utterly vanquished – retired from the field!

Dora, however, quite devastated. She had closed her mind to all rational discourse and been poisoned by her mother's arguments – 'still not too late to apologise' – 'everything could be made good' &c.

A 'jolly row' ensued. I fear even the neighbours may have heard it.

At all events, I did not recant; and since my wife found my opinions so uncongenial, I quit the house to 'take the air'. It is best to let heads cool after such heated exchanges.

Would that I had left it at that! I fear it was some spark of pure devilry that urged me on. For I caught a hansom on Pentonville Hill. I told the man –

No, I will write more to-morrow; I am far too tired. Must gather my thoughts. Doubtless all will seem better in the light of day.

One o'clock (a.m.). Wakeful. Tried brandy, to no avail. I fear sleep will be denied me.

I wonder, *did* Mary-Anne put the rat in dear Mama's room?

If so, she would rise in my estimation.

Wednesday, 29th January

Awoke with very bad head.

I should report that Mama Willis kept her promise and left last night. I do not regret taking a stand – anything else would have been unmanly. Dora herself now very subdued. She said at breakfast that she hoped I could 'make it up' with her mother, for 'Mama is very dear to me, even if her manner can be a trifle abrupt and unsettling.' I replied that I would give the matter full consideration, but that I could not – would not – be gainsayed under my own roof; and that I had been made to look a fool. Moreover, I said that the proper place of a wife, at least one deserving of the name, is at her husband's side, and not clutching her mother's skirts.

D. went very pale and quiet; but obliged to agree.

Enough!

Now – if I am to keep *my* word – I suppose I should write something more of what transpired after I quit Amwell Street. It is a tale in itself.

In short, I took a cab to Astley's to meet with Fortesque. I had no wish to wander the streets and required some distraction. It was, I think, an evil vexatious spirit which spurred me on.

Fortesque himself was in congenial, jovial mood; dressed in swell fashion with white Berlin gloves and an ostentatious jewel tie-pin. I soon recognised him amidst the crowds outside the building. He was accompanied by a young woman – perhaps a year or two older than D. – decked out *à la mode*, topped by a 'pork pie' hat with a feather that perpetually threatened to remove the eye of every passing stranger. Her features were, undoubtedly, uncommonly pleasing to the eye; but it is always ludicrous when girls of the milliner class ape the fashions of their betters – and the immense feather was, to borrow one of F.'s own phrases, *cutting it far too fat.*

I made excuses for D.'s absence, and was introduced to 'Elizabeth'(!). F. made no mention of that fact that I was wearing the same clothes I had worn at the office and spared me his usual wit. I should not be surprised, however, if he suspected some domestic disturbance. We then went directly inside, since F. had acquired box seats.

The boxes themselves were very good, with crimson hangings, plush chairs, seating two dozen persons. Half a dozen or so of the young men present, rakish sorts with a public-house swagger, seemed to know my two companions and exchanged knowing glances. I took them for University bucks, medical students or the like. The 'ladies' who accompanied them were definitely of the milliner and shop-girl variety. Not one of them possessed true grace or refinement, merely the splendid accoutrements of womanhood – dresses with fine lace flounces &c. – most likely made up by their own hands, in the small hours of the night, in the very mercantile establishments in which they toil for the benefit of others.

'Elizabeth' – no! I shall call her Betsy; I cannot bring myself to do otherwise – inquired 'how long have you and dear Billy been pals?' *Pals!* I told her that I had been in the office eight years and F. for two. She told me that 'he talks a good deal about you' and I returned the unlikely compliment. Then – thankfully – the first 'act' appeared.

Shall I hymn the delights of Astley's? The 'Eastern Imp' and his contortions; the pantomime performance of the clowns; the inevitable – the dismal – equestrienne and her flesh-coloured stockings, a display calculated only to appeal to a man's lowest instincts; the finalé of 'The British Fox Hunter' – a Spaniard, I'll wager, from his looks – perched astride two horses chasing *a live fox* three times around the ring. It is best to draw a veil. All these might, I suppose, provide some amusement to a youthful, uncultivated mind. It is no tribute, however, to the population of our great metropolis that such things can nightly 'draw' two thousand full-grown men and women. Betsy, meanwhile, proved quite 'game as anything', laughing at every tumble and acrobatic twist with ever-increasing vigour as Fortesque supplied her with champagne (at ridiculous expense – how can he afford such extravagance?).

I too indulged again in drink, perhaps a little too freely. It did nothing to lighten my mood.

I took my leave at ten o'clock or thereabouts, pleading a 'head'. I did not wish to linger. Fortesque shook my hand and, *sotto voce*, asked 'What do you make of her, then, old man?'

I *had* studied the girl all evening, since this was my avowed purpose.

Did I tell him that his beloved was a vain, commonplace little creature, so well-suited to her position in life that she could never rise above it?

No.

Did I tell him that – however beautiful – she could never be more than a mere ornament to a man's home; no better than an oil painting or piece of fine china? That all such blooms must fade; that she possessed nothing of the inner grace and spiritual beauty which are pre-requisites in a wife?

No, I did not.

Did I assert that *she* could no more manage a man's household economy, than I could perform the rapid evolutions of the 'Eastern Imp'?

No.

I said, rather, that he 'could not want for anyone better'. And I do not believe that I uttered a lie in this instance. For F. *is* quite blind to the mischief he will do himself, should he marry the girl; he seems quite incapable of understanding it.

No cabs to be had on the road outside. I walked back across Waterloo Bridge, still beset by black thoughts. It was, perhaps, a foolish hour to be walking abroad – at least, across the river – for the bridge, despite the toll, was infested by women of the lowest character. Several 'noticed' me; two of them all but bundled me back in the direction of Lambeth. I was obliged to raise my voice and mention the word – the magical incantation – that removes such nuisances in an instant – 'I will summon the police'.

'No need to come it so strong, my dear –'

'It's an honest mistake, eh? '

I determined not to slow my pace and take the first cab, but there were still none to be had. I kept walking, therefore, turning down along the Strand to Temple Bar. It was there, in the shadow of those ancient gates that I met with a strange coincidence.

The pavement was quite devoid of foot traffic but for two parties: a man and a girl, engaged in a heated argument. The man, whiskered, respectably dressed, had laid hold of the girl's wrists, and was attempting to drag her by main force away from the gloomy entrance. The girl, in turn, more shabby in appearance, violently resisted.

Such regrettable scenes are, of course, enacted nightly, on every thoroughfare in our great metropolis. But, on this occasion, I had cause to be astounded. For the girl before me was none other than the same female who had brought drink to my father's drink lodgings; the same 'Ellie' possessed of the dubious honour of his friendship and patronage.

What perverse Fate, I wondered, ensured that I should pass by at that very moment?

I composed myself and stepped forward; I could do little else. I asked the man what he was about. He was some ten years my senior; not powerfully built, but a little taller than myself. He immediately lambasted me, cursing my 'interference'.

I replied that any decent individual might 'interfere' on seeing a young woman so roughly handled. The man, despite his anger, much amused at this.

'This 'young woman' is a thief, *sir*. She has taken a shilling from me, on a shabby pretext. She is not a fit object for your chivalry.'

The girl protested.

'I ain't taken nothing and I don't want your shilling! I told you – I don't want nothing to do with you – leave me be!'

In fact, she now struggled so vigorously that the man was obliged to release her. Thwarted by my continued presence, plainly at a loss how to proceed, he swore an oath, abruptly turned on his heels, and strode briskly away. He paused only once, calling back over his shoulder, casting a contemptuous glance in my direction:

'I'd keep clear of that one, my good friend. She's not much to look at; and the game's not worth the candle!'

I did not demean myself by replying. It was plain from the man's words – indeed, from his manner – that it was not righteous anger that had motivated his actions, but an immoral purpose. The only question in my mind was whether his intended conquest was complicit.

What was I to do? I could not simply walk away. I inquired of the girl whether she was hurt – no, she did not think so – and if she knew me – yes, she said, although she had only just 'twigged it' as I stepped beneath the gaslight.

I asked what was the cause of the row. – 'I don't like to say.' – I pressed her; told her that she must.

'Perhaps you don't know it,' she said, with visible reluctance, 'but there's gentlemen who make it their business to bother a girl, if she's on her own; and promise her this and that for – well, I won't say – something in return. He kept at us all the way from Charing Cross. Only I never gave him no encouragement; not a word, I swear I didn't; but he wouldn't leave me be.'

Could this be the true story? I suggested that a girl on the street, alone, at such a late hour, might give an unfortunate impression.

'I can't help that, can I?' she replied. Moreover, she said it with such piteous, despairing exasperation that any doubts I had harboured, as to her own part in the affair, were at once removed. I asked her what had brought her to the Strand. She told me that she had had piece-work to deliver to her employer in Tothill Fields; that he would not wait until the morning; that she would not walk if she could do otherwise, but that she had to 'make shift for myself.'

I asked her where she was now going. – 'Back to my lodgings, in Whitecross Street.' – and she thanked me for my help and was about to recommence her journey.

I could not help but wonder whether she would not receive similar unwelcome attentions on the way. She replied that she 'didn't doubt it'; but that she had become accustomed to it and 'most of that sort of swell will take a hint, like, if you don't speak to 'em'.

I was immediately struck by her simple modesty and the stark contrast with the behaviour of the 'gentleman' who had molested her. I did, therefore, a foolish thing: I offered to accompany her home.

Why does a man's good sense take leave of him, when confronted with a young woman in distress?

I do not mean to imply that the girl's conduct belied my opinion of her. She accepted my offer with an unaffected gratitude; and she preserved a contemplative silence as we walked, only speaking when I made modest inquiries regarding her history and prospects.

Yet, such a risk!

What would anyone of my acquaintance have made of it – if I had been seen? Indeed, what might any stranger have thought? The disparity in our age; in our manner of dress; the lateness of the hour – all this could only lead to one unpleasant conclusion in the eyes of Society.

Yet nothing could be further from the truth. The girl even forbade me to walk further than Aldersgate, lest she be seen 'with a gentleman', since her landlady was 'most particular about her young women, and didn't want no nonsense.'

To think – when so many decry the morals of the poor – that a poor seamstress in Whitecross Street must be as Caesar's wife!

As to the girl's history, I learnt a good deal. Her proper name is Ellen Hungerford; she is sixteen years of age; resides with a 'Mrs. Bartholomew'. Her parents died 'of a bad fever, which took half of 'em in our court' almost two years ago. Her father lived in a large house in said court and let out rooms. It turned out, after his will was read, that he was merely a tenant and did not own the bricks and mortar. She has worked 'day and night' with her needle, ever since, for various masters.

'I can't see any way round it but to work, and work hard an' all.'

Poor little wretch!

As our talk drew to a close, I realised that she had made no mention whatsoever of my father. A remarkable tact for one so young. I could not, however, hold my tongue. I asked her, before we parted company, if she knew him well. She replied that she knew him 'well enough, I should suppose, on account of when he lodged with my pa'.

This, at least, sounded quite honest and frank, and did not support the boot-maker's gross suggestion of a closer attachment.

I then mentioned the boot-maker himself, and she conceded that she had been to his establishment 'cos your pa said he wanted the company; but I didn't much like it, nor the men and woman there, neither, and wouldn't go again.' I suggested that she might improve her own condition by improving her acquaintance; that a man who would take a mere girl to a gaming-house, might be a man whose friendship might best be shunned.

Her reply I shall now record *verbatim*, for I recall it all too well:-

'Well, I can't do that, sir, because your pa has been awful kind to me these last two years, with lending us money and all, and I reckon he ain't so bad as you think – exceptin' when he drinks too heavy.'

'Which is often enough.'

The girl gave me a knowing look. 'Would you think any better of him, sir, if I told you that he ain't hardly touched a drop since you last saw him?

I immediately replied that she did not know his full history; that such periods of abstinence were a mere prelude to renewed wanton indulgence.

'Well, that's as maybe,' she said, 'but since he started the church-going, I think your old man – begging your pardon, sir – I think he's changed his habits.'

Church-going!

On further questioning, she informed me that, only a day or two after I had paid my father's debt to the boot-maker, he had been reluctantly persuaded by a 'reverend' – one of the peripatetic sort of layman, who sets up shop on street-corners – to see Spurgeon preach his persuasive creed at the Metropolitan Tabernacle. Moreover, that, if not actually 'converted' by the experience, he had been driven to 'think on things pretty deep' and 'sign the pledge'. As a result, he had even managed to 'beg a favour from a friend of his' and find himself employment as a 'waterman' at a cab-stand.

And with that – quite convinced of my father's prospects for reformation – she bid me good-night.

Reform! The idea, of course, is quite risible. As for the promise of temperance, I can, even now, recall the veritable Bible of cards on the mantelpiece – each with their own worthy text – accumulated *each time* my father 'signed the pledge'. Moreover, what does a 'waterman' do, except to go in and out of the public-house, in order to provide beer for cabmen? The thought that my father could resist such temptation is quite ludicrous. For the girl's sake, however, I held my tongue.

I cannot help but find it remarkable that a mere girl – a harried specimen of young womanhood, honest and trusting, most likely doomed to spend her life in want and privation – can believe *him* a saint in the making. She even dared to suggest that, one day, I might 'pay the old man a visit and try to make things right between the pair of you'.

Woman – ever a creature of sentiment!

Of course, I shall not do anything of the sort. That road is too well-trodden; it leads only to misery.

Thursday, 30th January

I cannot abide the continued 'atmosphere' at home. Dora has said nothing more, but still v. subdued – hardly spoke at supper. I will write to Mama Willis at the weekend in terms of conciliation (if not apology). It is not congenial but something must be done.

Much thought regarding my father. I would do nothing for him; and much for the girl, Ellen. *She* displays many a good moral quality – honesty, loyalty, chastity – in primitive, unfledged and untutored form; but how can she retain them in his company? How long before he imposes on her trust and naiveté? She says he has been her 'friend' these last two years – that he has shown her kindness – but to what end?

Why should he cultivate her?

Is it a courtship? Is she to be his wife?

God forbid!

I could not voice such suspicions when we talked; it would have been indecent. Now they crowd in upon my mind. I can see no other explanation for his 'friendship'; it is not a quality he possesses in abundance.

What can I do? I possess no fortune; I can provide no money or position that might improve her lot; that might remove her from his influence.

Poor deluded creature!

I must banish her from my mind.

Saturday, 1st February

Today is a red-letter day!

I came home, a little before one o'clock, to find the good Dr. Antrobus quitting our front door. He plainly understood my concern, and assured me, in his customary laconic fashion, that 'nothing amiss – can't stop – you'd best speak to your wife'.

Astonished; found Dora in the drawing-room.

<u>I am to be a father!</u>

D. has known her condition – or, at least, suspected – since she spoke to Mrs. Antrobus, Thursday last. Mrs. A. possesses some experience of such things and diagnosed the signs instantly. She advised caution, however, until D. might be seen by a medical man, and volunteered her husband – *gratis!* – to confirm whether D. was *enceinte*.

The illness of the past fortnight is now explained!

My poor sweet D. has kept the secret – 'like a little treasure' she told me – these last seven days, not even admitting her mother into her confidence.

How dreadful, therefore, that we should have been at odds – much remorse!

She will write to Chelsea immediately; she cannot contain herself any longer. Now, at least, I suppose all will be forgiven and forgotten, in that quarter; and I am spared some personal difficulty in drafting a letter.

I must ask Mr. Hibbert if he will consider a modest advance in my salary. A child entails considerable expense.

CHAPTER FOUR

Inspector Delby glanced around the offices of the Crystal Palace Company, Moorgate. They were an ordinary affair, nothing like the magnificent public entertainment at Sydenham, whose profit and prosperity were their concern. There were no Florentine bas-reliefs upon the walls; no Byzantine mosaics on the floor. The offices were dry and dusty and lit by gas (a solitary sooty skylight admitting but little light) Their only 'historical curiosities' were a number of antique desks and bureaux, assigned to the more junior clerks. These were, moreover, articles whose age could be measured in decades, not millennia; and whose rusty hinges and ink-stained, scratched and pitted woodwork were an inconvenience, rather than a point of interest.

Delby estimated a staff of some twenty or so gentleman, young and old, crouched over books and papers, toiling in the studious gloom which is the lot of the London clerk. A few looked up from their work as the two policeman were ushered through the premises; most, however, kept their heads down.

'This way, sir, if you please.'

The inner office of Mr. William James Hibbert was more lavish in its furnishings. Here the gas shone bright, illuminating a mahogany desk, with a fine polish to the wood. Above a marble mantelpiece rested a painting of the Great Exhibition; on the floor below, a highly decorative Turkey carpet. In the centre, behind the desk, sat Mr. Hibbert himself: a comfortable, padded sort of gentleman, some sixty years of age, plump in the face, possessed of a respectable suit, and the habit of placing both thumbs in his waistcoat pockets.

He rose to greet his visitors.

'Very good of you to see us, sir,' said Delby. 'I expect you're curious to know why we're here.'

'I must admit, inspector, that I am a little concerned. I had a visit early this morning from a young constable, making inquiries regarding one of my employés who appears to have, well, vanished ...'

'Mr. Jones.'

'Indeed. I have been rather worried − it is quite out of character. And now I am visited by the Detective department. Whatever is the matter?'

'A good deal, sir, I'm afraid. I gather you've employed Mr. Jones here for a good few years?'

'Eight years, I should say,' replied Mr. Hibbert.

'What does he do, if I might inquire?'

'He is a senior clerk, with responsibility for share certificates and transfers. Has something happened to him?'

'Possibly; that's what we're attempting to establish. Did you – I should say, do you know him well?'

'As well as any of my men here.'

'And his wife?' said Delby.

'His wife? No, I regret to say that I have never had the pleasure of making her acquaintance. I am sure she is a charming young woman.'

'Was,' said Delby.

'Was?'

'I'm afraid we bring bad news. There is no pleasant way to give you the facts, sir. Mrs. Jones has been killed. Murdered; in her own home.'

'Good lord,' said Hibbert. 'How terrible.'

'As you can imagine, sir,' added Preston, 'we're very keen to talk to Mr. Jones, at the earliest opportunity. It's just that we can't lay our hands on him, at present. I don't suppose you have any idea where he might be?'

'Not at all. As I say, it is quite unlike him. But – his wife – now, surely you do not believe that he is capable of such an atrocity?'

'I wouldn't like to estimate the man's capabilities, sir, but I know that a young woman is dead; and that her husband has made himself rather scarce.'

Hibbert shook his head.

'I cannot – I will not believe that of Jones. He is a decent fellow; there must be some other explanation. I have personally placed a great deal of trust in him, and I have never been disappointed.'

'Is that so?' said Preston. 'How much do you know about the man's background, sir?'

'A good deal, as a matter of fact,' replied Hibbert, loftily. 'I would never employ a man without knowing something of his history.'

'Well, sir – anything you can tell us would be helpful. We haven't found too much, as yet, except that his father was far from respectable – an habitual drunkard and convicted felon.'

'I know that, my good man,' replied Hibbert. 'That is precisely why I hired his son.'

§

'I first came across young Mr. Jones,' said Hibbert, 'when he was no more than eighteen years of age. I was employed, at the time, as a broker on the Exchange and, once a week, I had the honour of giving a lecture at the Mechanic's Institute in Southampton Buildings.'

'I know the place,' said Delby.

'I spoke on *Funds and Leading Securities;* it was an introduction to matters of finance for the working man. I noticed a young fellow in the audience; who attended every lecture. He made a point of coming to talk to me, on several occasions, to elicit some particular fact, or confirm the answer to some question which he had formulated during my talk. It was plain to me that he had a lively mind; and a serious disposition. I made inquiries and discovered that he was to be found in the Institute's library almost every night, until it closed its doors; and often in the early morning, too.'

'This was the young Mr. Jones?'

'The very same. Clearly an earnest and hard-working fellow; something I found rather impressive in such a young man. Naturally, I congratulated him on his efforts to better himself and his dedication to the task.'

'And you offered him employment?'

'No, not at that time. I was not in a position to do so; but I gave him my card. I was pleased to learn, however, a few months later, that he had found a place at the London Joint Stock. He was little more than an office boy – but he had made a start in life. I felt sure he would do well. I believe I next came across him, quite by chance, outside the Exchange some three or four years later. He was dressed in a decent suit, silk hat; he told me that he had just been made a junior clerk.'

'He had done well for himself, then?'

'Indeed he had. A prime example of what, in these enlightened times, we would now call "Self-Help". You can, therefore, imagine my astonishment, when, only a few months later, I met him again on Cheapside, dressed in mere fustian. I assure you, inspector, you have never seen a man so deeply embarrassed; so terribly conscious of his appearance in the eyes of the world. He could barely look at me; I should think he would have avoided me entirely, if he had had the opportunity. It was clear that some dreadful reverse had taken place in his fortunes; but he would say no more than that he had lost his position, and was engaged as a waiter – a waiter! – at the nearby tavern. Now, inspector, I suppose another fellow might have left it at that; but my curiosity was piqued. So, shall I tell you what I did?'

'I can't imagine, sir.'

'I made discreet inquiries at the London Joint Stock. The long and short of it was that, a couple of months prior to his dismissal – for he was dismissed – Mr. Jones had prevailed upon the firm to take on his father. I do not know the precise details; it was a lowly position; but one in which the father was occasionally entrusted with the delivery of certain small sums of money.'

'Let me guess, sir,' interjected the sergeant. 'Mr. Jones senior was a thief.'

'He *was* a thief; but not a good one. Caught and convicted with in a month of commencing his new employment. Two years in Pentonville gaol. Mr. Jones, junior, also lost his place; and did not receive a character.'

'And this is when you first played a part in his career, sir?'

'Quite. I spoke to several persons at the bank. I felt sure that the boy had no part in his father's wrong-doing; and had suffered badly because of it. Indeed, why should a man on a decent wage – a man who had striven to raise himself up – implicate himself in such petty theft? I could find nothing to incriminate him; and a good deal in his favour. It turned out his father was a "reformed" drunkard. He had paid back the boy's ill-advised trust by stealing money to buy liquor and visit gaming-houses. I felt strongly that it was a dreadful shame to visit the sins of the father upon the son.'

'And so you offered him employment?'

'It was nothing; a small charitable gesture. The Company was but a year old; I put him on the lowliest rung of our commercial ladder, merely fifty pounds a year. I gave him six months' trial, and watched him closely. I was not disappointed. Never has a man worked harder to justify my good opinion. Indeed, you may take it from me, inspector: Mr. Jones is amongst the best of my employés, and has proved himself honest and reliable on every possible occasion.'

'You speak very highly of him, sir,' said the sergeant.

'I have every reason.'

'Can I ask,' said Delby, after a moment's silence, 'what is Mr. Jones's annual salary, at present?'

'I beg your pardon?'

'I have reason to think it may be significant,' said Delby.

'Well, I suppose there is no harm. It is a little over two hundred a year.'

'Forgive me, sir, replied Delby, 'I am not a man of business, but that is on the lower end of the scale, for a senior clerk?'

'We are not the Bank of England, sir,' said Hibbert.

'No, no. Of course not. Now – forgive me, again, I have various things I must ask – it will all become clear – am I right in thinking that Mr. Jones had a colleague here – a young gentleman named Fortesque?'

Mr. Hibbert's face darkened. 'Mr. Fortesque has left the company.'

'Of his own accord?'

'It is a sorry business. I am sure it can have no relevance to this dreadful … I mean to say, whatever has become of Mr. Jones.'

'Still, sir,' persisted the inspector, 'if you will humour me.'

'Very well. I asked Mr. Fortesque to leave.'

'On what grounds?'

'He had recently married,' said Hibbert, shifting a little uneasily in his seat. 'I discovered that his wife –'

Hibbert hesitated.

'You may speak frankly with us, sir,' urged the sergeant.

'Had loose morals,' said Hibbert.

'Ah, I see,' said Delby. 'Who brought that to your attention?'

'Mr. Jones. He informed me that he had seen the woman entering a house of infamous repute; moreover, that she was in the company of a man who was not her husband. Naturally, we had to let him go.'

'No question of further wrong-doing on Mr. Fortesque's part?'

'Not as such. But the Company has a reputation to preserve. It cannot allow such things to go unremarked.'

'I understand, sir. Reputation is everything.'

'Quite.'

'Unfortunately,' continued Delby, 'I fear you should have kept an even tighter rein on your employés.'

'Whatever do you mean?' asked Hibbert.

'I'm afraid, sir, I have some further bad news for you. We found in Mr. Jones's house a diary; a rather revealing and confidential document, if I may say so. It brings to light some rather unfortunate facts, which I'll wager you won't be too happy to hear. Tell me, is there a telegraph office near at hand?'

'Not ten yards down the street,' replied Hibbert, perplexed. 'But why do you ask?'

'Because I think, Mr. Hibbert, if you're at all concerned about the reputation of the Crystal Palace Company, you had better contact your directors.'

§

The two policemen walked out onto Moorgate.

'I believe our Mr. Hibbert was rather shocked,' said Preston.

'It serves him right,' replied Delby. 'The man's a humbug. He kept down Jones's salary, even when he moved up the firm, knowing he couldn't go anywhere else.'

'It all adds up, don't it, sir? Fortesque – the diary –'

'If you say so, sergeant; I am not so readily convinced.'

DIARY

Sunday, 2ⁿᵈ February

To church.

Discovered that my shilling had done its work; the warden, all smiles and servility, placed us in seats in the gallery. This will now be our spot, with a good view of the pulpit. The sermon rather good, entitled *Our Hope and Faith*.

Dora herself still 'a little seedy'. It was, I fear, most unwise to conceal her condition from me, even though her intention was to spare me any anxiety. The mental strain has robbed her of a good deal of nervous energy that might otherwise have been conserved. Her condition not helped by the fact that Mary-Anne returned late from her half-day – yet again! She had been 'out walking by the canal and got lost'.

Is this behaviour an unfortunate consequence of the argument with Mama Willis? Have I given Mary-Anne the impression that she is invaluable to us?

If so, I must disabuse her of the notion.

Monday, 3ʳᵈ February

Dora in better health.

At breakfast, we talked about 'our little guest' and she informed me that she would 'very much like a girl – to begin our family, at least'. I replied that I would not object to either sex, albeit that I expected that I should better understand the moods and tempers of a boy, and be better equipped to contribute to his rearing and management. D. suggested, however, that girls are less wilful and more susceptible to moral influence; and doubtless there is a degree of truth in this. Then came much amusing discussion on the subject of heredity. D. most flattering as to the particulars of my own appearance that she would want a boy to inherit. I replied that there were no qualities – mental or physical – in my dear wife which I would not wish for in my daughter.

Received a kiss!

It occurs to me as I write this – gloomy thought! – that a girl might be preferable. For, if I consider the question of heredity in its true light, then I am put in mind of my father, and all that has rendered him hateful to me. I have not inherited his weakness of character; but if there is any moral stain that passes from generation to generation, visible and active in some, passive and invisible in others, I should not wish to discover it in my own son.

Another 'family' matter: a letter from Chelsea. We are to expect a visit from dear Mama and Papa Willis. I must effect a reconciliation. Talked to D.; she remarked, in the course of our conversation, that it was 'such a shame' that neither of *my* parents had lived long enough to celebrate our marriage or its issue.

Yes – it is a 'shame' – no doubt of that!

Tuesday, 4th February

Dined at Gilroy's, alone. Fortesque has grown friendly with a young broker whom he met at the

Holborn Casino and has taken to lunching with him. I suspect he is attempting to ingratiate himself, in order to obtain a more lucrative position on the Exchange. It is a useless endeavour – he has neither the money nor the connections which might win him favour with City men.

In the afternoon, I sought an interview with Mr. Hibbert. I told him of my changed domestic circumstances; outlined my position as regards the new house &c. and asked him whether he might consider an increase in my remuneration. He offered me warm heartfelt congratulations and we drank a small glass of claret. As a result of my request, my salary will increase by six pounds pa., from the first of July.

It is not as much as I might have liked; but I am grateful to him.

Told Fortesque everything before I left the office; *his* good wishes couched in the most vulgar form. Dreadful! If he cannot raise his mind above the gutter, then even the little milliner is too good for him.

Mama and Papa Willis in the drawing-room when I returned home; their carriage waiting outside. Poor D., most anxious; all but wringing her hands! Papa W., however, had clearly prepared a speech – I recognised the peculiar posture of puffed-up self-importance which he adopts on such occasions, like a little cock robin – and he began by 'congratulating you, sir, on the commencement of a family, the finest institution ever blessed by God and man …' (there was a good deal more of this flummery) and finished with, 'I trust that any trivial misunderstandings which may have arisen between us, this last week or two, will now be placed in the proper perspective, and put aside'. Very dark looks from Mama Willis throughout! I replied that I was very sorry for *all that had occurred* during Mama W.'s stay; that I was *sure I would not want any awkwardness to arise between us.*

Such diplomacy!

Nothing more was required of me. A silent truce called on both sides, with immediate effect. Mama and Papa, however, despite Dora's entreaties, did not stay to dine, pleading a prior engagement.

One unfortunate consequence of Dora's condition is that we are bound to see more of them. Let us hope we can maintain our ceasefire.

Wednesday, 5th February

Dora now in good health; she has not felt 'off' since Sunday; it is cheering to see her quite recovered.

It occurred to me at dinner that I have put all thoughts of my MS. out of my mind. Such are the cares of a *paterfamilias!*

Nonetheless, I had expected to have received a letter; it has been a full week.

I shall write to Mr. Filks to-morrow.

Thursday, 6ᵗʰ February

Two items of post received this evening, both worthy of my pen, though for quite different reasons:—

The first was a letter from Mrs. Antrobus, inquiring after Dora's health, hoping that she is not feeling too delicate, and requesting our company at dinner on the 15ᵗʰ inst. Naturally, we shall accept.

The second letter appeared whilst we were at dinner and was delivered in a most mysterious and unconventional fashion, abandoned half way down the area steps! It was not noticed until Mrs. Galton quit the house. Mary Anne brought it up into the study for my attention: a rather shabby-looking envelope, blacked with various smudges, bearing the words 'MR JONES – PRIVATE' in uneven capitals.

I dismissed her and turned it over in my hands. It was not my father's writing. Was it, I wondered, the wretched boot-maker? Had my father broken his word and given him my address?

Inside I discovered a brief note, written in a poor hand.

Whitecross Street
5ᵗʰ Febary

    Dear Sir,

       This letter is to thank you for all your kind words and goodness; I will say nothing of it to nobody. I also wish to tell you, seeing how I wish I had done, that a certain party is waterman for the cabstand at the Cross Keys, Snow Hill, if you had a mind to go

see him there. He is not so bad a man as you reckon,
much better, and I know he will think a lot of it, and it
will do him good, if you do it and make peace. I hope
this finds you in good health, and good wishes,

E.

In short – a letter (of sorts!) in my father's defence,
from Miss Ellen Hungerford.

On reading it, I was both infuriated with the girl
– to naively expose me to such risk – the chance of
Dora reading her note – the misconstruction that
might be so easily placed upon its contents – the
gossip of the servants – and utterly astonished at
her devotion to my father's welfare. For she must
have come to the house herself and timidly placed
the envelope on the steps, too fearful to approach the
front door.

Of course, I realise now that it was foolish to be
annoyed. Doubtless, she is quite unable to foresee the
possible consequences of her action; nor contemplate
the invidious position in which she has placed me.

But what if she should write again; or appear in
person?

I can hardly begin a private correspondence with
her, no matter how harmless our actual relation. Nor
do I wish to parade about Whitecross Street.

Yet, something must be done; she <u>must not</u> come
to the house again.

One o'clock (a.m.). I have given the question a good
deal of thought. To seek the girl out – or to write to
her – would only expose me to the very risk – the

appearance of some unfortunate intimacy – which I wish to avoid.

I must, therefore, speak to my father.

Friday, 7th February

Bitterly cold day; rain in afternoon.

Worked diligently, but the letter from Ellen Hungerford weighed heavily on my mind. Indeed, I had planned, on quitting the office, to walk to Amwell Street *via* Snow Hill, but – feeling terribly cold – abandoned the idea and went home.

Dora had bought a new hat: white felt, trimmed with black velvet and ostrich feathers. She told me that she 'needed a new one for our dinner next Saturday'. Asked my opinion, I said I did not much care for the fashion; and that, to a mere masculine intelligence, the sacrifice of ten shillings for the sake of an article that would be removed at the front door seemed a peculiar extravagance.

I did *not* add 'and it recalls to mind a pretty, stupid young milliner, whom I met the other week, at Astley's'!

She will take it back.

Mary-Anne, meanwhile, is complaining of an odour in the kitchen and muttering darkly about 'drains'. Neither myself nor Dora can detect it. Let us hope she is mistaken – we cannot risk D.'s health.

I must steel myself and seek out my father to-morrow; come what may.

Saturday, 8th February

More bad weather; dreadful cold wind.

Held firm to my resolution, although obliged to work late into the afternoon: quit the office at five and walked directly to Snow Hill. It had already grown dark and I could not see my father in the vicinity of the Cross Keys, a poor-looking pot-house; nor was there a single cab waiting. The 'stand' itself was visible, albeit no more than a spot beneath a pair of gas-lamps, where straw had been piled and several large tubs of water were ready for the horses. I briefly entertained the notion of going inside the pot-house and making inquiries; but the chance of encountering my father, in his cups, surrounded by fellow 'lushingtons,' brought back too many painful recollections. I resolved, therefore, to wait to see if he might 'turn up' at his post. A quiet little coffee-house, respectable enough, was situated on the opposite corner. I took a seat by the window and kept my eye upon the road.

I had not long to wait. He emerged from the public bar some five minutes later, just as two cabs of the 'growler' type drew up by the twin lamps. I had intended to go directly and speak to him. In fact, I remained in the coffee-house for half an hour or more, watching him all the while. I had <u>not</u> intended to play the part of a spy. I can only say that it was a queer thing to observe him there, unseen; I fear it exerted a peculiar fascination.

I had, of course, expected to find him in his usual condition of intoxication. Yet he did not possess the lumbering, loose-limbed gait which marks an out-and-out drunk. At the very least, I had anticipated that he would 'share a drop' with the cabmen – but he did not partake. Rather, he performed his humble duties – the distribution of straw and water to the horses, the provision of tobacco and liquor to the men – with a remarkable urgency and efficiency. The faces of the half dozen men for whom he called up a cab also told an unfamiliar story: none were stirred into pity or revulsion; all was good nature and good humour. Thus I lingered in the coffee-house much longer than I had planned. The greatest surprise came when I finally stepped outside to meet him *and there was no stink of liquor on his breath.*

He met me with a smile and outstretched hand, which I reluctantly accepted.

'My boy! What a strange chance to see you here!'

I did not claim it was mere coincidence; I told him of my informant and how she would have me 'make peace'.

'Ah, that was wrong of her, dear boy,' he replied, shaking his head. 'You're not to be troubled; I've made that plain to her. But she's such a sentimental little thing; she has her own fancies about how such things should be between a father and son. I wondered why she was asking after where you lived in Islington – though I never had an inkling, on my honour!'

I told him that I would not speak of his 'honour'; and that I understood he had 'taken the pledge'. I did not say 'again' (though it took all my self-restraint). He understood me well enough.

'You're right to doubt it, my boy. You've got good cause. I have done it, though, and I'll stick to my guns this time around – mark my words.'

'In the event you are sober, and still employed here, a month from now, I might believe it.'

'There!' he exclaimed. 'There! You have said it, my boy! I shall prove it to you; one month from today!'

'I would rather,' I returned, 'that you merely told the girl that she must not interfere in my affairs.'

'She doesn't mean any harm, my boy.'

I told him that, by writing to me in such a fashion – so liable to induce suspicion – that she could only do me harm; that, if he himself had any gratitude for my recent kindness, he would tell her never to write to me again and impress upon her that any reconciliation between us two was quite beyond question.

His answer was both unexpected and unwelcome,

'Really, my boy? Not even if a month from now – I mean I should like it if –'

Then he hesitated; he must have seen the look upon my face. He might well falter! To think that, standing amidst the mud and muck, he fancied that a simple test of will – a month's sobriety – might stoke the some familial feeling in my breast! The very sentiments which he has quashed, by his every word and deed, since the day I was born!

It was only the arrival of a hackney that prevented me from speaking my mind.

'This gentleman wanting a cab, Georgie?' called out the driver.

I said that I did. To play my part, I even pushed the customary penny into my father's hand.

A mark of how low he has sunk – a man once considered, long ago, a 'gentleman' – that he accepted it with gratitude.

I have done what I can.

I can only hope I hear no more from the girl.

Midnight. I cannot sleep. Will try brandy.

Half past Midnight. The brandy is no use. It is some perverse freak of conscience that keeps me from sleep. I have neglected the final part of my account. I am loathe to write it; but I suppose I must and then I may rest.

On the journey home, I asked the cabmen if he 'knew the old man at the stand'. I had a mind to quiz him about my father. He said that he'd 'known him a month or so'. I said that I expected such fellows were bad sorts; very partial to drink. He replied that *they were, as a rule, but he'd never known him touch a drop, even when he'd been stood a glass.*

I have been proved wrong. I must admit it to myself. He has taken the pledge; and stuck to it, for longer than I have known before.

Of course, it will not last. He will begin again, his wretched thirst redoubled.

Then he will drag the poor confiding girl down with him.

Sunday, 9th February

An unfortunate start to the day.

Mary-Anne asked her mistress whether her half-day (not due for another week) might be 'brought forward', on account of 'visiting a sick relation'. Dora immediately suspected an untruth, both from the girl's demeanour and that fact that she had never heard anything of the relative in question. (Mary-Anne is given to reporting every item of uninteresting gossip regarding her family, former acquaintances and such like). She informed Mary-Anne, therefore, that we could not allow such a lax arrangement.

'Mightn't the master not agree to it, though –'

D. 'regularly flummoxed' (as Fortesque would have it) by such impertinence and came directly to me. For here was proof of the very difficulty I had suspected; that the girl had come to consider herself beyond reproach.

I immediately went downstairs and spoke to her in the strongest terms, such that there might be no mistaking the proper relation between master and servant. I informed her that few other employers would permit two half-days per month; that she was paid amply for her work; that if she found her situation unsuited to the demands placed upon her by her family, she might look elsewhere.

This, I think, served to remove any complacency; for she came to church with a quiet penitence never before witnessed.

Perhaps now we may manage a few days of domestic harmony!

Spoke to Dr. and Mrs. Antrobus outside the church; also saw two other 'acquaintances' amongst the general congregation: namely, two of the uncouth journeymen who papered our hall.

One raised his hat to me. Doubtless they hope for more work.

Tuesday, 11th February

A reply from Mr. Filks in the morning post.

I confess, a disappointment. It acknowledges receipt of the MS. 'with warm thanks for your choosing *The Gent.* [sic!] as the receptacle for your literary ebullitions' but concludes 'I am obliged to report that "our cup runneth over" at present, with the effervescence of several dozen lively young minds, all awaiting our consideration, your own piece amongst them,' and that 'we are unable to provide a more *satisfactory* reply until we have had opportunity to read them all, in their entirety'.

It is a courteous response; I am sure it is nothing less than the truth.

Still, it *is* rather *unsatisfactory*.

It seems I must wait!

Thursday, 13th February

Fortesque is an utter fool.

He informed me before lunch – most grave and serious – that he has decided to 'take the plunge and ask Betsy for her hand' and that he will do it to-morrow, on Valentine's day, 'seeing as how I can't think of a better time to hook a girl'. I did not attempt to dissuade him (it would be a vain effort) but counselled a long engagement. In turn, he confessed that his own father hadn't 'taken too strong' to his intended; that he planned to keep the engagement a secret from his family and 'get hitched just as soon as I can get the licence.'

The folly of youth!

He will enter into this terrible engagement because the day of the year is 'propitious'.

Then he will eschew the reading of banns – and any opportunity for sober reflection – simply to spite his father!

His only hope of future happiness is that the girl may refuse him; an unlikely outcome. How much misery in the world is caused by such poor matches; and how fortunate am I?

Mindful of this, after I quit the office, I went to Rimmel's, Cornhill, and bought a perfumed, illustrated "Sweetheart" for Dora's valentine (2s.).

Friday, 14th February

It has been a day of terrible embarrassments, which I shall not look back upon with much pleasure.

The day began well enough. I awoke at six and gave much thought to my 'secret' delivery of Dora's valentine. In the end, I placed it discreetly upon the dining-room mantelpiece, so that it might be noticed at breakfast. I soon realised, however, that I had been too discreet – D. did *not* notice it. I was, therefore, obliged to drop hints ('Had there been any post yet?' &c.) until I could no longer contain myself and said, quite plainly, that there 'might be something for you, on the mantelpiece, that came *very early*'. D. expressed surprise; and, I am pleased to say, upon finding the valentine, blushed exquisitely. I could tell she was most pleased; and we had a very droll exchange about her 'admirer'.

I *did* wonder whether a reciprocal token of affection had been cleverly hidden by my wife; indeed, I felt sure it must. This self-conceit, however, was my undoing and the cause of the day's first disaster. For, just before I quit the house, I chanced upon Mary-Anne in the hall, and noticed an envelope in the pocket of her apron.

'I expect that is for me?' I said, in a confidential tone.

She pulled out the envelope – bearing the tell-tale decoration of a heart – as if it had somehow fallen there by accident, without her knowledge. Foolishly, I took her stammering and confusion to mean that she had been caught out, instructed by D. to conceal a card in some suitable place. Ignoring her protests, I snatched it from her fingers with an mock exclamation of triumph.

Imagine my consternation, therefore, to discover a 'comic' valentine, featuring a fisherman, a mermaid entangled in his nets, and a verse commencing 'If you were a fish …'!

Then to realise that the card was addressed, *"To M.A."*

I could not help but wonder who might be author of this dubious compliment (a juvenile prank by the butcher's boy or his ilk?). I restrained myself, however, and merely remarked that *I had obviously been mistaken.*

Mary-Anne, of course, turned *Bright* crimson.

I hurried to the office, thoroughly chastened by the encounter. There was much talk, amongst the juniors, of *their* cards (F. still bent upon his proposal – the poor wretch!) and little in the way of work. I returned home at the usual hour. Awaiting me on the hall table was a single item of post, addressed to 'Mr. Jones'.

This, I felt certain, was *my* valentine!

The content of the envelope – which had been cunningly sent by penny post – was a card, a woman's face in silhouette, surrounded by powder blue lace. It bore the verse:-

To thee my heart
Beats with
Affectionate Passion.

I went straight to Dora; I showed her the card and said that I, too, could muster 'a single admirer'; that 'my many gifts were not wholly unappreciated by womankind,' &c. &c. Indeed, I gave her much good-natured chaff, of the sort in which we had both indulged earlier in the day. She, however, seemed to find less humour in our shared joke. It was only after dinner – when we sat together by the fire – that I discovered the truth of the matter. I noticed that she had made no progress with her needle; and that, every now and then, she rubbed her eyes, as though attempting to dispel a tear. I begged her to confide in me and, though she refused at first, she finally relented.

'I know it's silly, my dear,' she said, 'but I did not send that card.'

Thus my poor sweet dear wifey – blameless creature! – had kept a solemn silence, throughout the evening, yet all the while feared that her husband was the object of another's affection! She confessed that she had forgotten the day entirely – quite natural, given the interesting condition that preoccupies her mind – and had not thought I would appreciate a belated token of her esteem.

I reassured her that the card was, most likely, the work of the same juvenile mind that had resolved to torment Mary Anne; that I had not given any woman, with the single exception of my wife, any cause to address me in such extravagant terms; that I trusted she could not doubt my devotion.

It was, however, only when I threw the offending item into the fire, that her nervous equilibrium was restored; and only my sworn oath – that we shall never again celebrate the festival, even in jest – that regained her good humour.

What moral is to be drawn here?

That the amatory instinct – at least, in the female – is not to be trifled with; indeed, that we might do better to do away with 'St. Valentine' altogether!

I cannot conceive who might have played such a trick.

Saturday, 15ᵗʰ February

Dined with the Antrobuses, eight o'clock.

Discovered, too late to express my disapproval, that Dora had not returned *the hat*, an article which soon entailed much ridiculous fussing concerning its application, and all sorts of difficulties regarding its removal.

The vanity of the sex!

The complement of other guests was the same as for St. James's Hall; namely Mr. & Mrs. Wynne-Smith, Mr. Poulford and Mr. Taunton. Introductions were made, for Dora's sake; then we proceeded downstairs to dine. The meal itself was perfection: Palestine soup; red mullet; sweetbread cutlets; roast fillet of veal; plum pudding, ices; also, good sherry and port; and a man in livery to wait on the table (hired for the occasion).

I cannot claim that the conversation transcended the commonplace, though it was lively enough and entertaining. Mr. Antrobus becomes no more garrulous after a hearty repast, or a glass of port; Mr. Wynne-Smith, on the other hand, rather inclined to lawyers' gossip, the sort of thing which means little to one unfamiliar with the Inns. Mrs. Antrobus, naturally, discoursed a good deal; but on what topics, I find myself quite unable to recollect, with the exception of some talk of planning a journey to Sydenham. For Mr. Antrobus claims never to have visited the Crystal Palace, neither during the Exhibition or at Sydenham (I had thought no such a man existed in all of London!). I ventured that, if it suited them to travel by rail, I could easily obtain seats for a small party in our Directors' coach.

Mr. Poulford and Mr. Taunton, meanwhile, said little in the ladies' company; one suspects that the nephew's visits to his uncle are performed more out of duty than love. Both became a little more animated when we men absented ourselves for cigars. Taunton once more recounted his speculation in property (tedious). Poulford, on the other hand, was inclined to discuss the 'Extraordinary Disappearance of a Lady' reported in this morning's *Times*. I have read the article since returning home and it seems to me an utter nonsense. The suggestion that a young woman was rendered insensible on the railway, at some point between King's Cross and Leeds, by the use of chloroform – and then abstracted from the train, together with her luggage, without her assailants garnering the slightest notice – too incredible to be believed. This, however, did nothing to stop Mr. Poulford lecturing us on the various practical uses of the drug, with considerable fervour, for some ten minutes. (It is a fine thing for a young man to display the fruits of his *knowledge*; it would be *wisdom*, however, on occasion, to keep them hidden)

We came home at eleven; I remarked to D. that the evening had gone well. She agreed but then added that she 'did wish Mrs. Antrobus might have something in her house that was not quite perfect'. I asked what she meant by such a comment; it seemed somewhat mean-spirited, after we had been treated so well. She explained that, should we reciprocate – as we ought – we are, at present, 'quite at a disadvantage' in every particular of glass, china and plate that might be required. I suggested that we possessed nothing of which we should be ashamed; she informed me that I was 'a *man*,' and possessed of 'not the slightest idea.'

I do have, however, a good idea of the expense of new glass, china and plate.

A very pleasant evening, nonetheless. It gratifies me immensely that we are mixing in good society.

Sunday, 16th February

To church.

The sermon, *On the Felicities of Scripture*, not to my liking; doubtless very *deep* but I could not penetrate it.

Mary-Anne all but ran from the house at the stroke of midday. We have heard nothing more of the 'sick relation' – plainly nothing more than the flimsiest pretext. Dora suspects that she has acquired a 'young man'. For my part, I cannot imagine what aspect of our maid's character or appearance could engender a romantic entanglement. She did, at least, return home in good time. When she brought tea to the study, I took the precaution of reminding her that we took an interest in her moral welfare, and that we both hoped there was nothing in her Sunday outings to which a respectable person might take exception.

She assured me that there was not, although her manner was rather impertinent. I could hardly say more on the subject.

For tuppence I would give the girl her notice.

Midnight. A dreadful turn of events, which has so disturbed my mental equilibrium that I feel obliged to take up my pen.

I had not intended to write of it until to-morrow; yet I cannot find sleep. I find myself in need of a confidant, even if it is only the mirror of my own conscience.

<u>My father</u>, of course, is once more the cause of my misery; it has ever been thus and I shall never shake myself free of him. I shall only find peace when he has paid the debt of nature; and yet – what hope of that? He seems to possess a terrible resilience.

Enough. I shall merely record the facts of the matter.

It was a little after half past ten this very evening, that we heard the door-bell. I accompanied Mary-Anne, as the hour was so late – Dora already in bed – and no visitor was expected. We were met by a <u>police constable</u> who inquired after 'Mr. Jacob Jones'. I dismissed Mary-Anne and ushered the constable into the dining-room.

I had a fairly good idea of what I might learn, before a word was spoken; and I was not proved far wrong.

My father – it transpired – had been arrested outside the Wheatsheaf public-house, Goswell Road, two hours previously, for an assault on the person of one William Halifax ('a boot-maker of Greek Street, Soho'). Awaiting the magistrate, he had prevailed upon the sergeant at Old Street station-house that a certain 'respectable gentleman' of Amwell Street, Islington, would *vouch for his good character.*

Did I, therefore, wish to attend the police-court in the morning, and say something in his favour?

I did not inquire as to the nature or cause of the argument; doubtless another bad debt. Indeed, it was plain to me that the request for my presence in court was a flimsy pretext to obtain my the attendance of my wallet!

The policeman demanded an answer and so I gave him one. Namely, that Mr. George Jones *was* a relation of mine; but that I had no wish to vouch for his character. Moreover, that I would be *unable* to do so – since I knew him as a confirmed drunkard, who had all but beaten his own wife to death, and had been gaoled on half a dozen occasions.

The constable, much embarrassed, thanked me for my time, and left.

To think, that he would have me stand before a magistrate! Such gross presumption!

Indeed, why should his past crimes go unnoticed? With luck, the constable will report my remarks; and then he will be committed for a month or two; perhaps for longer. At least, then, I shall know a modicum of peace.

I told Dora – who had risen from her bed – that the man had come concerning Fortesque. I could think of no better excuse; for I have mentioned *his* errant behaviour to her on many occasions. I said that it was F. who had be involved in some trivial *fracas*, and who had asked me to speak for his character at the police-court.

'Will you do it?' she asked.

I told her that a man must pay the price of his own actions; that I would not be his nurse-maid.

She said nothing; I am sure she thought me too hard.

Of course, she does not know the circumstances in which my own character was forged.

If she did, then she would think me a saint.

Monday, 17th February

I slept but fitfully during the night.

It was, perhaps, a measure of my mental abstraction that, performing my toilet, I nicked my chin with the blade of my razor, utterly ruined my shirt, then proceeded to knock over my shaving water. I then spoke harshly to Mary-Anne, who made a clumsy business of cleaning up the spill.

Quit the house at eight o'clock.

I found the City Road busy as ever, awash with the early morning tide of clerks and artisans. It is not uncommon for females to mingle with this crowd of working men: some are the wives of the artisan or mechanic class, despatched upon particular errands; others are flower-girls, match-sellers and the like. As I crossed the canal bridge, one young woman hurried up to me. I instinctively assumed that it was one of the latter tribe and I had ready my customary word of reproof. It was only when her hand rested lightly on my arm that I realised it was none other than Ellen Hungerford.

'May I speak with you, sir?'

I was immediately conscious that she must have been following me – from Amwell Street! – with all the dangers that implied. Yet my anger was assuaged by the realisation that her shawl, wrapped tight around her head, served to partially conceal a black eye. My father, I felt sure, had given it to her in the same drunken fit during which he had set upon the boot-maker. I felt a twinge of sympathy but maintained my steady pace.

'If you'd only listen a moment ...' &c.

She spoke a few words; and I swiftly gathered that she had come to plead for my interference in my father's case. I told her plainly that nothing would modify my opinion of a man, if he deserved the name, who could set about a young woman with his fists; that it was a peculiar weakness, all too common in the female, to forgive and forget such abuse far too readily, to blame 'the drink' (dread recollections of my mother!). This, however, seemed to perplex her greatly, until she came to a sudden realisation.

'Oh, Lord! This?' she said, touching her face. 'No, you don't know nothing. It weren't your pa – he ain't so much as sniffed a drink – it weren't his fault at all ...'

I had already resolved to terminate our interview but there was something so pathetic and urgent in this plea, that I drew the girl to one side, and listened to her story. I cannot account for it; I suppose that I felt a degree of pity.

I will try to recall our conversation in full –

'He ain't been drinking, sir,' she said, with great emphasis. 'I'd know if he had.'

'Then how have you suffered that injury' – she self-consciously raised her hand to her brow, as if to shield her bruises from my view – 'and why is he before the magistrate?'

"Cos of me, sir.'

I could not fathom her meaning, though she seemed somehow ashamed of herself.

'You?'

'Well, it ain't my fault, in one way of looking at it; but I suppose it is me. You know Mr. Halifax, what he owed the money?'

'Of course; he has my three pounds; and I gather he is the man my father has assaulted.'

'Well, he is that,' she admitted, 'but there's things you don't know, sir.'

'What do you mean?'

A delicate colour suffusing the girl's cheeks. She spoke hurriedly, nerves in her voice.

'I saw him – Halifax, I mean – last week. I was in town and he followed us and we got to talking. He said he'd taken a fancy to me, that time your pa lost his money; that he couldn't "shake me out of his head." I remember him saying those words particular; I didn't like 'em much.'

I could not help but recall the words the boot-maker addressed to me.

I know a few highly respectable gents who'd pay good money–

'You know that such men are to be avoided. We have spoken of it.'

'Just! Only he kept pestering us, see? He knew where I lived, and all, though I don't know who told

him. He turned up and starting waiting for me —
there on the street — three days in a row. Your pa
walked me home one evening; your pa told him to go
hang, but he wouldn't have it. And then, Saturday
night, when I got back to my lodgings, he was in my
room. He'd told the deputy that he was my cousin —
probably given her a couple of shillings an' all — and
she'd let him wait.'

The girl's voice faltered as she spoke. It seemed
indecent to ask the question; and yet, I was sure, she
wished to place me in her confidence.

'What happened between you?'

'He kissed me,' she said, her repugnance quite
audible, 'before I had the chance to say anything. I
didn't want him to. Then he said all sorts; foul things,
I won't say 'em out loud. Then he tried to —'

I told her that there was no need to say the words;
that I understood her meaning too well.

'But I wouldn't have none of it, see? I fought him,
though I never knew I could fight a man so hard; and
I screamed. I kicked up such a fuss that the deputy
came to the door and said she'd call the police, if he
didn't hook it. And that's when he gave me this.'

She gestured shyly towards the bruise on her face,
wincing at the memory of it; acutely conscious, of the
temporary disfigurement of her features. I asked her
what this had to do with my father's imprisonment.

'He got all fired up. I never seen him so angry. He
said it was his own doing; that he should never have
taken me to the man's house. Then I had to tell him
that I'd lost my lodgings and all.'

(I expressed incredulity at this. But I was informed that the landlord's deputy had pondered the matter and decided that she 'did not want such goings on in a respectable house' and had summarily evicted her tenant. Such admirable discretion!)

'Anyhow, your pa went out looking for Halifax; and he knew where to find him. He hit him, too – I ain't denying *that*, everyone saw it – but a Peeler saw it happen, and nabbed him before anything had got started. I s'pose it's better for him he *was* nabbed. Halifax would have done for him.'

I said nothing, lost in thought. The girl, however, tried to take my arm.

'Don't you see, sir? Your pa weren't to blame, was he? Not really. Won't you go to the magistrate? It's only St. Luke's – it ain't too far to go, is it?'

I weighed it up in my mind. All the while, the girl's eyes pleaded with me. I thought of my own encounter with the odious boot-maker, and how I myself had yearned to strike him down.

'Won't you go, sir? They'll start the hearings at ten o'clock.'

'You might bring a charge against Halifax yourself,' I suggested.

The girl positively cringed at the idea. 'Not me, sir. He'd do for me. Your pa won't say nothing against him, neither, not in court; he wouldn't dare.'

'Then – if everyone is so afraid of this man – what can I do?'

'I don't know – whatever you can, sir.'

I yielded to her entreaties; I could not resist. I said that I could talk with her no longer – I was already late for my work – but would attend the court. In turn, she thanked me with such genuine warmth and sincerity that I recalled with some regret my own unsparing words to the policeman the previous night, and wondered if they might somehow be undone.

Thus began the day!

I am too tired to write more; it will have to be to-morrow.

Tuesday, 18ᵗʰ February

I still find myself utterly confounded by the events of yesterday, though I have now had ample time to contemplate the folly of my actions.

In any case – to continue my narrative – I arrived at work a little late; but not so late that I was obliged to apologise for my tardiness. I knew, however, that I could not attend the police-court without absenting myself for an hour or more; and so I presented myself to Mr. Hibbert and told a story which was as close to the truth as I could manage: namely that I had witnessed a brawl the previous day and that I had been asked by the police to appear before the magistrate in the capacity of a witness.

It was at ten o'clock, therefore, that I mixed with the rabble outside the court, awaiting the appearance of an usher who might admit us into the little court-room. I would have happily paid sixpence to secure a seat; but no-one was forthcoming until the last moment. Then came a rush; a headlong surge of bodies into the building. Whilst it may be that some, like myself, had a connection to a particular case, it was plain that others merely attended for the sport of it. At length, I worked my way to the fore (many complaints – 'no scrouging!' &c) and found a court clerk who informed me that my father's case was the second to be tried that day.

His appearance in the dock – he arrived only a few minutes after I had spoken to the official – was unutterably shabby. In himself, he appeared quite downcast and his very features assumed the aspect of a criminal before a word was spoken. The boot-maker was also present. His attire, however, was that of a gentleman, perfectly neat and fastidious; his expression severe and confident, with only a small bruise on his cheek to show for my father's attack. Had there been a case to answer, I have no doubt that the boot-maker would have won it, on his looks alone. My father, however, merely confessed his guilt and, when asked what was the reason for the assault, or whether he might present any mitigation, said that he had none, except that he 'did not like the man, and may have been drunk.' The magistrate, in turn, was brisk and not given to moralising. The sentence – a forty shilling fine or three months imprisonment.

I saw his face fall as he contemplated gaol. I let him hang for a moment, then I stepped forward and paid the fine.

Was I a fool to do it?

I could not help but notice the look of utter surprise on my father's face, when I came up to the bench. This, at least, told me that he had not connived with Ellen Hungerford to procure my presence. Nor was there any sign of her in the court.

Yet – again – again! – to be throwing money down that bottomless well!

I left the place hurriedly – I had no wish to speak to him – and, within seconds, I felt pangs of self-recrimination. No wise man would spend two pounds in such a fashion. But it was <u>not</u> that I wanted so much to keep my father from gaol; nor was I convinced of his 'reform'; nor, indeed, did I think that one dubious act of 'chivalry' could atone for all his wrongdoing.

No – I must admit this to myself – if I acted for any rational cause – if it was not sheer lunacy – it was for the sake of the girl; because *she* had begged me.

Which only goes to show that all men *are* fools when they indulge such whims. For I received a letter in the post this very morning. It came from my father. Amidst all the usual nonsense, it contained his 'sincere thanks for your unsolicited interference' (well he might thank me – to be spared three months in Pentonville!) and one dire piece of information, which foreshadows a consequence so unfortunate and unintended that I would rather have done nothing. Indeed, it is so painful to me that the words are indelibly inscribed upon my memory:

If you were concerned for the welfare of dear Ellie, who finds herself without a roof over her head, you may rest easy. She has consented to stay with me until she can find better lodgings. I shall rig up a curtain and bed and we shall make the place quite cosy between us!

A curtain!

The girl places *this* trust in him. Doubtless she considers this another example of his kindness towards her.

But what if this arrangement is the prelude to a seduction?

What if he would have her share *his* bed?

I cannot banish the idea from my mind.

Midnight. It is the boot-maker's fault; my own thoughts have become tainted by his vile suspicions – the thoughts of a man who himself would happily violate an innocent girl.

If she succumbs to him, then she is lost; if she does not, then he will pay her back – it will begin with liquor, and end with his fists, until she is ground into dust.

CHAPTER FIVE

The interior of the public-house was filled with smoke, a dense fog of cheap tobacco, that hung in grey garlands about the low ceiling. The prevailing scent, however, was not that of the numerous clay pipes which puffed away, producing the swirling clouds, nor the burning coals in the hearth, but the smell of stale beer and sweat.

Inspector Delby surveyed the room. He had been warned by the local constable that The Wheatsheaf was a 'low public', an old establishment, beloved of working men who eschewed the gas and gilding of newly-built gin palaces. He had not, however, expected such an unnatural gloom, and rather disliked the sensation of peering into the semi-darkness.

'Makes you want to get a bull's-eye and shine it in all their faces, don't it, sir?' said Sergeant Preston quietly.

'I am not sure I would care to make the inquiry,' said Delby. 'Did you find anything?'

'You were right, sir. This is the place. He comes here most days. The landlord pointed him out. Nice as pie; at least, when I started talking about him holding on to his licence, come the next sessions.'

'You had better lead the way.'

The sergeant nodded, and directed Delby towards a small deal table in the corner of the adjoining room. It had two men seated on either side: one was small and wiry; the other possessed a distinctive burly physique and was smartly dressed. The smaller man rose as the two policeman approached, and hurriedly darted past them both. The sergeant raised his eyebrows, as if to say, 'I might catch up with him, if you like'; but Delby shook his head.

'Mr. Halifax, is it?' said the inspector, as he approached the table.

The boot-maker glanced upwards, in theatrical surprise, as if he had not seen the two approach.

'You have the advantage of me,' he replied.

'My name is Inspector Delby; this gentleman is Sergeant Preston. Detective department.'

The boot-maker nodded. 'I took you for Peelers.'

'Then you're a sagacious individual,' said Delby, dryly. 'May I sit down?'

'As you like.'

Delby sat, facing Halifax. The man seemed quite unperturbed.

'I expect you're wondering why we're here,' said the sergeant.

'I expect you'll tell me, when it suits you,' replied the boot-maker, with a shrug.

Delby smiled. 'My! You don't give much away, do you, Mr. Halifax?'

'If you say so, then I suppose I don't.'

'Well,' continued Delby, 'that's a fine policy, I should suppose, in a general way, but not in this case – not with me. So let me tell you what I know about you, sir, and then, you can decide if you feel like talking and being civil. Now, I understand you're in the boot-making line, Greek Street, Soho.'

'You're not wrong.'

'But I gather you keep up an evening trade as well.'

'I can't imagine what you mean,' said Halifax.

'I'll speak more plainly, then. I've heard that twice a week, there's a little get-together above your premises, where certain parties amuse themselves with a game of cards, or the roll of a dice; and I've heard that money passes hands – handsome amounts of money.'

'Nonsense.'

'Really? I've also heard that you used to do a little in the way of boxing – is that right?'

'Now, *that's* common knowledge.'

'Quite right. But I've also heard you're a regular gent amongst the "fancy" if anyone wants to set up a bout; that you can always find a couple of likely men, and you'll give good odds too.'

'You've "heard" that, have you? I don't know who's been spinning these falsehoods, Inspector. Gambling and prize-fights! I'm a respectable individual.'

'Falsehoods?' said Delby. 'Well, perhaps you can tell me, then, what a "respectable individual" is doing in such a dark corner, in such low company.'

'I ain't one for airs and graces, sir. Simple as that.'

Delby shook his head. 'Very droll. Now, let's talk like men, eh? I know who you are, *sir*, and I know what you do for a living. Now, maybe you can get away with a good deal in Soho, if you don't give the magistrate any trouble. But, unless you want Scotland Yard shutting down your little gaming-ken, you'd better play fair with me.'

The boot-maker fell silent for a moment.

'What do you want, anyhow?' he said, at last.

'Now that's more agreeable. I just want a few words, Mr. Halifax, principally concerning a young lady by the name of Ellen Hungerford.'

The boot-maker took a gulp from his bottle of porter and rested it back upon the table.

'What about her?'

'Well, suppose you tell me if you know a girl of that name.'

'I might.'

'Now,' cautioned the inspector, 'remember what I said.'

The boot-maker shrugged. 'Perhaps I do remember the name. I reckon she came to my house, just the once, end of last year, together with an old pal of mine.'

'With George Jones?'

'That's the one, God rest him.'

The sergeant smirked. 'Good friend, was he?'

'Good enough,' said Halifax.

'Ever see her again?' asked Delby.

'No,' said Halifax, weighing his words carefully. 'Not sure if I ever did.'

'You see, Mr. Halifax,' said Delby, 'I'm struggling to keep this talk pleasant and friendly. Because I know you did see her again. For one thing, I know you hung about her lodgings, and tried to get familiar with the poor girl. That's why your *good friend* Mr. George Jones assaulted you. For another, I happen to know you took her out on the town one evening, a couple of months later, to the Argyll.'

Halifax frowned, for the first time visibly unnerved. 'Who's been feeding you these lies? What's this all about?'

'A murder.'

§

'You say the girl's involved in it?' said Halifax, having listened to a carefully abbreviated account of Dora Jones's demise.

'I have good reason to believe so,' replied Delby.

'Well, on my life,' averred the boot-maker, 'I've got nothing to do with the business.'

'The murder? No, I suppose not. I'll grant you that. The "business", as you put it, well, I think you do, after a fashion. You can't deny you took an interest in Ellen Hungerford.'

'Hardly knew her.'

'Still, you took a fancy to her; wouldn't leave her alone, by all accounts,' said Delby.

'Not true.'

'We need to find her. If you have the slightest idea –'

'Listen,' said Halifax, 'you know more than me, by the sound of it. If she's run off somewhere, then I haven't the slightest clue. I've not so much as laid eyes on her for two months since –'

'Since you attempted to force her into prostituting herself?' interjected Preston.

'I did what?' said the boot-maker with a derisive snort. 'I told you already, my friend, someone's gone and fed you a proper story. This is all nonsense.'

'Do you deny that you assaulted Miss Hungerford in her lodgings in Whitecross Street?'

'Whitecross Street? Never set foot in the place.'

'It is on record that George Jones assaulted you on the night of the sixteenth of February, outside this very house. He thought that you'd tried to rape her.'

'I don't care what he thought. The man laid into me – Lord knows why – and I would have set him right, if I'd been given half a chance. Most likely he was drunk.'

'Ellen Hungerford told Jones's son that you tried to rape her; that Jones was trying to protect her honour.'

The boot-maker raised his eyebrows, then broke out into uncontrolled laughter. The two policeman, in turn, exchanged confused glances.

'Forgive me, gents,' said Halifax, regaining his composure. 'Only, it's damned funny!'

'Do you see me laughing, sir?' said Delby.

'Ellie Hungerford was a cheap whore, Inspector. I knew it; George Jones knew it all right – my word, he did! She was the sort who'd screw her own father for tuppence. Her honour – my word!'

And, with that, a broad smile spread across William Halifax's lips; until he could contain himself no longer and, once again, burst out laughing.

DIARY

Thursday, 20ᵗʰ February

The 'Extraordinary Disappearance of a Lady' (one 'Mrs. Buxton') is now explained in the press, in a manner which must be most unsatisfactory for Mr. Poulford. Far from being abducted by a gang of unscrupulous villains, the woman in question merely *did not take the appointed train*, and removed herself to lodgings in Barnsbury – wherein she has only been discovered by the work of a detective. Her unlikely claim is that she fell ill and was unable to communicate with her spouse or his family. No explanation is given as to why she should have hidden herself away in the first place. There is undoubtedly 'more to it' – I pity the husband – but it will <u>not</u> involve chloroform.

Mary-Anne complains once more of the drains. I have made my own investigation in the kitchen and the garden; regrettably, I now think that she may be correct.

I shall write to the house agent.

Walked home from the office this evening along Goswell Street, then Goswell Road. I had half a mind to pay a call upon my father and have it out, regarding the girl.

I thought better of it.

Friday, 21ˢᵗ February

Two invitations received today, neither to my liking.

First, a letter came from Chelsea, requesting that we pay a call at the weekend and partake in Sunday lunch.

Second, at the office, Fortesque informed me that he *is* to be married. The milliner has reciprocated his sentiments; a licence has been taken out; their union is to be celebrated a week on Saturday. We dined together at Gilroy's for lunch, and he asked me whether I should like to attend. I pleaded a prior engagement (nb. one must now be arranged!). Fortunately, we are not such 'pals' that my refusal might be deemed an insult.

It pained me to dissemble my true feelings and wish him 'every happiness'. I do not think, therefore, that I could bring myself to actually bear witness to such a misalliance.

Also, a reply came in the evening from Mr. Phillips, regarding the drains; he will send a man to inspect them on Monday.

Saturday, 22ⁿᵈ February

A fine day; mild weather for the time of year.

On returning from Moorgate, I had a chance meeting with Mrs. Antrobus in Claremont Square, accompanied by her maid, laden down with baggage – bandboxes &c. – alighting from a cab. She informed me that she had been on a 'spree' in the West End, and 'bought so many perfectly useless articles, that I shall never wear – but they will show one such *lovely* things!'.

How fortunate for her that she is married to the good doctor – would that I could afford Dora such licence!

She then remarked that she had intended to call on myself and D. and ask whether we might 'make good' our promise of a visit to Sydenham. Not for her husband's sake – 'Dear man! To see the Crystal Palace? I declare, he is almost a hermit! He would sooner stare at the walls of his own drawing-room than the Pyramids or the Parthenon!' – but for her own, in order to attend the forthcoming Saturday Concert (Mendelssohn).

I readily agreed to the outing. The music will also be to our liking; the tickets should be easy enough to obtain; and – a stroke of luck – here is the 'prior engagement' which forbids us attending F.s' nuptials (!).

I left Mrs. Antrobus in good spirits; but returned home to a dreadful odour in the hall.

There can be no mistaking the source. Mary-Anne complains bitterly of the kitchen. Doubtless the warmer weather has made matters worse.

It occurs to me that I may have to send D. away; she cannot be exposed, in her condition, to such a miasma.

Sunday, 23rd February

To Chelsea.

Dined with Mama and Papa W.; the spinsters Harris; a Miss Pierce (niece); and D.'s brother James (some twenty years her senior), just returned from India and planning a 'grand tour' of Europe. I was pleased to make his acquaintance. He gave a remarkable account of Hindoo magicians and all sorts of primitive superstitions that flourish amongst the common people there.

Mama W. provided a sumptuous roast; only her welcome was a trifle *cool*. I let that pass and said nothing out of turn – though, I confess, I said little – and Dora most happy and content.

Back at home, D. talked incessantly of new curtains for the dining-room. I did my best to dissuade her but I can tell the responsibility of returning Mrs. Antrobus's hospitality weighs heavy on her mind.

I have looked again at our finances, all the accounts &c; it is not good. With all the expense entailed by the new house, any further outgoings must all come from our savings – the money *she* brought to our marriage – and what would Papa W. make of that!

Midnight. Again I find myself committing my darkest thoughts to paper, when, by rights, I should be sound asleep.

It is ridiculous what peculiar association of ideas may operate within one's own mind. Tonight, the question of 'curtains' has led me, by a tortuous path, back again to thoughts of Ellen Hungerford.

And yet, why should I continually worry concerning the moral peril that hangs over one poor girl, when there are thousands of such creatures in our great metropolis?

Indeed, what if she has already fallen?

It is not my responsibility to safeguard her; and yet *he* is *my* father.

That is the nub of it; a tie that cannot be severed.

It is a miserable thought.

Monday, 24th February.

The house agent's plumber came today, as promised, and left his report with Dora. It appears that rats have damaged the principal drain near the kitchen, and this is a cause of noxious effluvia permeating the soil, leading to the foul odour. The drains themselves are in poor condition, and a good deal of the underground pipe must be replaced, as soon as possible.

We are, at least, fortunate in that work can commence on Wednesday. The smell, however, is unlikely to diminish until the work is completed.

I have instructed D. to write to her parents and inquire whether she might spend the remainder of the week in Chelsea.

Tuesday, 25th February

Dora left this afternoon (with three trunks and a valise!). It is convenient, as she will see more of her brother before he goes to France.

I myself shall remain and 'weather the storm' under Mary-Anne's tender care – a 'bachelor husband' once more!

Wednesday, 26ᵗʰ February

Met with the plumber, by the name of Wincher, before I quit the house.

I have heard it said, in jest, that men grow to resemble their dogs. Mr. Wincher, on the other hand, has a good deal of the rat about him, being an agile, wiry man, with particularly small and acute eyes, that are given to darting here and there, even as he converses. Whether his affinity to his mortal enemy – and he had a good deal to say on 'that miserable animal' – is innate or acquired, it is impossible to guess. He assured me, at least, that I 'should not notice he was there'; and that sending away my 'missus' was 'the kindness of a gentleman;' but that I wouldn't find anything in his work that would 'upset a lady's sensibilities'.

I can only assume that the man is entirely unacquainted with the sex. For, on returning this evening, I found the near portion of the garden – some five or six square yards of ground – resembling nothing so much as an open cesspit.

I cannot adequately describe the aroma; but it has permeated the entire house and not a room is free of it. I have instructed Mary Anne that the kitchen must be thoroughly lime-washed, once the work is completed. I fear it may be needed throughout the house.

Thank God that D. has left!

One o'clock (a.m). Again, I begin a fresh page when I had intended to lay down my pen until the morrow. It is becoming a habit – an undesirable one.

Indeed, looking back at my words, these last few weeks, I do wonder whether a man may write too much of himself into his diary; whether a noble intention – to catalogue one's innermost thoughts for posterity – may ultimately provide endless opportunities for future recrimination; whether it would be better if all one's deeds and thoughts were confined to the dim cupboards of memory. Without a doubt, I fear that this evening will be one in which I shall find cause for self-reproof. For, at half past ten, I informed Mary-Anne that I intended to go out, on the pretext of 'taking the air'.

A pretext? There is no other word.

I had made no definite plan as to my 'night walk', yet I soon turned my steps eastwards. How easy it would be to say that I then came to Goswell Street *quite by chance*— were it not disingenuous to call such things 'chance' or 'an accident'. For the wretched preoccupation which has nagged at my mind this last week drew me inexorably onwards, to Pear Tree Court and my father's door.

The idea took a more solid shape as I walked. I determined that I would visit my father and Ellen Hungerford unannounced – inspect the room – and observe whether there might be anything immoral in their mode of living. If I found the girl untainted by her association with my father, then the promise of money for rent, or some other form of relief, might induce her to quit the place. If not –

(Well, I cannot say what I should have done!)

I ascended the steps and knocked; received no answer.

I had screwed up my courage to such a degree that I was tempted to try the handle. Yet, I reasoned with myself, what if I should have come across the girl, sound asleep within, and she should take fright?

My resolution waned and, reluctantly, I retraced my steps, back to Goswell Street. It was there, however, that Fate intervened: I caught sight of Ellen Hungerford.

She was some two hundred yards distant, visible beneath the monster gaslight of a public-house. She kept her head bowed down, her eyes on the pavement. I might have accosted her there and then. Yet the very sight of her – unaccompanied, modest and defenceless – made me utterly ashamed of all my suspicions; and the fact that I would have to explain my presence, most disagreeable.

In short, I lost all courage!

I hurriedly crossed the road and concealed myself in the entrance to the opposing alley. I could not help but see her face, before she turned into the narrow passage to Pear Tree Court. Her skin was terribly pale; I felt sure her expression contained far less life in it than when last we had met. I even heard her give our a terrible croaking cough, before she turned the corner.

Once she had gone, I left the place and walked home.

It was a fool's errand from the first; and I am glad that I did not pursue it.

Of course, if she must live in such a terrible den, then she will pay a price; sickness and suffering abound in such places – I know *that* too well.

Besides, if she has actually fallen ill – if it not *his work* that has reduced her strength – then what aid can I offer? She is young and vigorous. A mere cough – what is that?

And yet –

Damn my wretched cowardice; am I not a man?

I <u>will</u> do something.

Thursday, 27ᵗʰ February

Awoke early; little sleep – much thought concerning EH. Breakfasted, then spoke to Wincher before leaving the house (nb. received assurances that the work will be complete to-morrow).

On reaching Moorgate, I found that I had a good deal of business to transact. This left little time for lunch and I did not leave before six, quite exhausted.

On my departure, however, I did not waver from my firm resolve: I walked straight to Pear Tree Court.

I climbed the bare boards up to my father's door and knocked. I had guessed that my father would be at the cab-stand, and hoped that I might chance upon Ellen Hungerford 'at home'. I was not disappointed. After a few seconds delay, the girl opened the door. To my surprise, she was accompanied by a pungent stench, reminiscent of a butcher's yard. The source of the aroma was not difficult to ascertain: behind her, two dozen or more fresh rabbit skins were laid out on the floor of the room. To one side lay a greasy blunt-looking knife, to the other a large paper bag, containing a mass of grey down. The air itself, meanwhile, was thick with the fine white hair, and particles of it adhered to her hands and face.

Her first expression, upon recognising her visitor, was one of surprise, though she greeted me nicely enough. It was swiftly followed by a crimson flush and lowered lids. She was plainly ashamed of her appearance, and the dismal labour which she was pursuing – though, in truth, the modest ruddy bloom on her cheeks conferred an unlikely degree of charm on her otherwise bloodless features.

I asked her what she was doing, though I had some notion of the work that was laid out on the floor.

'Fur-pulling. I get ninepence for two dozen skins.' – 'I thought you were adept with a needle. That will pay better, surely?' – 'The place I got work, in Tothill Fields, they say they've got enough local girls now. I ain't found a new master, not yet. So I take what I can get.'

There was little complaint in her voice; rather, a quiet and weary resignation. I told her that I feared she was not accustomed to it; that it had made her ill. She did not deny the charge; indeed, she coughed as she spoke, sending a flurry of white down – noxious stuff – billowing from the arm of her dress, as she covered her mouth.

She asked, with her customary untutored politeness, why I had come.

What could I answer?

To see if my own father had assailed her virtue?

I could not be so frank as that. Nonetheless, I had already surveyed the room; and discovered a good deal: a makeshift curtain of thin cloth hung from a second line of cord; and there was a small bed on either side, by the back wall – though, in truth, the 'mattresses' of blankets and rags hardly deserved the word. Thus, having satisfied myself on these points, I told her the truth: that, having become familiar with her history, I found myself increasingly interested in her welfare; that I would do something to improve her condition; that *this* was not a suitable place for any young woman to live, if she could do better; and much *could* be done.

She demurely replied – bless her! – that she *did not want charity* and, begging my pardon, that she could *shift for herself.*

Then it occurred to me – did she fear *my* motives? A dreadful thought!

In any case, unknowingly, by her proud refusal – covered head-to-toe in filth from her labours – she only confirmed my opinion of her good character and stimulated the very instinct which urged me to help her. In fact, her reply was not unexpected and I had my own response prepared. I believe I can record it word for word:

'It is not a question of charity,' I said, 'but of assisting you to find your own way in the world. You have been a good friend to my father, and I would help you. Now, my father-in-law is a prosperous draper in Regent Street; he keeps a good number of needlewomen under his roof. If I were to recommend you to him, I am sure a place might be found for you – if not immediately, then in due course. It would be a regular wage and, if your work was good, then, after a few years, you might do very well for yourself.'

The girl's face expressed open-mouthed astonishment at this simple proposal. (How pleased I was with myself to have thought of it!) The suggestion of a salaried position clearly fell beyond any hope she had cherished for her prospects in the world. If I had offered her the hand in marriage of the Prince of Wales, I cannot imagine she would have been less surprised.

It would be otiose to record her expressions of gratitude, but they were forthcoming. It was necessary, however, to check them, and explain the only possible objection to my plan.

'You must realise, however,' I said, 'that I could not make the true circumstances of our acquaintance known.'

Her face told me that she did not understand.

'I mean to say, that my position in society and my father's are irreconcilable; that I have, therefore, allowed my wife and her family to labour under certain illusions, regarding my own parents.' – 'What do you mean, sir?' – 'They believe I was orphaned whilst still a young man. I do not take any pride in the deception, but it is for the best.' – 'They think he's dead?' – 'Precisely.'

In an instant, I could see that she now thought less of me; and less of my suggestion. How could it not be so, when a man makes such a remarkable confession? Yet what a palpable sense of relief one experiences when one tells a fellow human such a secret – one that has never been divulged to another living soul!

'It is for the best,' I repeated – how often have I told myself so! – 'and if we were to carry out my proposal, we would have to decide upon a suitable story, to explain our connection. I might say, for instance, that you were the child of my mother's old servant, fallen upon hard times; you would have to tell the same tale.'

'I shouldn't care to lie, sir,' she said, cautiously.

I assured her that no harm could come of it. She thought on it for a moment, and pronounced:

'I don't think I can, sir.'

I asked her why not.

'I'm helping your pa with the rent, and I wouldn't want to let him down.'

I could stomach her baulking at deceit, but this ridiculous objection irritated me. For it suddenly seemed quite plain that she did not comprehend what a chance I had taken, in coming to talk to her – what risks I proposed – solely for the sake of her own welfare.

'Damn his rent – he may take care of it himself.'

I had not meant to curse; I offered my apologies. She, in turn, shook her head, an air of solemn, silent disappointment about her, like a child who plays with a toy in a shop, only for it to be replaced on the shelf, out of reach. I encouraged her to speak – for it was plain to me that something more than the rent was on her mind – but she refused. When I persisted, she finally gave way.

'Beggin' your pardon, sir, but I know your opinion of him and I wouldn't want your help neither, if it was done just to spite your old man.'

Such candour!

I gave her every assurance that it was not – though I could not bring myself to spell out the truth: that I <u>did</u> wish to remove her from his presence; that it was not a question of spite, but a fear for her own well-being. She took the opportunity to plead my father's case.

'He can't take care of the rent himself, though, sir – the landlord's raised it again – and if he can't sleep nowhere decent, how can he work? – and if he can't work – well, it's an awful shame – if only –'

Her speech had become staccato and urgent, quickening with every word, until she was obliged to draw breath.

'Well,' she continued, 'I suppose it don't matter, anyhow.'

It was an awful thing to see the spark of hope which I had kindled snuffed out by such scruples. I begged her to reconsider my offer; and she took my words at face value, falling quiet again, deep in thought.

'Could you not help *him* instead?' she said, at last. 'He is your flesh and blood, when all's said and done.'

I told her that my father was beyond such help; that I certainly could find no-one willing to employ him and his position at the cab-stand must remain the summit of his ambition; moreover, that I had been badly burned once before, and had no wish to put my hand back into the flame. She looked back at me with a hint of reproach.

'Couldn't you, though, sir? It's just I know of something –'

Foolishly, I encouraged her to continue.

'There's a cabbie, what you pa knows from the stand; he wants a sub to run his hansom of a night. Says he'd give it to your pa in a second, let him have half of the fares, if only –'

'If what?'

'He wants a surety, he calls it, sir. Ten pounds.' – My face must have revealed my thoughts, for she continued, with much expression – 'Only think how well he could do! He'd have the money to pay you back in no time.'

I told her that my father had a knack of losing money; that, if any flowed in his direction, it was liable to run through his fingers like water.

'Oh, but he ain't touched a drop of liquor,' she pleaded, 'and it's been ever so long! If only you'd help him. It'd do him such good, too; keep him going straight.'

I did not doubt the girl's sincerity, or her earnest desire to help him. In the end, after I had spoken a little more, it came to this: that she would accept nothing for herself unless I gave my father some similar opportunity. I do not mean to say that she had planned or schemed to conduct such a bargain; rather it was merely the result of her own peculiar naïve sense of justice to a man she considered her 'friend'. It was plain that, however much I might cajole or persuade, she would remain steadfast; and thus defeat my entire object of removing her from her present way of living.

Must I confess that I yielded? That I conceded the very point on which I had thought I should never waver?

For I told her that I would help my father, for her sake, if she would allow me to apply to Papa W. on her behalf.

I cannot now believe that I did it.

Is there some secret portion of my heart that would still place trust in a man who has utterly failed me, not once or twice, but in almost every instance? If there is, I suppose it is only the eloquence of her pleading looks, her desperate words, that have revealed it to me.

In any case, I have given her *my* word – that my father may have the cab work, if ten pounds will acquire it. If he prospers, all to the good; if he fails, then she shall have an object lesson – one that cannot be denied.

And, all the while, she will be safe in Papa Willis's work-room; and I will have done my best by her.

I shall write to Dora first thing in the morning; it must all be arranged, before I lose my courage.

Friday, 28th February

Awoke before dawn, possessed of a peculiar restless energy.

The letter to D. preoccupied my thoughts and I set about it immediately. It took longer than I had thought, for I was at pains to practice no greater deceit than was required; and took care with every word.

Of course, it is still a deception, for all that, albeit one that serves a noble purpose.

My Dearest Dora,

I trust you are well, and that Chelsea agrees with you. Mr. Wincher's work here is almost done, as you will see to-morrow.

I had not intended to write again, but I should very much like for you to speak to your father on a matter that has come to my attention.

I received, on Wednesday evening, a letter from a young woman, some sixteen years of age, the daughter of a certain Mrs. Hungerford, who once held the position of cook in my parents' house. I knew the mother well – a respectable god-fearing woman – and recalled that she had quit my parents' employment to marry an older man, a half-pay captain. The daughter's letter – the girl is called Ellen – informs me that she was the sole product of that union, but that she lost her father when she was only a mere child (though she is little more than that, even now!) and her mother some eighteen months ago (it is unfortunate that I heard no news of her death at the time). She then found herself without friends, relations or money, and, like so many friendless girls, she has since earned a meagre living in the metropolis, by her skill with the needle.

(I believe she has found my address – or, rather, that of our old house in Clapham, since the letter was

sent on – from a letter I sent to her mother some years ago.)

The import of her letter is, of course, a plea for our charity. She says that her mother spoke fondly of my parents (I do not doubt that) and, though it shames her to write in such a fashion &c. &c.

As you know, I do not believe in relieving mere beggars; but I have taken steps to ascertain the truth of the girl's account, and to inquire as to her morals and character. In all respects, I have heard nothing to her detriment, and praise from those who know her well. I would do something to relieve her present condition.

Your father's business employs a good number of needlewomen. Will you speak to him and inquire whether a place might be found – on trial, naturally – for such a girl? Of course, we might merely give her a little money, but to find her a place would be infinitely preferable, and more likely to improve her future prospects.

I am sure you would agree with this course of action, my dearest; for, though we owe the girl nothing, we might, nonetheless, do her a great service. Moreover, you possess the sweetest, most charitable nature I have ever encountered.

You may tell me your father's reply in person – tomorrow! It seems an age since I last looked upon your face, and I long to see it before me once more.

Your devoted husband, &c.

For good or ill, I believe it is well done.

I posted it on the City Road. I have also made arrangements at the receiving-house near Old Street for them to keep anything that comes addressed to Mr. J.H. Jones – thus I may now correspond comfortably with the girl and collect any reply, in complete safety.

If she follows my instructions, she will make some arrangement whereby I can meet the cabman who offers my father *his* opportunity, and write in the next day or so.

I wonder – is all this a form of madness?

I have persuaded myself that I am justified in deceiving my wife and father-in-law – to what end?

To help a young girl – in a fashion that, if discovered, is liable to generate the worst suspicion – that will bind me even tighter to my father, whom I have so long endeavoured to cut loose. For I will not benefit from it; and, unless my father exceeds every expectation, I shall surely lose a good sum of money, of which I have every need.

Indeed, the *ten pounds* must, perforce, come from D.'s money; that is the worst of it.

Yet I have <u>done</u> something; and I feel easier in myself, more so than I have for many weeks.

Poor Dora! I do not deceive *myself* – it is a bad thing to lie to one's wife, on any account – and I *would* tell her everything; if only I could be sure that she would understand.

Saturday, 1ˢᵗ March

A pleasant start to the day – much sun – heralding spring.

Dora arrived by cab at noon (a little late, given our planned excursion to Sydenham, but it would have been churlish to remark on it). I must admit that I have never seen my dear wifey look so pretty nor lively. It was not merely a case of *absence makes the heart* &c. but rather a pleasing bloom to her features – Mother Nature's blessing on the mother-to-be – and her unselfconscious delight, expressed in every movement and gesture, at returning *home*. She was pleased to discover, too, that the garden had been returned to its natural state (Mr. Wincher having completed his work yesterday evening; the odour in the house now thoroughly dissipated).

I did not mention EH, but Dora herself – whilst Mary-Anne was unpacking – was curious about the 'poor needlewoman' and so I told her something of her character, the condition of her lodgings &c. – omitting any mention of *a certain party*. D. very sympathetic. (Papa W., moreover, has provided the name of the 'Lady Superintendent' at his premises in Regent Street, to whom EH may apply this coming week – very good.)

We then fell to talking about the afternoon's outing. D. very excited to see Palace once more but barely had time to change her day dress before Dr. Antrobus called – punctual to the very second – and announced that our hackney was waiting. We set off, therefore, shortly after one o'clock.

I was seated opposite Mrs. Antrobus and, as we conversed, it occurred to me that her day dress was rather pleasing to the eye (if a mere *man* can judge!) and that something similar – if it could be afforded – might suit my dear wifey. It is remarkable, however, how quickly one may revise one's opinion! For, as Mrs. A. stepped down to the pavement at London Bridge, I noticed that her skirts were was looped-up at intervals at the hem, so as to reveal a scarlet flannel petticoat beneath! Dora, sensible to my astonishment, waited for a quiet moment and informed me, *sotto voce*, that such display is *the fashion*. I told her that if *my* wife were to possess such an article, I should have something to say on the subject. (Dr. Antrobus, of course, is a more cold-blooded creature; and if he *has* anything to say, I doubt his wife will hear it!)

We made our way through to the platform without difficulty. The train itself was busy but the Directors' coach was most comfortable and not over-crowded. It was not long before we left London Bridge, steaming along the viaduct, past the sooty garrets and slates surrounding the station. Dora and Mrs. A. engaged in a light-hearted speculation as to the inhabitants of the various little rooms, whose interiors could be glimpsed momentarily amidst the smoke. Neither of them, of course, *knows* such poverty and hence it acquires a certain romance. Indeed, the day-to-day lives of such people are – thankfully – as remote to D. as the struggles of the Hindoo or African savage.

The arrival at Sydenham itself was a 'crush' – as always – and the corridor from the station seemingly endless. Nonetheless, we had time for a brief stroll around the fountains before entering the Palace. I had obtained seats in the upper gallery, which provided an excellent view of the transept, although D. required her parasol against the sun. I asked Dr. Antrobus what he made of the Palace. I did not hear the reply in full – the performers were taking their seats – but it included the word 'greenhouse'. I *believe* he spoke in jest; but I would not care to lay odds.

Whatever his opinion, I do not believe anyone could find fault with the music. Indeed, the sound of two thousand souls singing in harmony has an expressive power which cannot be equalled; and the chorale – 'Lord, let us hear they voice' – mighty and sublime. I observed that Mrs. A. was positively transfixed by the potency of the performance; Dora, too, visibly affected. It was only when the concert was finished that I realised D. had rather 'wilted' under the glass roof despite her parasol – too shy, poor thing, to complain of it! – and was in need of sustenance. We made our way, therefore, through the crowds to the Refreshment Department and took a shilling tea, whilst the good doctor went off to investigate the Technological Museum, a recent addition, much lauded in the press.

'My husband,' remarked Mrs. Antrobus to D., 'prefers minerals to divine music. Really, it is too much.'

This was said with a smile – but I could not help but wonder if she felt some sense of genuine grievance that her spouse did not share her native enthusiasm for the arts. She then regaled us with several humourous anecdotes to further illustrate his curmudgeonly temperament. I was, however, somewhat distracted by Dora's appearance. She seemed distinctly pale and listless, though she professed herself 'quite all right' and begged that I did not 'fuss'.

On the doctor's return, we began our walk back down to the station. The gas had been lit and there was a certain fascination in surveying the illuminated gardens and walks. However, the path was clogged with <u>every</u> class of visitor – including some still supping sandwiches and ale – all bent on the same errand. I began to realise that we had left at the worst possible moment. It was with some difficulty that we entered the station, and it cost us a great deal of trouble to progress down the platform to the Directors' coach. I might, even then, have pressed for finding a cab, regardless of the difficulty or expense, since Dora now appeared quite drained – a fact which Dr. Antrobus himself remarked upon. The possibility of turning about, however, was entirely denied to us, by virtue of the sheer volume of passengers crowding the train. At last, with D. clearly quite exhausted, we were just about to board our carriage, when a porter blocked our path.

'Only two seats left inside, sir.'

I do not believe I have ever felt such acute embarrassment.

'We have tickets for the Directors' coach,' I insisted.

'I'm sure you do, sir. But there's only two places. If you could try second class?'

I will not chronicle the remainder of our conversation; further comment is quite redundant. The man did not budge, and the train was due to leave within minutes. It was left to Dr. Antrobus to suggest – what else could we do? – that we give our wives the two seats and find ourselves places further down the platform.

Mrs. Antrobus, however, interjected.

'My dear, how can you suggest such a thing? It is quite plain that Mrs. Jones is not at all well,' – D. weakly protested – 'and if anyone should accompany her it is a physician. What if she is taken ill – on the train – or at London Bridge? Who will care for her?'

'Do you intend to travel in second, my dear?' said the doctor, showing the merest hint of surprise.

'Mr. Jones can be my chaperon. Indeed, I am sure there is nothing that goes on in *second*, or even *third*, that does not occur in *first*.'

And thus – though I myself had hardly spoken a word – it was decided that I should abandon my wife!

The crush for *second* was no better, a general scrimmage taking place all along the platform. In fact, I myself would have abandoned the attempt altogether, and waited for the next train, had not Mrs. A. herself seen an opening in *third* (!), rushed headlong into the crowd, and somehow found room in the carriage.

(Had Fortesque been present, I am sure he would have pronounced her 'game' without any hesitation!)

The train then pulled out. I did my best to retain a vestige of dignity but it was not to be managed. Indeed, I was advised to 'cheer up' by a mechanic, obviously in spirits, who then offered me a bottle of porter 'to share with yer missus'. Needless to say, my embarrassed reply – a halting explanation of my proper relation to Mrs. A. – provided nothing but general amusement.

How I despise being made a fool!

The only crumb of comfort is that, in the course of our journey, conversing with Mrs. A. above the general hubbub, I made mention of my MS., and my hopes for its eventual publication, which induced her to ask if she might read it for herself. Indeed, I believe she was impressed by my efforts; and, unless I flatter myself unduly, it did something to raise me up a little in her opinion.

Fortunately, by the time we reached London Bridge, to be reunited with Dora and the worthy doctor, D. herself seemed considerably recovered. Dr. Antrobus, meanwhile, suggested that it was merely a case of over-exertion; recommending a day's rest and no further outings 'where there might be such crowds'.

From the tone of his voice, I fear that, in future, he will abide by the same prescription for himself and his wife. D. assures me, however, that he was kindly and considerate on the train. Moreover, that she does not think he believes that I was at fault, but 'rather blames the porter'.

Let us hope so!

Mrs. Antrobus, at least, did not seem overly discomfited by the experience of *third*. I remarked on it to D. after supper. She, in turn, confided an interesting fact – a choice piece of gossip – that might account for her *sang froid* under such trying circumstances. Mrs. Antrobus was once an actress!

It is, undoubtedly, a tribute to Mrs. A. that she has entered into a good marriage; and I myself do not entertain that peculiar prejudice which certain folk bear against any woman who has set foot on the stage.

Nonetheless – an actress! It explains a good deal. (nb. Have written to EH.)

Sunday, 2nd March

To church in glorious sunshine – the sermon *On Job's Resignation*. Then back home to inspect the garden, which will need keeping in check during the summer months (more expense!). Spoke briefly to our neighbours and remarked on the unseasonably warm weather.

Dora, meanwhile – still a little fatigued and not inclined to go out – all but ordered me from the house. Informed me that, with Mary-Anne on her half-day, she might at least read a book 'without any nuisance or interruption'; that I myself should 'not fuss about the place'; that I would do well to exercise.

I took it into my head, therefore, to follow the course of the New River up to Stoke Newington to the reservoirs by Green Lanes, and thus escape for an hour into 'the country'.

The walk itself was pleasant enough – how rare and welcome is the pure unfiltered light of the sun in our dismal metropolis! – but the brickfields were much in evidence (more so, even, than last summer, when I walked the same route with D.). There seemed hardly a patch of ground along the way that had not fallen to the speculative builder. It was only when I spied the great pumping-station that prepared plots yielded to green fields; only as I approached the reservoirs themselves that I observed any semblance of rusticity (the gardens of the old cottages visible all along the Lanes, and Hornsey Wood looming behind).

I tipped the man at the gate-house and resolved to walk 'clockwise' along the footpath by the river, then back around the two lakes. I soon came across several other 'city folk' engaged in the same recreation; then a gang of ragged small boys, no doubt living nearby who, by the state of their clothes, had just washed themselves in the water (surely a practice to be discouraged on sanitary grounds!). It was a few hundred yards further on, however, when I saw two brawny labourers approaching. They wore 'Sunday best' – ill-fitting suits and collars – and had a pair of young women in tow. The path was narrow and I was about to stand aside and let them pass, when, to my astonishment, I recognised three of the party. The men were the same two employés of Mr. Saunders whom I last observed at St.Mark's; and one of the women was *no other than my own housemaid!*

The older of the two men wished me a good afternoon, and I replied in kind. The deep embarrassment occasioned need not be recorded. I would have preferred, at least, to have been spared the giggling of the two females, and guffaws of the men, once they assumed I was out of earshot.

(The mystery of Mary-Anne's valentine and the identity of her 'lover' now explained!)

I recounted the incident to D. on my return, with every intention of giving the girl her notice, if only for the insolent laughter which prevailed after my departure. However, after some discussion, my dear wifey – good, sweet-natured D.! – persuaded upon me to relent. For she made me confess that, with the exception of the laughter, I had observed nothing improper in the girl's behaviour, nor that of her companions – no sign of liquor, nor any display of immodesty – and that it was, most likely, only a primitive consciousness of the awkwardness of the situation that had occasioned their amusement.

'What is she to do with her holiday, in any case,' said my D., 'if she wants to find a husband?'

Such solidarity in sentiment – when it comes to matters of 'romance' – is, I suppose, to be expected of the sex. Nonetheless, I called for Mary-Anne in the evening and told her that – whilst the half-holiday was her own – she must conduct herself properly at all times, and that I would certainly not brook followers in the kitchen or hanging about the area.

'No, sir.'

She might well have added 'Three Bags Full, Sir'.

I did not, however, pry any further. In truth, I hope it is an engagement – if the brute would only offer her marriage then we might be relieved of an encumbrance!

I thought a good deal, too, on the question of EH during my walk. I shall visit the receiving-house to-morrow; there may be a letter.

Monday, 3rd March

Fortesque is married.

He placed a slice the wedding cake in my hand as I sat down at my desk this morning, then recounted the whole affair during lunch at Gilroy's. It was held at a small church near Aldgate. Everything and everyone involved 'prime' 'slap-up' 'first-rate' &c. &c. followed by a 'regular blow out' at a tavern in the Borough.

I would happily have been spared the details and was grateful to find our conversation cut short by the unexpected arrival of the young broker with whom F. has formed an acquaintance. The broker is a man by the name of Gresham, smartly dressed but somewhat after the 'swell' fashion. He begged my indulgence, and then took F. aside and they held conference for several minutes. F. very pleased with himself upon returning to the table. Indeed, I rather fear he has been inveigled into some financial speculation — for brokers always have some new scheme. Fortunately, it is not my affair.

Left the office at five; walked home along the City Road; nothing at the receiving-house.

I found Dora at home, quite herself. We went together, therefore, to pay a quick call on Mrs. Antrobus, with a precious cargo in my little brief-bag. For Mrs. A. had visited earlier in the day, and expressly reminded D. of my promise to let her read my MS. I have now entrusted it to her care and she promises faithfully to read it before the week is out.

I wonder what she will make of it?

Tuesday, 4ᵗʰ March

Dora, having recovered her strength, has suddenly acquired a great appetite – 'eating for two' &c. – and complained at supper that she will grow terribly stout 'like a prize pig'.

I replied that it was rather to be expected, a remark to which she took peculiar exception.

I should not tease her so!

Wednesday, 5ᵗʰ March

At lunch, another astonishing announcement from Fortesque: he is to rent a house – six rooms and basement – in Upper Holloway!

I asked him how this might be managed – for his wage is quite insufficient – and he informed me that he had 'come into a little unexpected capital,' (an inheritance?) and 'thought Betsy would take to somewhere respectable'.

It is more, I fear, a question of how the residents of the district – in the most part, *utterly* respectable – will take to 'Betsy'.

Back home via City Road and again the receiving-house: a letter!

Pear-tree Court
4th March

Dear Sir,

This letter is to thank you again for your kindness.
I have wrote to Mrs. Prendergast at Willisses and she
says to come on Thursday and make a trial. I will do
my best – my word of honour I shall – and cannot do
no more.

I have spoke with your pa and _he_ is truly grateful
and sends his best regards. The cabmans name is
Wilfred Dennis and he says he will come to the Angel,
Islington, or any other place that might suit, and that
you can write to him at 12 Ampton Place, King's
Cross.

Your best health and all good wishes,

E.

I shall write directly but I will not pay the cabman
until she has had her interview and – with any luck
– secured a place.

Thursday, 6th March

A second letter at the receiving-house this
evening, sooner than I had expected.

Pear-tree Court
6th March

Dear Sir,

This is to tell you that I saw Mrs. Prendergast
this morning and she says that I will do and must
start on Monday. There will be board and lodging

and twelve pound a year.

I will not forget your kindness to do such a thing as I never dreamed of for me when there is no ties between us, excepting your father on whose account I know you shall be seeing Mr. Dennis, for which I bless you too. If you should like, I will write again and tell you how I like my place, but only if you should like.

Your servant,

E.

I cannot adequately describe for the great relief I experienced upon reading this news. How gratifying it is to know that my plan – so fraught with danger – has been carried out; that the girl's welfare is now in safe hands.

It only remains – regrettably – to acquaint myself with the cabman and afford my father another chance to 'prove himself.'

It will not be the Angel, however; I should not wish to be recognised.

Saturday, 8th March

Left Moorgate at two o'clock, caught the 'bus and met with Mr. Dennis (by prior arrangement) at the Cock, Fleet Street.

I found him to be a stocky little man, no more than fifty years of age, with craggy features and a somewhat argumentative manner, given to jabbing his finger in my direction to illustrate the most trivial point. Hearing him talk, there could be no doubt that

he had 'fought the battle of life' long and hard; and
that, from an unpromising start, he had done well
for himself. He informed me that he owned both his
own horse and cab – 'on account I never liked owing
nothing to nobody' – and possessed a share in half-
a-dozen others. He declared himself 'minded to do
business' with me and, indeed, he seemed a practical,
business-like fellow, albeit of an uneducated variety.

I could not imagine, therefore, why he should
place such confidence – ten pounds or no – in my
father.

I hinted as much. He replied that he had 'never
known a better waterman' and that although 'half
the subs and night-workers in the cab trade are out-
and-out villains, sir,' he was certain my 'old man'
would be 'on the square and pay out on all the fares'.

Is it possible that my father *has* changed?

In any case, our conversation continued:

'Would you like to inspect the cab, sir?' – No,
I said, I would not. – 'Would you care to see my
licence?' – To this, I said yes. For the cabman had
seemed discouraged by my previous answer, and was
most anxious to produce his *bona fides*. – 'And did you
require a receipt, sir?' – Yes, I informed him, I did,
then gave him my cheque.

Thus, with a firm shake of the hand, our business
was completed.

It is quite foolish – I cannot quite explain it – but I
returned home in high spirits; so much so that Dora
remarked upon it at dinner.

I rather believe I should be grateful to Ellen
Hungerford. For what greater satisfaction is there

than improving the lot of a fellow human being? She will now benefit from her industry, rather than suffer for it; and as for my father –

No, I will write no more. I dare not hope.

Tuesday, 11ᵗʰ March

Bad weather; cold again.

When I returned home, Dora inclined to talk about her condition. She has been writing to her mother this last week or so, and received a good deal of advice concerning her confinement, a monthly nurse &c., though it is quite premature to discuss such matters. Indeed, in my opinion, it has generated a rather morbid disposition in my dear wifey, which I must endeavour to dispel – but how?

I was pondering this very question, after D. had retired, when Mary-Anne knocked on the study door. She informed me that a cabman had rung the area bell – deep in reverie, I had not heard it ring myself – and, despite the late hour, wished to speak to 'the master of the house', since he had found an item of lost property, which I might wish to claim.

For a few moments I was perplexed, until the truth dawned.

I put on my coat and went outside. There, on the pavement, stood a hackney and its solitary driver, who had descended from his seat, and tethered the horse's reins to the nearby lamp-post. He was wrapped in a heavy oil-skin cape and a hat which all but concealed his features. Nonetheless, I recognised him instantly as my father.

I demanded to know what he meant by coming to the house. In truth, I had but one question on my mind – the same question I always used to ask myself as a child – 'is he sober?'.

'My boy!' he said *sotto voce*. 'I would speak to you, that is all.'

I *was* gratified – I cannot deny it – to discover that there was nothing of the drunk in his manner; nor any foul stink of liquor about his person. Nonetheless, I reminded him that I had forbidden him to come to the house; that it was rash in the extreme &c.

'I have only come to thank you, my boy, for all you've done –'

I interrupted this speech and told him that the only thanks I required was that he did not trouble me again, except to repay the ten pounds which I had expended to secure his future employment. I would happily have left it at that, but he persisted, placing his hand on my arm.

'No, no, my boy, listen to me. I will have my say – you can't deny me. I know I've been a dreadful trial to you all these years; I can't deny any of it and you haven't deserved it one iota. But what you've gone and done this last week for me and the girl – well, you've been a true Christian, my boy, and so I just wanted you to know that I'm keeping to the pledge – just like I said I would – and I'll try to do better by you. I'll try as hard as any man could. Now, I know, by rights, I shouldn't be here vexing you – and I won't stay a minute longer – but I couldn't drive this horse a mile more, not without coming and giving you this.'

As he spoke, he reached inside his coat and handed me a small silver locket.

'Won't you open it?' he asked.

I did as he suggested. The clasp stuck, but it came apart at last to reveal a delicately painted miniature of a young woman.

'That's your mother, my boy. Not long after we were married – better days. I've been saving to get it out of the pawnbroker's these last couple of months. Lord knows it's been in and out often enough. It's about all I have left of her, rest her soul. Now, I'd like you to have it; keep it safe.'

My mother!

I fear that I could not help myself; wordlessly, I shed a tear. For I have had nothing to remember her by these twenty years – I had felt sure that all had been lost – and the last time I saw her face –

To see her again, young and radiant, a woman possessed of beauty and charm – the effect cannot be described.

My father said no more, except to bid me goodnight. For my own part, I felt hardly able to speak, and said only a few solemn words.

I look at the portrait now, by the light of the candle on my desk. The inscription reads,

To My Sweet Georgina, my true love.

Better days, indeed!

I cannot dwell on them; my own memories of that marriage, and its conclusion, are far from sweet.

And yet, surely tonight is a presentiment – the merest hint – that I have been wrong; that *even my father* may yet redeem himself.

Can it be believed?

Wednesday, 12ᵗʰ March

Dora once more fretful about her confinement &c. though it is several months distant.

She came into the study after dinner and said that I 'was not to be angry' (are there any words less likely to ease a husband's mind?) but 'might we not forego a monthly nurse, my dear, and just ask Mama to stay a week or two instead? I am sure I would be much more at ease with Mama, and she will want to get to know the child —' &c. &c.

I replied that I was not 'angry' but I did not see how one could 'get to know' a new-born babe, a creature possessed merely of the promise of character and intellect; as yet utterly unformed in every particular. Nor, I added, did I consider Mama W. to be an adequate substitute for a nurse.

(Indeed, will *she* sit through the whole night while the infant cries? Will *she* tend to the needs of mother and child — and all the disagreeable work that may entail — *without complaint?* I very much doubt it!)

D. said nothing in reply but retired early to bed. It is fortunate for her constitution that we avoided a row.

Of course — D. does not realise it — this is the direction to which all Mama W.'s advice will tend: that only *she* possesses the requisite experience; that only *she* should hold any sway over her daughter. She is inclined to poke her nose into everything.

In any case, I have now thought of a way to improve D.'s spirits: I shall propose a few days at the sea-side. I am certain it will be of great benefit to us both, both mental and physical. Mr. Hibbert always praises Broadstairs; I shall see whether something can be arranged.

Thursday, 13ᵗʰ March

Dora not at breakfast; then, this evening, retired early. I asked if she was unwell, but she vigorously denied it.

I would not have believed it of her, but it seems that she has fallen into a sulk over the subject of her dear Mama.

I will not give in to such blackmail.

Friday, 14ᵗʰ March

The <u>worst</u> of days.

I returned from the office to learn that Dora was in bed. I thought nothing of *that*. Indeed, I did not go and see her, thinking it better to let her rest, if rest was required.

An hour later, however, Mary-Anne came to me and said that, though she did not want to contradict her mistress, *had I not better call for the doctor?*

I did not understand her, and said so.

'Ain't she told you, neither, sir?' – 'Told me what?' – 'Begging your pardon, sir, but she's been bleedin', these last two days and not said nothing. I've seen it in her laundry. Now, I just went to fetch her some water. She tried to hide it, but there's blood again, lots of it, too, and I reckon she's cramped up –'

I wasted no time in going to Dr. Antrobus.

It was all done by nine o'clock; a full bucket of ice to stem the bleeding.

The half-formed stillborn child was a strange little thing; a tiny doll, no bigger than my hand. It seems it would have been a boy.

It is only by the Lord's mercy – and the work of the good doctor – that my poor wife lives.

The doctor offered me a crumb of comfort before he left: that the child would never have grown strong and firm-limbed; that it would only have suffered all the more, had it lived.

'It is Nature's providence, my poor fellow. Let that and your faith be your consolation. Indeed, your wife will recover her strength, and may yet bear another child.'

Two o'clock. D. terribly silent and still; she will not sleep.

I shall send for her mother in the morning; I do not know what more I can do for her.

CHAPTER SIX

'You just don't believe it, sir, do you?' said Sergeant Preston, as the cab came to a halt on Amwell Street.

Inspector Delby stepped down onto the pavement. 'It is hard to believe that a mere girl … Now, wait, who's this?'

The object of the policeman's curiosity was a fine Amempton carriage, in red and gold, that drew up behind the cab. Its interior was obscured by black window blinds. The driver promptly descended from his seat, and opened the door, revealing a woman seated inside. She had a full matronly figure and was dressed in full mourning, with a veil concealing her face. Taking the driver's outstretched hand, she stepped down onto the pavement.

'May I help you, ma'am?' asked Delby, as the woman turned towards him.

'I suppose you must be the policeman in charge?'

'Inspector Delby,' he replied, feeling rather obliged to stress the first word, slightly offended by the woman's haughty tone.

'You spoke to my husband earlier today, Inspector. I am the poor girl's mother.'

'Mrs. Willis?' said Delby, surprised. 'We did not expect you here, ma'am.'

'Nonetheless,' said Mrs. Willis, 'I have come. I suppose one should observe the proprieties; but I will not immure myself in the house until … ' – her voice faltered – 'Of course, my husband, as you may gather by his absence, does not approve. He assures me he will never set foot here again; he cannot bear the thought of it. All the same, he shall not gainsay me in this.'

'In what, ma'am?'

'I have come to see my daughter.'

'See her? Are you sure you wish to do that, ma'am?' said Sergeant Preston, after an awkward silence. 'Her condition … it is not pleasant … well, I mean, for a member of the fair sex …'

'Pleasant? I do not imagine it is "pleasant". Tell me, there will be an inquest, will there not?'

'Yes, of course.'

'And a dozen or more strangers will come and gawp at her.'

'The coroner is obliged to do his duty, ma'am.'

'I do not deny *that*, sir. And I hope you will not deny me. I should like to see my daughter.'

The inspector paused for a moment.

'Very well.'

§

Delby glanced at the clock on the bedroom mantelpiece. He had paid it no attention on his first inspection of the room. Unwound, it had ground to a halt, as if united in mechanical sympathy with its mistress. Just below it, the corpse of Mrs. Dora Jones lay perfectly still, in front of the fire.

'I am afraid the room must not be disturbed, ma'am,' said the inspector, gingerly. 'I'd rather … well, I'd rather you did not …'

Mrs. Willis, who had stooped down to touch her daughter's face – the skin as cold and pale as bone china – rose up and resumed the stiff-backed resolute posture which had marked her progress through the house.

'She will be returned to us, after the coroner's inquest, I trust.'

'Unless – forgive me, ma'am, but it is only fair that I give you warning – unless the coroner should request a *post mortem* examination.'

'You would hardly have to be a surgeon, Inspector, to see what he has done to my poor girl!' exclaimed Mrs. Willis, indignantly.

'No, ma'am. I expect you are right.'

She looked down once more at her daughter, then turned away.

'Very well. Now take me back down.'

§

'I have already lost two of my children, Inspector,' said Mrs. Willis, seated in the drawing-room, sipping from a hastily-prepared cup of tea. 'One at her birth, another – my second boy – was taken after only two summers. In each case, I comforted myself that it was God's will; that their little souls had risen up to Heaven because He had a purpose. But this – this is not His work – her young life foreshortened – it is the work of a devil in human form.'

'Who do you mean, ma'am?'

'I can tell, sir, that you know full well who I mean. Her wretched husband. I trust that every effort is being made to apprehend him?'

'Every effort, ma'am.'

'That is something, at least.'

'It might help me in that endeavour, ma'am,' continued the inspector, 'since you have come, if I could ask you a few questions. Would you object?'

'Of course, if it might do any good.'

'Well, to start with, ma'am, I gather you yourself were not on good terms with Mr. Jones.'

'Doubtless my husband has spoken of it. I always thought the marriage would be the ruin of my poor girl – to be the wife of a mere clerk – and one without prospects, at that – but this – this horror –'

'I am sorry to distress you, ma'am,' said Delby, changing tack. 'Tell me, how did your daughter meet Mr. Jones? I suppose you can recall?'

'Of course, though I can hardly see how it might help you. We took her with two of her cousins to the Regent Street Polytechnic to attend a public lecture by a scientific gentleman. I saw no harm in it; nor would there had been, if a certain individual had not seated himself besides our party.'

'Mr. Jones, I take it?'

'He fell into conversation with one of the young men – though they had not been introduced – and inveigled himself into our company. I did nothing to encourage any intimacy between the pair of them, I assure you of that. But the harm was done.'

'In what way, ma'am?'

'We met him again in Chelsea, the following week, on the King's Road – "quite by chance". I knew it the moment I saw him there – he had set his sights on my poor girl!'

'He was in love, perhaps,' suggested Delby.

'I trust you are not so credulous in other matters, Inspector,' retorted Mrs. Willis. 'Love, indeed! If he were a mere boy, I might credit it. Besides – even if I were to allow it – what sort of man pursues a match that is plainly to his advantage, and his alone?'

'But your daughter thought highly of him?'

'My Dora was a sweet, trusting child, sir. She had never received the attentions of a determined man – an older man – the letters, the little gifts – it turned her head. On every occasion that I interfered,'– she sighed, exasperated by the recollection – 'well, I am sure all that can be of little importance now.'

'I am just trying to understand the nature of the fellow, ma'am. If he is to be found – at least, if he is to be found alive – it may assist us to know such things.'

'"Alive", sir?'

'Mr. Jones left a note, indicating that he intended to do away with himself.'

'Too cowardly to face the gallows; it does not surprise me.'

Delby fell silent, gathering his thoughts before speaking again.

'Tell me, how did he treat your daughter when they were married? Was he violent towards her on any previous occasion?'

'Not to my knowledge,' conceded Mrs. Willis.

'I see,' said Delby. 'Well, now, I hope you will forgive me, ma'am, if I may proceed to touch on a delicate subject; it may be very pertinent to our inquiry. Your husband told us that your daughter suspected her husband of a liaison with another woman.'

'Dora did not "suspect" him; she knew it for a fact.'

'When we spoke to your husband, ma'am, he implied –'

'My husband, Inspector, does not know everything that passes between a mother and her daughter. She first confided all the dreadful details to me. I told her to speak to her father on the matter of divorce. If she only spoke of 'suspicions', it was to allow her husband to retain some vestige of his reputation.'

'Can you tell me these "details"? I do not mean to pry, ma'am; it may be relevant.'

'Of course,' said Mrs. Willis. 'In fact, I have brought something to show you.'

She reached into the black reticule which lay on her lap and retrieved a piece of folded paper, handing it to the policeman. Delby examined it closely. It was the briefest of letters, which had been written in an uncertain hand, the ink smudged in several places.

> *Dearest Mama,*
>
> *I have been so rash to listen to your advice – I am quite driven mad by it – I have seen them together. I did as you said – I gave them the opportunity – and – all is lost!*
>
> *How much better if I did not know!*
>
> *I will not say what I have seen; but, Mama, I have seen them <u>together.</u>*
>
> *Now you must counsel me – what is a woman to do, if her husband cannot keep sacred the natural relation between man and wife?*
>
> *What must I do?*
>
> *Your daughter,*
>
> *D.*

'There is no date, said the policeman. 'When did you receive it?'

'The thirteenth of last month. The following week, she spoke to her father.'

'Did you learn the woman's name?'

'No. She refused to reveal it; she was utterly loyal to him, you see, even though he had deceived her. Foolish, foolish girl!'

'She was plainly very distressed by the whole business.'

'I hope you do not mean unbalanced, Inspector. She was in her right mind, I can assure you of that. A little nervous trouble, but nothing more. Don't you see? That is why he did it – my poor girl had discovered his sordid little secret!'

Inspector Delby frowned.

'I'm sorry, ma'am,' said the policeman, 'but I'm afraid it's not that straightforward. Indeed, this rather confirms Mr. Jones's version of the events in question.'

'I do not understand you, Inspector. I thought you said you were still searching for him. Were you deceiving me? Is he in custody?'

Delby shook his head.

'My apologies, ma'am, I did not mean to mislead you. You are aware of the fact that your son-in-law kept a diary?'

DIARY

Sunday, 16th March

Yesterday, I had the undertaker's man come and remove the stillborn child, before Dora might look at it. I feared the sight would only unnerve her; and she <u>must</u> conserve her strength. She has not asked after the child, and I myself have said nothing. The undertaker's man informed me that it would be buried today in a grave at Abney Park 'with a few other little ones,' (for which I have paid 10s.) and receive a prayer from the curate (2s.). If, in future, D. should ever wish to see the spot, then it can be arranged.

Dr. Antrobus visited again this morning. There is some good news: he believes there is no impediment to D.'s full recovery, barring lack of sleep and proper nourishment, and the *will*. He has prescribed his own mixture of opium and spirits – that will suffice for *sleep* at least – but what of the remainder? Cook has been energetic with soup, broths &c. but to no avail. Likewise, Mama W. – who has taken up a permanent residence on the 'made-up' bed in D.'s room – seems unable to effect any change.

Tuesday, 18th March

D. still too weak to leave her bed and, worse, shows no inclination to rouse herself.

In the meantime, I pass my evenings in the company of Mama W. and Mary-Anne; and try to prevent them coming to blows over my poor invalid wife. Mama W. has lost none of her distrust of the girl, and takes every opportunity to enforce petty discipline concerning D.'s meal-times and toilet. Mary-Anne, upon the other hand, can only conceal her true sentiments by approaching her domestic chores with that peculiarly female outpouring of emotion, that sets up a rattling and clattering of our 'goods and chattels' throughout the house.

I should speak to M-A; but we cannot afford to lose her now; a new maid would be too much for D. to endure.

Wednesday, 19th March

Mrs. Antrobus has brought carnations, which have brightened D.'s room and visibly cheered her.

Mama W. tells me that D. has taken some soup.

Thursday, 20th March

Visited Old Street. A note from EH at the receiving-house, accompanied by a small parcel – most unexpected – wrapped in brown paper. Uncertain of the contents, I took the precaution of opening both items in a respectable public on the City Road.

> *Regent-street*
> *16th March*

Dear Sir,

I have written this seeing how you said you should like to hear something of how I get by in my new place.

Sir, I like it well enough. I share a room in

*common with eleven other girls who is mostly older
than me but I don't much mind that. Mrs. Prendergast
has charge of us and she is hard on those girls that
dawdle or chatter but I am proud enough to say that
she finds no fault with me nor my work as yet and
says I shall do well for myself if I work hard.*

*On Sundays we have time to read the Bible
and go to church then two hours free. Thursdays the
evenings are free and we can visit our friends — only
I do not think I have many. Also one Saturday in the
month. I often think of your kindness towards me
and so I have used my time to make you a gift. I asked
Mrs. P. if she thought that was right and she said it
was right by her and that your wife might like it.*

*Sir, if you should ever see me again, I should tell
you how much I am grateful to you. And I will always
be,*

Your Servant,

EH

*P.S. The Mrs. said I might have the lace for
nothing.*

Mystified a little by 'the gift' and the postscript, I
opened the parcel. It contained a lace doily.

A ridiculous token but I cannot deny that I was
gladdened to receive it (and to find no mention of
my father). It demonstrates that I was not wrong in
my estimate of the girl's character and industry; nor
in relying upon the beneficial effect of finding her

employment; and that – for all the risk to myself – I *have* done her a great service.

Dora, meanwhile, seems a little stronger and has been moving gently about the house. She lacks, however, a certain vital spark.

My poor wife!

Friday, 21ˢᵗ March

A thing I should not have thought possible – a row between Dora and her mother!

I was not at home to witness the spectacle, but it was duly reported to me by Mary-Anne, who felt honour-bound (with, one suspects, an attendant degree of personal satisfaction) to alert me to the 'atmosphere' in the house.

The remarkable fact is that there was no particular cause for disagreement. As far as I can judge, Mama W. had removed Mrs. A.'s carnations, on the grounds that they were 'past their best' and Dora asked for their return. This trivial spat led to a state of affairs in which Mary-Anne 'found the missus crying her eyes out,' and 'Mrs. W. with a face like thunder, sir, so that I thought she'd strike me down, as soon as look at me.'

(Most remarkable of all, perhaps, is how Mary-Anne's dislike of my mother-in-law is sufficient to make me my *confidant!*)

I later asked Dora herself what had passed between them but she merely said that I must allow for her 'moods' and that she had already apologised. She spoke most plaintively, saying that it was 'terribly hard for a person to be watched all day long' and that she was 'not a prisoner, as far as I know' and 'had done nothing wrong' and would I not just let her alone, &c. &c. and seemed to grow increasingly despondent, until tears welled up and I was obliged to leave her room.

There can be no misfortune more deleterious to the female constitution than that which has befallen my poor wife. It has clearly played upon her nerves.

Saturday, 22nd March

Mrs. Antrobus paid a call in the afternoon and Dora felt well enough to receive her in the drawing-room, in the company of her mother. Later, after a couple of hours' repose, D. came to dine with us downstairs.

I asked whether Mrs. A. had brought any news. D. looked distracted for a moment – as if the very idea was a novel one – then replied:

'She said that I was to be sure to tell you that she is reading your manuscript, my dear, and thinks it very good.'

Upon any other occasion, my wife would have announced this with some pride. Yet, she spoke utterly without animation, her voice quite flat, seemingly quite heedless of what she had said, or what anyone might make of her words. I remarked that she might have mentioned it to me earlier; this provoked no response.

Mama W. offered the opinion that Mrs. A. was 'a clever woman' (one suspects that she does not consider this a virtue in a female) and that she had plainly done well for herself *as regards her marriage*.

I held my tongue – and we ate the remainder of our food in silence.

Nothing further from D. all evening. It is a terrible thing to see my little woman in such low spirits; I pray that she finds the strength to raise herself up.

Sunday, 23rd March

To church. The sermon, *The Fruits of Grace*, well read.

Met with Dr. Antrobus – polite inquiries after D.'s health – and Mrs. A. who remarked once more on my MS., saying that it is 'such a diverting little book' &c. I replied that it was hardly a book, as it had not been published. Mrs. A. said that she felt sure 'if there were any justice in the world' that it should find a publisher; that I was 'so terribly clever'; that she would 'see it in print within the year'.

(Most flattering, of course. But if the woman was not given to such ridiculous hyperbole, one might trust her judgment a deal more.)

After we had returned from St. Mark's, Mary-Anne demanded an interview. She reminded me that she had not taken her half-day last week 'because of the missus' and asked whether she might 'just have an hour or two, to-day, on account'.

Her unstated purpose, of course, was to meet her *beau*. I informed her that, with her mistress in her present condition, I could not allow it. Met with stony silence; then more of her irascible clattering about the house.

When D. is well, I shall press her to find another girl.

Two o'clock. A dreadful revelation!

I had thought, after Dora's mishap, that we had received our full share of domestic misfortunes.

No, it is too late to gather my thoughts. To-morrow −

Monday, 24th March

I have spent much of to-day − when, by rights, I should have had my mind on matters of business − pondering whether I ought to document what transpired last night; and whether it should be a *full* account. I have come to the reluctant conclusion that, if there is to be any merit in these pages, it will only be to the degree that they record the truth − even if that truth may encompass the grossest misconduct.

It began a little after one o'clock in morning − when I happened to wake from sleep. I cannot say whether it was any noise in the house that stirred me; but it was the distinct sound of a woman's cry outside the house − a sharp exclamation, expressive of pain − that roused me to complete consciousness. I got up, pulled back the curtain, and peered down through the gap between the shutters.

At first, I convinced myself that I was dreaming. For I saw the figure of *my own maidservant*, wrapped in the same tatty shawl she normally reserves for marketing, *walking down Amwell Street!* She seemed to walk a little awkwardly and it took no great leap of imagination to surmise that Mary-Anne had just quit the house and tripped on the area steps; that it was she who had cried out and disturbed my slumber.

My first thought was that I should go down to the kitchen and await her return – and dismiss her on the spot. For what *good* cause could she have to quit the house? However, as I continued to observe her progress from the window, she came to an unexpected halt, some distance down the road. It was plain from her manner that some nocturnal assignation was planned at the very spot where she stood; and that her lover (who else?) had not yet shown himself. It seemed ridiculous, therefore, to wait in the house when – if I acted swiftly – I could put a stop to her mischief. Thus, I put on my clothes and hurried outside.

(What Dora or her mother would have made of my absence – had they woken – I cannot imagine! My fury made me utterly reckless!)

When I finally stepped outside onto the pavement, I realised that my quarry had vanished. Nonetheless, I walked down the hill until I came to the place where I had last seen her – at the confluence of four roads (where Amwell Street becomes Upper Rosoman Street) by the works of the New River Company. It seemed impossible to divine which direction she had taken, until I happened to notice a gap in the works' railings. Two of the upright struts of metal had worked loose, or been worked upon; the rail was broken; and atop one of the adjoining spear-points, there was a scrap of red wool that precisely matched the colour of Mary-Anne's shawl.

It became plain where the girl had gone. Determined to pursue her, I hurriedly squeezed through the gap myself.

Beyond the railings were a set of small wooden out-buildings, dimly illuminated by a single gas-lamp. I hesitantly explored their limits – suddenly conscious of my own trespass – taking cautious steps, lest I encounter a night-watchman. Then, hearing a woman's voice, I peered round the corner of one of the larger out-houses.

I could make out the figure of Mary-Anne, shrouded in shadow, *in company with the labourer.* She stood with her back to a wall, *her skirts pulled up to her waist.* He, meanwhile, lavished lewd kisses on her face; her throat; and, even as I watched, roughly pushed and pulled at her body. It was a brutish seduction but one in which there could be no doubt – even in the half light of the gas – that she was utterly complicit; for there no suggestion of ignorance or unwillingness; nor any doubt that she responded to him in every movement.

What was I to do? I confess that I had not imagined to find the girl abasing herself so utterly and abjectly; the very thought of stepping forward and speaking out – of interrupting their intimate coupling – quite revolted me. I turned around in silence, therefore, and retraced my steps homewards.

I came back to the house with every intention of waiting out Mary-Anne's return in the kitchen. Indeed, I believe I relished the prospect of such a confrontation. Yet, as I waited, I began to consider the possible consequences of a 'row'; and my head began to cool.

First, it occurred to me that if Mary-Anne were dismissed without notice, then Dora would be suddenly deprived of her principal prop in domestic matters; that finding a suitable replacement might take some time; and that the whole business would place a terrible strain on D.'s nerves. Then another idea struck me. As things stood, would not the choice of a new maid, *de facto*, be decided by Mama Willis? If *that* were the case, then was there not every chance that any new girl would become that woman's agent; bending to her every whim; thwarting me on every occasion?

Then came the final consideration – the thought which has hovered on the edge of my mind these last ten days – which ultimately overturned all else and induced me to pity the wretched sinner.

If Mary-Anne had not come to me, to call for the doctor – would Dora have lived?

Here, then, is what I did –

I left the kitchen and returned to my room, waiting until I heard Mary-Anne return and creep up the stairs. Opening my door, I accosted her as she ascended the steps to the attic.

'What are you doing up at this hour?' I said. 'I thought we had burglars.' – 'Beg your pardon, sir. I was feeling poorly and wanted some cordial.' – She looked in the finest of ruddy health and told the bare-faced lie without a hint of remorse or shame. – 'Then you had best go back to bed and lie down.' – 'Yes, sir.'

She began to go up the stairs, but I called her back.

'I could swear that I heard someone scuttling about the area a short while ago. You did not see anyone?' – 'No, sir. There's no-one about, I'll swear to that.' – 'Well, all the same, I think we must make double sure. Speak to the constable when you next see him come by the house; and I think we must have a proper Chubb lock put on the door, and I shall make sure it's locked when I retire.' – 'Yes, sir. May I go now, sir?' – 'Of course.'

I will not deny that it gave me some small pleasure to observe her face. She could not quite hide her disappointment; and she did not realise I could read her thoughts:

Will he leave the key downstairs?

Of course, it cannot be left at that. Neither pity nor gratitude has clouded my judgment to such a degree. For I would have been right to summarily dismiss her – quite within my rights. Moreover, if she has *fallen* – indeed, there can be no doubt of *that* – then who knows how far such moral pollution may spread its pernicious influence?

It is only a reprieve; as soon as Dora is recovered, Mary-Anne must be given her notice.

Tuesday, 25th March

Already I regret my unspoken generosity towards Mary-Anne; for the very sight of her both reminds me of her wrong-doing and provokes all manner of unwelcome conjecture, that comes unbidden to my mind.

How often *has* she thus abused our trust?

Has the labourer led her into vicious habits or is it merely an aspect of the girl's base nature that, hitherto, has lacked an opportunity for its fullest expression?

A man should not be obliged to consider such things at the breakfast table!

Yet, I am quite hamstrung, for this very morning Dora *gave her mother notice to quit.*

Such a course would be natural enough – indeed, most welcome – were D. to have recovered every faculty, but she has not. Nevertheless, Mama W. will leave to-morrow and – *mirabile dictu* – has made no fuss about her peremptory dismissal. I can only conjecture that she fears the effect that another blazing row might have upon her daughter. Certainly, there can be no doubt that a peculiar weakness still afflicts my poor wife's spirits. Indeed, there are times – particularly in the evening, after dinner – when every movement (nay, every word!) seems to betoken an unimaginable mental effort which, in turn, induces a deep lethargy that no words or tokens of encouragement can dispel.

We must, therefore, manage with Mary-Anne until such time as D. is better, no matter how disagreeable the prospect. A new servant would be too great a burden; I dare not remove any prop to my wife's recovery.

Thursday, 27th March

D. still very low; the house dreadfully quiet.

The business with M-A − still most awkward. Must banish all thoughts of it from my mind.

Friday, 28th March

A surprising letter arrived in the afternoon post from *Mrs. Prendergast*, on the subject of *Ellen Hungerford*, addressed to *Dora!*

> Regent-street,
> 27th March
>
> Dear Mrs. Jones,
>
> *I hope you will not think me forward in writing to you, on a subject what I know must be dear to your heart.*
>
> *I have the privilege of being Lady Superintendent at Willis's and recently received a certain Ellen Hungerford into our 'little family' of employées: a poor but deserving girl whom you were so kind as to recommend in the capacity of needlewoman.*
>
> *I thought it right, since you possess an interest in Miss Hungerford's well-being, to acquaint you and your husband with her progress in the work-room. You will be gratified to learn that she has acquitted herself admirably. She is quick-witted, lively, very much 'a worker' and already produces the quality of work for which Willis's is rightly famous. I would even venture to predict that she has the capability to elevate herself, in due course, to the shop-room − for she has a good womanly figure, if yet fully formed,*

and her features are neither too interesting nor too plain.

There is but one barrier, however, to her self-improvement: a want of cultivation and education which, at present, would render her unable to engage in that lively and charming social intercourse with the client which is essential for shop work. I have encouraged the older girls (for she is amongst the youngest here) to begin to gradually correct any points of manners where she presently falls short; and I shall endeavour to provide guidance whenever I am able. The question of education, however, is more difficult, and I hope you will not consider me importunate if I suggest that together we might provide Miss Hungerford, and the other girl's in your father's establishment, with further opportunities for their betterment.

I have been considering for some time, for instance, whether a small library (secular and religious) might be established in the work-room, to afford the girls more profitable leisure in the evenings. I wonder if you would agree with me that this would be a very worthwhile enterprise? It has also occurred to me that we might also arrange a Saturday afternoon visit to the Polytechnic, once a quarter. Indeed, so much could be done to improve the minds of our young women.

I am considering establishing a subscription amongst friends of our girls for this very purpose, which would benefit not only Miss Hungerford but all our employées.

I feel sure you will agree with me that this is a worthy cause and I wonder whether you might like to

> contribute a small sum at the commencement of the scheme?
>
> Yours respectfully,
>
> Mrs. G. Prendergast.

It is an awkward, importunate letter, but perhaps we are obliged to give *something*. I do not approve, however, of the woman writing to D. It is a roundabout, feminine way of appealing to the purse-strings of Papa Willis – she does not go to him directly but plainly hopes that he will hear of her efforts through his daughter.

Of course, she cannot know of Dora's condition; and the present unlikelihood of stirring any emotion within her breast. Indeed, she merely read the letter once over, then handed it to me, and said I might do as I wished.

I suppose I shall send something.

Saturday, 29th March

A visit from Mrs. Antrobus. She took tea with myself and Dora at three o'clock.

I confess, I am very grateful for the little attentions she has paid to D. since her mishap (today, she brought a miniature china vase, filled with *pot-pourri*, which D. has now placed in her room). Her brief visits are the only 'medicine' that seems to kindle a spark of life in my poor wife. For there is something naturally *lively* about Mrs. A. such that – in the manner of the mesmeric – one feels that some portion of her vital influence is conducted through the aether.

There were two topics of conversation. The first was on the matter of servants. In short, Mrs. A. has lost an item of jewellery – in fact, several items over the course of a year or two – and suspects her maid of pilfering. Whilst she has no particular proof of the theft, she has decided to give the girl notice. (I need hardly record that I said nothing about our 'servant problem'!). Much talk, therefore, on the subject of finding decent girls, the use of registries &c. &c. and the 'horrors' inflicted upon a variety of friends and acquaintances by incompetent and ill-disposed domestics. Dora contributed only a few words – all that is required with Mrs. A. – but listened attentively; I held my tongue.

The second subject was much more to my liking – namely my MS. Mrs. A. has finished reading it and considers it 'as good as anything by Mrs. Braddon or Mr. Wilkie Collins'. Again, such *extravagant* praise only serves, in my estimation, to belie the sentiment which has been expressed. Nonetheless, there can be little doubt that Mrs. A. took some pleasure from the book; and her comments on particulars of character and location – with special praise for my description of the Thames – prove that she has read it in full. Whatever her flaws, Mrs. Antrobus is undoubtedly an intelligent woman – surely I may yet find 'an audience'?

(nb. Nothing as yet from Mr. Filks at *The Remembrancer* – should I write to him a second time?)

Mrs. Antrobus left a little after four. I was disappointed, however, to find the restorative effect of her presence was short-lived. For D. retired to her bed before dinner – 'quite exhausted' – and did not come down again. I visited her room before I retired, expecting to find her asleep. I was surprised to find that she had not slept and was tearful and miserable. Worse, she had convinced herself, in retrospect, that Mrs. Antrobus found her 'ridiculous' and 'weak-willed' and 'pitiable' &c. &c. and that her conversation had actually been peppered with little slights and insults (needless to say, all of which quite escaped my notice!). I informed her that I doubted Mrs. Antrobus would ever make such judgments concerning her friends and neighbours; but, quite unaccountably, this only rendered D. the more wretched. She informed me that 'a man cannot see such things' (a *mere* man!) and insisted that she would not see Mrs. A. when she next called. When I then tried to console her, she informed me – her husband! – that she 'could not bear to be touched', was 'utterly tired' &c. &c.

Two weeks have passed since she miscarried the child; yet it seems that any physical or spiritual communion between myself and my poor wife is still quite impossible.

It is a sorry, unnatural state of affairs.

Sunday 30th March

Dora began the day by coming to my room and apologising for last night's outburst. My poor wifey looked so pretty and contrite that, I must confess, any atom of ill-feeling was instantly dispelled. The effect was, however, utterly ruined when she proceeded to make a confession ... that she has not taken the doctor's opium and spirits since her mother returned to Chelsea!

The unfortunate consequence of this abstention is that she *has not slept* – 'no more than an hour or two, I fear, my love, each night, and, for the rest of the night, all I can do is to lie still and quiet.'

No wonder, then, that she has not recovered!

I asked on what grounds she decided to forego the remedy. She replied – quiet and timid – that it increasingly produced an unpleasant 'sinking' sensation; and that the mixture was inclined to summon 'the most awful nightmares'.

I replied, sensibly enough, that the latter was a most childish objection; and that the drug was the one medicine that seemed to aid her recovery.

More tears, &c.

I remained firm; and spoke harsh words. She agreed to resume taking the mixture.

Poor foolish creature!

More thoughts crowd my mind regarding Mary-Anne and Ellen Hungerford, and the contrast between them. The former has squandered her best opportunity in life; and given away her most valuable possession. (Why should that surprise me in the slightest, when I have reluctantly come to know every weakness of her character?) EH, on the other hand, is industrious and uncomplaining, untainted by her association with the worst of men, and now may profit by her own endeavour and rise up in the world.

Have sent Mrs. Prendergast five shillings.

Wednesday, 2nd April

Fortesque has moved to Upper Holloway. This morning, his crowing about the new house quite unbearable. I was obliged to tell him I did <u>not</u> require to be informed of 'Betsy's' opinion on each of the rooms, the length of the garden, the superb gentility of the neighbours &c. Indeed, I am now half-inclined to pay a call and see it for myself. For he is either guilty of gross exaggeration or *has* come into a good deal money; I rather suspect it is the former.

The whole business placed me a bad temper. When F. went to lunch, I took the opportunity to inspect the deeds and registers, which I should have done today regardless, as we have commenced the new quarter. I found the numerical register had not been updated for two months. I warned him, on his return, that this was shoddy.

F. suitably cowed – thus I exerted my authority!

I also spoke to Mr. Hibbert, at long last, on the subject of Broadstairs (for now there is all the more reason to give D. a change of air). He has recommended a respectable little property, which he has rented in previous years, and has graciously given me a week's leave, 'at such time as may suit'.

I will wait until the weather improves and then broach it with Dora; I am convinced it may help her.

D. herself a little better than yesterday.

Thursday, 3rd April

Fortesque more subdued today; most satisfactory.

Left office at five. Walking back home along the City Road, I found myself come unexpectedly face-to-face with a young woman. She was dressed in sober brown cotton, trimmed with white lace; her hair pulled tight back, concealed under a plain straw bonnet, which also partly hid her features. I was about to apologise for interfering with her progress when I recognised the creature before me – a picture of respectable working womanhood – *as none other than Ellen Hungerford!*

The change wrought in her appearance by three weeks at Willis's – a tribute to the care of Mrs. Prendergast for her employées – is truly remarkable. For, with the provision of proper nourishment, and the addition of decent clothing, all that was rough-edged and care-worn in the girl's features has now become smooth and rosy; and her eyes now speak of a blossoming health and vitality, of which formerly there was only the merest suggestion.

I should have chastised her for (once again!) lying in wait for me in such a fashion – quite contrary to what was agreed between us, and *decidedly* contrary to the behaviour Society demands of a respectable young woman, of any class. Yet I could hardly bring myself to say a word on the subject. For, although she remained as demure and unpretending in her speech and manner as ever, she could not hide her own pride in her new appearance, nor the satisfaction she took in my own astonishment at her metamorphosis.

Indeed, although she said that she had merely come to thank me in person for all that I had done – 'for I did so want to see you, sir, and a letter ain't the same thing at all, is it?' – I could not help but think that she was gratified by the effect she had produced. It also occurred to me, as she spoke, that Mrs. Prendergast's assessment that she might suit the shop-room (which I had assumed to be a species of flattery, designed to elicit our subscription) was not ill-founded.

She walked with me along the road a brief distance and gave me a frank and satisfying account of her occupations at Willis's. Her only complaint was that the other girls teased her, on account of her 'slang way of speaking, like … but I don't take it to heart, sir, and it ain't badly meant, I don't reckon, and they'll learn me, I suppose'! Mrs. Prendergast's ambitions for her entering the shop-room, meanwhile, wistfully dismissed as 'not likely!'

We parted company after the canal bridge. I was disappointed by her inquiring after my father (though I suppose that only natural). I replied that I had heard nothing further from him.

At home, I thought it wise to tell Dora of the encounter; for there was no harm in it. Indeed, although she does not know the entirety of the facts (God forbid!), I even hoped that she might take an active interest in the fruits of her own charity.

D., however, hardly said a word, preferring to fuss at her needle-work, rather than engage in conversation. The self-same piece, a sampler, was her occupation all evening. It was only when she went to bed that I realised, despite her industry, that she had made no progress whatsoever in the work – that she spent several hours doing little more than picking and unpicking the threads.

Friday, 4th April

Tried, in vain, to raise Dora's spirits. Proposed that we should seek out a lively entertainment to-morrow evening. I picked out half a dozen likely candidates from the *Times* and read them to her over supper. I said that I should prefer either Mrs. Macready, or Mr. & Mrs. Matthews 'At Home' (Haymarket!) but I did not scruple to include 'Professor Jacob, the Wizard Ventriloquist and Improvisatore' or 'The Secrets of Spirit-Rappings Revealed' (a measure of my desperation, that I would consider patronising such nonsense!).

D. said immediately that she 'did not have the head' for going out. I replied that she could not know how might feel to-morrow night; that I thought an outing might do her good. She replied that she supposed that she would go, *if she must* and that I must choose.

With such enthusiasm, what a merry evening it will be!

Saturday, 5th April

Left Moorgate and went directly to Austin's ticket-office, Piccadilly, and obtained two seats for Mrs. Macready's entertainment (7s.).

A foolish investment, since I returned home to find D. had taken to her bed, informing Mary Anne that she *had a head, begged not to be disturbed and did not think she could go out this evening.*

I cannot describe my irritation on hearing this news. For I was quite certain that all that was required was an effort of will.

What was I to do?

In the end, I paid a quick call on Dr. Antrobus and asked if he and Mrs. A. might enjoy the tickets. He conceded that *'a night out' might please his wife* and took them off my hands. I asked him, during our conversation, if he had any further advice on the management of D.; he also suggested sea-air.

I will say nothing to D. as yet, but we shall holiday in May.

Eleven p.m. D. has just come down and apologised for the wasted tickets &c. I told her how I had disposed of them. She said that she *was* determined to get better; that I should not think too badly of her; was sure that I was angry and that she could not bear it.

I did not 'lay it on too thick'; said that I was not angry; that I too only wished for her full recovery.

We finished our conversation, I think, on better terms.

Sunday, 6th April

D. seemingly more herself. Went to church. Sermon on *Charity and Grace*; that prompted renewed thoughts of Ellen Hungerford.

EH much on my mind since Mrs. Prendergast's letter. I should very much like to further her education, such that she might become fit for shop-work. I spoke briefly to D. on the subject. She appeared to pay some attention to my remarks – gratifying.

Mary-Anne, meanwhile, has taken her half-day – and what that may signify, I do not care to contemplate.

Monday, 7th April

A remarkable improvement.

Dora came down early to breakfast and said that she wished to speak with me. In brief, she said that she knew that I was not happy with her these last weeks (I demurred and said that I understood the cause of her suffering full well); that she was still most sorry for missing the theatre (I said nothing); and that she would like to do more, if she could only find the strength (a sentiment which I endorsed). All this was, of course, perfectly pleasing to me; but little more than a recapitulation of our talk the night before last. She then went on, however, to add that *she had thought all night about that poor needlewoman, Miss Hungerford*; that *she herself would like to meet her*; and, it had occurred to her, *might we take her to the Polytechnic ourselves?*

I cannot adequately describe what feelings this suggestion induced. The simple fact of my dear wifey taking an active interest in the welfare of another human being – having been entombed in the house, dwelling on her own misfortune, these last three weeks – quite overwhelmed me. It was so much to my liking that I rose to my feet and kissed her on both cheeks – which produced such an agreeable blush that, for a moment, I felt sure that I had caught a glimpse of 'my' Dora – the true Dora – once more.

Naturally, I cautioned her regarding several points; not least that EH is a simple girl, who can never aspire higher than the shop-room or perhaps domestic service. But she replied that she had gathered as much; and that, for precisely that reason, she thought that we might do EH the greatest good.

My dear wife! How many others of her class would condescend to put into action the tenets of Christian charity – *in propria persona* – for that most derided and traduced of creatures, a humble needlewoman!

I wasted no time in writing two letters: the first, I sent to Mrs. Prendergast, putting forward D.'s suggestion: namely that we accompany EH on a visit to the Polytechnic, to attend a lecture on a suitable subject. In addition, I wrote that if the attempt should be a success – if she appeared to profit by such exposure – then the effort might be repeated.

The second letter, I sent to EH, by our confidential arrangement. I have given her notice of what is planned. I have also made clear – though it need hardly be stated – that *no mention can be made of my father* and that she must maintain the fiction concerning her mother being in my family's service (to which end, I have supplied some additional requisite information).

With luck – if the girl can be thus moulded and improved – this will be the last instance of such subterfuge; and all future relations between us – if any exist – will be irreproachable.

Midnight. It is too late for second thoughts. Yet, to rely on the girl's silence – to place her in proximity with my wife – it now seems to me quite foolhardy. My enthusiasm at seeing D. *revived* made me reckless.

I hope no harm will come of it.

Brandy!

Tuesday, 8th April

A letter from Mrs. Prendergast in the afternoon post. She writes that EH is due to take this Saturday afternoon as leisure; that she is willing to take up any opportunity for self-improvement which we may offer her.

Dora most pleased. Nothing from EH herself.

Wednesday, 9th April

Dora still afflicted by lingering bouts of tiredness. Nonetheless, she is throwing herself into preparations for Saturday with all the enthusiasm she can muster. She has even selected two instructive pamphlets (on the principles of domestic economy) from her own little library, which she intends to donate to 'our poor needlewoman', and some pieces of old lace which 'I suppose she might care to work up into something fancy'.

She has also chosen the event: a Mr. Plumptre ('lecturer, Oxford and London') reading from '*Julius Caesar*, the works of Tennyson and other modern poets' and 'delineating the art of versification in all its forms'; to take place at the Polytechnic, 3pm. I remarked that it sounded rather 'light', to which D. rejoined that she was sure *something light would suit a young needlewoman precisely.*

Thus does the female mind intuit obvious truths, which may lie hidden from male reason!

I have written to Mrs. Prendergast with the details.

Thursday, 10th April

A note from Mrs. Prendergast – all is arranged.

Still nothing from EH herself; I had expected a reply.

Friday, 11th April

At last, a letter at the receiving-house.

> *Regent-street*
> *10th April*
>
> Dear Sir,
>
> *I am thankful for all you have done for me, and Mrs. P. should not like it if I did not go, so I shall see you on Saturday at the Polly, though I am feared I shall say something wrong and you shall not like it.*

I know you must think me a silly girl but I suppose
your wife is a lady and I do not think I should tell
her stories. I will not say nothing, though, and keep to
what you have told me for all our sakes.
I will always do what you ask of me.
Your servant,

EH.

This reply stirs mixed emotions. For it is a shameful thing to be rebuked – and it *is* a rebuke, even if she did not intend it – by the very girl for whose benefit I have worked so hard. Yet there is something so plain-spoken and honest in her (she assuredly does <u>not</u> possess that love of secrets and intrigue which comes so naturally to some of her sex) that I cannot help but admire her native integrity. For I *am* asking her to practice a deception, however good my motives. Indeed, I fear I have become so adept at maintaining an overweening lie – the concealment of all traces of my own history – that I presume too readily on the connivance of an innocent girl.

What a fool I am – to place myself in such unnecessary danger!

If Dora should ever suspect what I have contrived to keep secret –

I would write to her again; but it is too late for that.

Lord! Will she keep her word?

CHAPTER SEVEN

Inspector Delby sat alone at the desk in Jacob Jones's study, gazing out into the back garden. The disordered sheets of the diary, which had once littered the desk's surface, were now neatly arranged into several piles of paper. The inspector's own pocket-book, meanwhile, pencilled with notes, lay open beside them.

Sergeant Preston knocked loudly at the door, disturbing his superior from his brief moment of reverie.

'Any luck, sir?'

'No, I fear not. A little bit of luck is just what we need. We must find both Jones and the girl. That is the long and short of it.'

'We'll find them, sir, don't you worry.'

'Do you think so? We have made little progress thus far. Meanwhile – for want of anything better – I am obliged to sit here, reading through all this self-regarding scribble, in the vain hope that it may contain some vital clue.'

'Well, sir, if we didn't have the diary –'

Delby rubbed his forehead, waiving his hand dismissively. 'I am well aware of that; the affair would be even more of a mystery. But we are no further, for all Mr. Jones's compulsion to document every aspect of his existence.'

Preston fell silent. Delby frowned, but made an effort to recover his temper.

'Come, sergeant, I do not mean to sound quite so defeated. Now, have you spoken to the neighbours again, as I asked?'

'Yes, sir,' said Preston, adopting the same brisk tone he reserved for speaking in court. 'Several parties, sir; mostly servants. It all confirms what we thought anyhow: Mrs. Jones was killed Friday. At least, that's the last time that anyone saw or heard anything of her.'

'Be more precise, Preston. Who is this "anyone"?'

'Sorry, sir. In particular, I'm talking about the cook next door; name of Donaldson. She's the last one that saw any sign of Mrs. Jones. She recalls seeing the doctor's wife, Mrs. Antrobus, come round to the house to visit her. Heard her talking to Mrs. Jones on the door-step and thought it queer –'

'There was no maid. Mary-Anne Bright, had been dismissed the day before.'

'Precisely. Anyway, she puts that at about two o'clock, Friday. She saw the woman leave about half an hour later.'

'And what about Dr. Antrobus and his wife?' asked Delby. 'We need to speak with them. In the absence of any other line of inquiry, it is becoming rather pressing.'

'I know that, sir. Both of them have been out all day. It seems that he's seeing a patient in Mayfair.'

'He left no name or address with the servants?'

'The maid's new, of course; she doesn't know a thing. As for his missus, she's visiting a sick relation in the country. They should both be back this evening; I've told the girl to let us know.'

'Then I suppose we have to await their return,' said Delby. 'Well, let us forget them for now – continue.'

'Well, like I say, sir. It seems Mrs. Jones died on the Friday. Now, no-one has seen *Mr.* Jones since, neither, except – and this is what I came to tell you, sir – I just got through talking to a few of the cabbies at the Angel –'

'Jones took a cab?'

'It seems like it. I found one fellow who said he'd taken a man from the corner of Amwell Street to London Bridge that very night – about ten o'clock. So I showed him Jones's photograph – that little daguerreotype I found in the drawer – and he reckons that it was the same man.'

'Did he take him to the bridge itself, or the station?' asked Delby.

'He dropped him off by the station – Tooley Street – but he's not sure if he saw him go inside. Can't recall if he had any luggage, neither.'

'That does not help us. Did he notice anything in his manner?'

'Just that he was in a hurry, sir,' said Preston. 'Nothing more.'

'Did he say anything to the man?'

'Only "London Bridge."'

The inspector shook his head. 'A curious journey for a man supposedly intending to do away with himself.

Where the devil was he going? Do you still have Jones's photograph?'

'Of course, sir.'

'Good. When we are done, give it to one of the men and put him in a cab to London Bridge; perhaps one of the clerks may recall Jones buying a ticket. If he took a train, I should like to find out.'

'You and me both, sir.'

'And what about Ellen Hungerford?'

'She was definitely here that day, too. The cook again – she definitely saw her later in the afternoon – after Mrs. Antrobus had been round. She couldn't say the precise time, mind you.'

'Anything more?' asked Delby.

Preston looked at his note-book.

'Told me that she noticed Ellen Hungerford go down the steps to the kitchen – she didn't know the girl's name but she knew her by sight – assumed she was on some errand. No idea if she went inside or not. She didn't see her coming back up the steps, though that might have escaped her notice – she was too busy with putting a crust on a pie.'

'Not that busy, from the sound of it. Now, one moment, what's this?'

Their conversation was curtailed by a constable appearing at the door with an envelope, plainly intended for the inspector.

'Are you expecting something, sir?' asked Preston.

'I should think it is a note from Sergeant Brentwood at the Yard,' said Delby, taking the delivery and opening it. 'I inquired after any suicides in the last three days; in London and a hundred miles about. He has been combing the newspapers for me. Hmm. Apparently he has found a couple of cuttings.'

'Then you do think Jones might have done for himself?'

'It's as well to be —'

Delby's voice trailed off. It was plain that his eyes had lighted on something in particular.

'Sir?'

'In this morning's *Daily News:* "A Mysterious Disappearance. A full suit of clothes, including a shirt, trousers, cuffs and collar, were found on a beach at Broadstairs, Kent, on Saturday. The find prompted great speculation amongst the local people that a man had gone to the beach to take his own life. Drags were procured and a careful search made for a body in the area where the clothes were found; but no body was recovered. There was nothing to identify the owner of the abandoned articles, with the solitary exception of a silver locket in the pocket of the man's trousers …"'

'You think it might be Jones?'

'I do,' said Delby, who turned away abruptly, and began rifling through the pages of the diary on the desk. 'Here, read it for yourself.'

Sergeant Preston took the proffered article. He swiftly realised that his superior had neglected to read out the final sentence.

'"This locket bears the inscription *To My Sweet Georgina, my true love*,"' said Preston. '"If this is familiar to any reader, they may contact the station-house at Broadstairs."'

'It's familiar, all right,' interjected Delby, holding up a page from the diary. 'Here! The miniature of Jones's mother.'

'So he went all the way to Broadstairs,' mused the sergeant. 'Suicide, though – do you credit it?'

'I am not sure,' replied Delby. 'Leaving his clothes on the beach might be a mere blind.'

'Or the fellow went and drowned himself.'

'You had better get the train down there yourself,' said Delby, after a moment's reflection. 'Someone must have seen him; spoken to him. Ask at the station; boarding-houses; talk to whoever came across the damned clothes.'

'What about you, sir?'

'Either Jones has drowned himself or he has manufactured this discovery. If it is the latter, he has had two days to plan his next move. In either case, I should be surprised if you actually find him waiting to be apprehended in Broadstairs. Therefore, I think it behoves me to remain in London. Besides, if nothing else, I still wish to see the doctor and his wife at the earliest opportunity.'

'You think they might have some idea about where we might find Ellen Hungerford?'

'I rather fear, Preston, that is our only hope.'

DIARY

Saturday, 12ᵗʰ April

Dora awoke before dawn and could be heard pacing about her room. At breakfast, she confessed that, during the night, the visit to the Polytechnic had slowly assumed a rather fearful aspect in her imagination; that she had woken plagued by a host of anxieties (all quite trifling). I remarked that this was a natural consequence of her seclusion in the house for so many days; and that the outing might well serve to stimulate and invigorate her. This seemed to provide some reassurance; for she agreed with me and told me that she was determined, for both our sake's, to *seize the day*.

I returned from work at two. Our cab had been ordered for half past the hour and arrived promptly. Dora was a little dilatory in coming down – a question *of the right hat* (!) – but, at last, we set off. A victory of sorts! I remarked how fine it was to step outside with *my lovely wife on my arm* and received a kiss for my trouble (How welcome was this small token of affection!). D. herself, meanwhile, grew more lively and excited – more like her old self – with every yard of our progress down Pentonville Hill.

EH was waiting for us outside the Polytechnic. She stood sentry upon the pavement, unaccompanied, a short distance from the functionary employed to take visitors' shillings. I noticed that she watched the road from beneath lowered lids, not daring to catch the eye of passing strangers. Nonetheless, even as our cab approached, a pair of young men looked pointedly in her direction. Doubtless they hoped that it might be the prelude to some species of flirtation. I was gratified to observe that not only did she give them no encouragement – God forbid! – but her manner and her dress did not embolden them to renew their effort.

'Is that the girl?' asked D. – I replied that it was. – 'She is rather pretty.'

Pretty! It is a peculiar characteristic of the sex that every woman, on meeting another female, passes some judgment on her beauty – whether she admits it or not – regardless of her class or station. I could not help but remark on it. D. replied, quick as lightning, that it was a peculiar characteristic of men to pretend that they did not.

Much laughter!

(And how much did this resemble my dear wifey of old!)

I paid the cab, then hurried to make an introduction and pay for our tickets – for a large crowd was gathering for the lecture. EH herself as quiet as a mouse – barely audible above the noise of the street. D. seemed most pleased with her. My own nerves were also swiftly calmed. EH displayed a considerable degree of native shyness in the presence of 'a lady' and limited her answers to a handful of words and no more.

'I am pleased to meet you, Ellen.' – 'Thank you, ma'am.' – 'I understand your mother was with my husband's family?' – 'Yes, ma'am. She was, ma'am.' – 'For many years?' – (here, I confess, a pang of anxiety!) 'A dozen or more, ma'am.' – 'And then she married?' – 'Yes, ma'am.'

And so the conversation progressed – until my dear wife *herself* had re-told the very story in which I had schooled my unwilling conspirator (with only a 'yes, ma'am' or 'no, ma'am' to correct it!). It was fortunate, nonetheless, that we had but a short time before the lecture began. Thus, with polite inquiries all but exhausted, I led the way up the steps, through the marbled hall, and into the theatre.

Mr. Plumptre proved to be an elderly gentleman, with a professorial mien, who did little to breathe life into his subject matter. Nonetheless, even as she took her seat, a child-like reverence was visible in EH's face. I do not doubt that she felt it an honour merely to set foot in such a splendid hall of learning. Moreover, on hearing Shakespeare, if she did not understand each word, it was plain that she intuited the sentiments expressed, and enjoyed the beauty of the Bard's language.

The lecture itself finished at half past four. Mr. Plumptre then took the opportunity to announce a sequel to the proceedings: 'at the same hour, seven days hence, consisting principally of a discourse upon scenes from Shakespeare's Stratford and Old London, presented with the aid of an oxy-hydrogen lamp and slides'. Dora, to my great surprise (and disbelieving delight!) immediately insisted that we attend. She then inquired of EH whether she 'might like to see the pictures and hear another talk?' I interjected that EH would not be permitted a second afternoon's leisure, at such a short interval. D., however, declared this 'Nonsense!' and said that she would write to Mrs. Prendergast and 'make arrangements'.

(Thus EH herself had no say in the matter!)

We quit the Polytechnic with D. in high spirits. Having bid EH goodbye, she professed herself convinced that our experiment in philanthropy had 'opened the poor little creature's eyes to the better things in this world'. Meanwhile, as we waited for a cab, I had begun to harbour a new hope that my dear wife, with a little fresh air and useful activity, might soon be returned to herself. The outing seemed to have wrought a complete transformation; a beneficial effect which no amount of doctoring or nursemaiding had hitherto accomplished.

Yet how swiftly may one's most cherished ambitions be overturned!

For, minutes after we had begun our journey homewards, my poor D. began to lose that renewed vitality which had animated her at the Polytechnic. A silence fell between us; her face remained turned to the window; her back, formerly resolute and stiff, seemed to slacken and slump against the seat.

I asked her if she felt quite well, and she replied that she had over-exerted herself.

Then – worse still – as we travelled through Bloomsbury – to my utter consternation – she suddenly let out a low moan, like the sound of wounded animal, and burst into tears.

Utter confusion!

On returning home, it was all I could manage to bring her indoors and carry her to her bed. I asked if she required the doctor; she replied that it was 'merely tiredness and fatigue' and demanded 'rest'.

What was I to do? I feared that no rational explanation might be wrung from her lips, whether by her doctor or her husband. Yet, after supper, I visited her room and, finding her wide awake, at last the truth came out.

It was not mere 'tiredness' that had prostrated her. Not long after we entered the cab, she had spied a young woman from the window – a coster-woman, no less – *with a little boy in her arms.* The sight of the ragged little boy – inconsequential enough – had 'sent such a miserable chill through my soul,' and 'placed such muddled and unnatural thoughts in my head, that I almost lost my senses.' – 'What thoughts?' I asked. – 'Vile thoughts. That it was a terrible thing that my child had died while hers had lived. That I would rather have seen her child dead than mine.' – 'It was an unfortunate fancy, nothing more.' – 'No, Jacob. You cannot imagine how I felt at that moment. Lord forgive me! *I truly wished it dead.*'

She said no more, but broke into tears. I could offer no solace. What can a man say to such things?

Sunday, 13th April

D. too weak for church; remained in her bed all day.

I spoke to Dr. Antrobus, after the service, and told him all that had occurred after the Polytechnic. He assured me that it was a question of over-exertion; and that such irrational fancies were not uncommon in females delivered of a stillborn child; that all such things will pass, given time.

I pray to God he is correct.

Tuesday, 15th April

D. in bed much of the day – the same dismal lethargy has a grip on her once more. Mrs. Antrobus has been to read to her – kindness itself – and left a note, assuring me that 'time will heal' &c. &c.

Where do people acquire such wisdom? I am far from certain that it is borne out by fact.

Wednesday, 16th April

Dora a *little* brighter; came down to breakfast.

An unfortunate turn of events, however, at the office. The day began with Fortesque arriving in a dreadfully sour mood; quiet and sullen. I asked him – by way of making conversation – how he now found living in Holloway. He replied that it was 'all right, I should suppose' and then said nothing more for the remainder of the morning.

This was remarkable in itself – and so out of character for F. that I wondered if he might be unwell. I waited until lunch and then invited him to Gilroy's. This, too, he refused, saying that he had no appetite (again, a first!). But – as luck would have it – it was in the chop-house that I uncovered the root cause of his misery. I am not one to pay heed to City tittle-tattle, but I overheard a piece of gossip at the adjoining table: that a broker on the Exchange had 'cut and run' after a series of disastrous speculations – most likely frauds – that he had left behind a mountain of bad debts; and – here is where I pricked up my ears – that the man's name was *Gresham – viz., the self-same young broker whom F. first met at the Holborn Casino!*

I hurried back to the office, neglecting my customary cup of tea, and immediately took F. to one side. Once I mentioned the man's name, a floodgate was opened. As I feared, F. himself confessed that, with the folly of youth, he had fallen victim to one of the broker's fraudulent schemes. He had bought worthless shares in a mining company, on the man's personal recommendation, *to the value of one hundred pounds* (!). He felt certain that he now could not pay his rent past the second or third quarter; moreover, that his 'dear Betsy' would desert him; and that, now I had learnt of his mistake, he feared he would lose his position.

I assured him that the latter contingency, at least, need not occur; that a foolish speculation with his own capital was not the Company's business. He looked up at me – as if relieved of a terrible burden – and heartily shook my hand, and called me 'the most decent fellow in London'!

It is a dreadful thing to see a young man ground down; and I could not, in good conscience, add to his troubles. It is only be hoped that he has been chastened by the experience; and, if anything remains of his inheritance, that it will not be squandered.

I returned home at six. Went upstairs and spoke to Dora – still 'low'. She told me, however, that she had written to Mrs. Prendergast and asked whether we might take EH to the Polytechnic a second time. I questioned whether this was wise; but she replied that she was 'determined to rise above things'.

A good sign?

When I then returned downstairs to the study, I found an envelope waiting for me on the desk. Mary-Anne informed me that it had been delivered by hand, earlier in the day. I recognised instantly my father's script and felt the familiar pang of trepidation as I opened it.

It contained two items: first, a note that simply read *In part payment. G.J.*; second, a pair of bank-notes to the value of two pounds.

Thus my father – it can be no other – has performed a miracle of sorts. Never, since I was a small boy, have I received a scrap of money from his hands; never has any debt been repaid – except in misery and disappointment. Under any other circumstances, it might be a cause for some small private celebration – yet, with Dora ill, I cannot bring myself to be cheerful.

But still – two pounds.

We may yet 'rise above things'!

Thursday, 17th April

Mrs. Prendergast has agreed that EH may attend the Polytechnic a second time.

It *is* a good thing that Dora is enthused at the prospect – but I worry for her health.

Friday, 18ᵗʰ April

Met with Mrs. Antrobus on my return from Moorgate. She had spent much of the afternoon in Dora's company. I said that I hoped that my poor wife was not placing too great a demand on her time. It is a tribute to the woman (after a fashion!) that I can vividly recall the conversation which followed:

'My dear Mr. Jones, it is your sweet Dora who has been obliged to look after me! So, you see, it is your poor wife with whom you ought to commiserate.'

'How can that be so, ma'am?'

'It is quite true, sir, you have my word on it. Shall I explain? Now, you must tell me if you can believe it – you recall, perhaps, my difficulties with Martha?'

I did not recall the name. She was obliged to remind me that it was that of the servant, whom she had suspected of theft.

'Well,' she continued, 'let me say that, these last three weeks, I have said nothing more to her on the subject. In fact, even when we did speak, I merely told her that she did not suit and must work out her notice. But I have not been easy in my own mind – not at all – and you can imagine the atmosphere in the house!'

I asked if – granted her reasons for the dismissal – she intended to give the girl a character.

'There, Mr. Jones, you have the nub of it. Should I, or should I not? It was, after all, only my intuition that guided me. I had no proof of wrongdoing. But then it came to me last night! A master-stroke! And this morning – can you imagine it, my dear Mr. Jones? – I laid a trap!'

'A trap?' I said, incredulous.

'Can you credit it?' she replied, smiling, with a touch of self-pride in her voice. 'Shall I tell you how I went about it? I let it slip that I had lost a brooch – a very pretty valuable little silver article, that belonged to my dear mother – that it had become detached it in the street when I last walked to Highbury to see my cousin.'

'I do not follow you, ma'am.'

'Why, I hid it under the drugget, in the drawing-room, by the fire. You would know the spot, I am sure – you have stood there yourself.'

'But surely she would find it there?'

'Precisely!'

I perceived that the plan was a clever one – that if the girl were honest, she would return the brooch; that if she were not, it would vanish.

'And – what do you think, my dear sir – no sooner had Martha cleaned the grate this morning, than it was gone!'

I congratulated her on her ingenuity; but that was not the end of the matter. She had gone directly to the girl – not waiting for either her husband or a policeman – demanded the return of the jewellery and the girl's immediate departure from the premises. The worthy Martha, however, had denied all knowledge.

'Can you imagine the bare-faced mendacity of it, Mr. Jones?' – Unwelcome thoughts of Mary-Anne! – 'Can you imagine a young woman so brazen? In any case, I told her that I would fetch a constable. She said that I "might well do as I liked!'"

'I trust you found one?'

'Our local man. Now, he is a very nice young fellow, and quick on his feet. He came directly and – I could hardly believe my eyes – he had to drag her up the area steps to effect an arrest – screaming like the proverbial banshee. You may rest assured that I have never been so mortified! Such a spectacle! So I hope you see now, dear Mr. Jones, why your wife has been comforting me – indeed, it has been a terrible trial! I do not believe I have yet recovered.'

I inquired if I might walk her home – which she declined – and we bid each other good-night.

Inside, Dora was ready to repeat the whole story to me; most disappointed to discover that I had heard it all; was it not so terribly unfortunate for Mrs. A. &c.

I did not vouchsafe my own thoughts – that, contrary to her protestations, Mrs. Antrobus was precisely the sort of female rather enjoyed a spectacle – a seeker after sensation! – that she liked nothing better than recounting the story, and would cheerfully tell it to her astonished friends and acquaintances for weeks to come.

D. in general is somewhat improved. She has made herself busy about the house; talked with enthusiasm about 'seeing the little needlewoman once more.'

Saturday, 19th April

An awful day.

Returned from the office at two – expecting to find D. ready for our trip – only to discover her in bed with 'a terrible head'. I asked if she might not rouse herself; but she assured me that she could not; she had *hoped all morning* for recovery, but she had only become much worse.

I remarked that it would be a great nuisance to go to Regent Street and inform Ellen Hungerford. She replied that the girl *should not be disappointed on her account*; that, if it were too late to despatch a message, I might simply take her to the lecture myself.

This seemed to me a foolish plan and, instead, I concentrated all my efforts at persuading her to assay the cab ride – if nothing more – for the good of her health. This, however, proved a wasted effort. Every attempt at suasion only encouraged her to plead for 'the poor disappointed needlewoman' – deflecting all my entreaties. Worse, fixing on the idea, she became doubly insistent that I attend the Polytechnic 'for Miss Hungerford's sake', working herself into such a paroxysm over 'our duty to the little needlewoman' that she visibly exhausted herself. At last, since nothing else would placate her, I found myself obliged to agree.

Thus it was that, *at my wife's insistence*, I met Ellen Hungerford on Regent Street a second time. I can recall our initial conversation – the most banal exchange – with absolute clarity (and I will record it here, as it is required in my defence!).

'You're alone, sir?' – 'My wife is indisposed. She was, however, most insistent that you should not miss Mr. Plumptre's lecture. I promised her that

I would see to it. In any case, I trust *you* are well, Ellen?' – 'Very well, sir, thank you.' – 'Good, well, I believe it is nearly time. We had better take our seats, if I am to give my wife a good account of the afternoon.' – 'Yes, sir.'

No more was said!

We followed the crowd and took our seats in the theatre. The room itself was already in semi-darkness – all but one window obscured. Mr. Plumptre took to the podium and, after a few introductory words, the final blind was shut and the lime-light ignited. I confess that I turned to look at my companion, when the first slide was placed before the powerful lens. The scene before us was commonplace enough – an ancient house in Shakespeare's Stratford – but there was no doubting the wonder in the girl's eyes at the brilliance of the light and clear delineation of the subject.

An <u>innocent</u> glance. Yet, was it then – as she turned her head and her eyes chanced to meet mine – that a fatal misunderstanding arose? Or was it the fact of Dora's absence? For it was some five minutes later that she shifted slightly in her seat and – in the darkness – *she placed her hand to rest gently on my own!*

What monstrous confusion had prompted the girl to act thus? Had I given her any encouragement? No, I had not. In neither word nor deed! A thousand thoughts raced through my mind. Did she imagine that I had brought her to the place for an immoral purpose? Surely not! Worse – much worse – was *that* the supposition of every man and woman who had seen us enter the hall?

I pulled my hand away and turned to look at her. Never – thank the Lord! – have I seen a truer picture of confused and wounded innocence. It seemed clear to me that the gesture was the naïve and thoughtless expression of youthful sentiment, unplanned and spontaneous. Foolish, yes; but born of tender feminine feeling – not least a degree of gratitude for all I had done for her – and not, *in itself,* immoral. Indeed, the only immorality that could result would be if one more wise and worldly were to exploit such naivety.

Was she not a mere girl?

Thus, I whispered a discreet admonishment; that *such things are not proper.*

Nothing more, I think, was required; and anything more would have only drawn notice and occasioned further embarrassment. Yet, in truth, I cannot claim that I passed the remainder of the hour in a spirit of relaxation. Nor, indeed, when the blinds were opened, and we had quit the theatre, did Ellen Hungerford venture to look me in the eye.

I hesitated for the right words.

'I hope we are still on good terms, Miss Hungerford,' I said, at length. 'And I trust that what passed just now may be quite forgotten.'

'Oh, yes, sir!' (with much emphasis; for I could tell she was very sorry for her foolhardy act.)

'It would be wise, however, if we did not meet again under such circumstances. But perhaps, on occasion, you may still write to me – or, better still, let us say my wife – and tell us of your progress with Mrs. Prendergast.'

'Yes, sir.'

'Very well.'

And – with that awkward exchange – I bid her good-bye.

D. was still in bed on my return. She asked – though with little enthusiasm – whether 'the little needlewoman' had enjoyed the lantern slides; I replied that she had.

What else was I to say?

Midnight. I find it difficult to put the events of the day from my mind; and I struggle with the question of whether, in some small part, I am to blame. The unintended intimacy of a darkened theatre has doubtless led to many a romantic misapprehension; and I know in my heart that I myself have *done* nothing wrong. Nor have I done anything which might have induced the girl to form some mistaken attachment – except to take a kindly interest in her well-being and her future.

I must be truthful, however, and confess that it is not only the *deed* that concerns me.

For the touch of girl's hand – the merest stroke of her fingers – stirred a dreadful yearning in me – the sort which cannot easily be satisfied.

I had not thought myself prone to such weakness – for I do not fool myself it is anything else – and fear I must value myself the more cheaply for it.

If only all were right between Dora and I –

Monday, 21ˢᵗ April

It is remarkable how swiftly gossip may become 'news'.

For, though he has yet to be caught, or convicted of any crime, the young broker's fraud – the bogus company &c. – is now the property of Fleet Street, the name of *Gresham* appears in every newspaper and the allegations against him (which appear to be legion!) are banded about throughout the City. Fortesque, in consequence, in low spirits; he fears that 'his Betsy' may abandon him, once she learns of the money that has been lost (a fine wife!). I remarked that he might yet thrive, despite the loss of his inheritance, if he only were to adopt a more frugal and economic mode of living.

He replied that he would 'think on it'!

Dora is still 'not herself'. Indeed, she is hardly ever in that blessed condition. It is true that, on certain days, she can rally; the tide ebbs and I see a glimpse of the lively young woman whom I married. Yet, seemingly, the tide always turns; then the lethargy predominates.

Mrs. Antrobus is due to call to-morrow; but that is only a temporary tonic, whose effect soon vanishes. The only possible remedy is a spell of sea-air. The weather is still too cold for Broadstairs – but I think we may go soon.

Tuesday, 22nd April

Mrs. Antrobus came this afternoon and regaled Dora with talk of her new servant, a girl by the name of Catherine, who – D. informs me, secondhand – is the most slovenly and sluttish creature to be imagined. Mrs. A. – harsh, unforgiving and exacting mistress! – has all but decided to end her week's trial and 'try her luck' a second time.

Meanwhile, our own 'difficulty' persists. For Dora relies utterly upon Mary-Anne; and, in her present condition, she could no more 'try her luck' at a registry-office, and instruct a new girl in managing the house, than dance a jig.

Thus, for Dora's sake, I submit to a viper in our midst. And, when my mind's eye turns to what I witnessed that night – when I catch the girl's eye at some unexpected turn, when she comes down the stairs, or she appears from the kitchen – I can only attempt to blot it from my conscience.

Thursday, 24th April

I returned home this evening to find Dora in possession of a letter, 'concerning Miss Hungerford.'

My heart skipped a beat!

For there was something so distressed in D.'s tone that I half fancied the girl had posted a letter herself, containing some foolish girlish apology for what had happened at the Polytechnic (which, however it might be worded, could only cast doubt upon my own actions) or, worse still, a confession of her true history. I took the piece of paper from my wife's hand and I was relieved to discover it came from Mrs. Prendergast. The contents, however, caused me considerable dismay. I have copied it herein.

Regent-street,
24ᵗʰ April

Dear Mrs. Jones,

I hope you will not object to me writing to you once more, on the subject on Ellen Hungerford.

I am afraid I must convey a piece of disagreeable news which can give her friends no satisfaction. I must inform you that, although it troubles me deeply, I have been obliged to give her notice; she will leave our employment on Saturday 26ᵗʰ April.

The facts of matter are straightforward and I trust, having heard them, you will not consider that I have acted unwisely or counter to the interests of Willis & Co. For Miss Hungerford returned, last night, from her evening's leisure, in tears, with a dreadful laceration across her cheek. To my horror, it resembled the sort of mark that might be left by a blow with a whipcord or belt. Of course, I had no wish to speculate on such matters and demanded where she had come by such an injury. I had expected and hoped for some innocent explanation. She not only refused to give me an answer, but has maintained the same stubborn refusal all night. I trust, therefore, that you will appreciate I have little alternative, if only for the maintenance of good discipline, to remove her from our employment. Furthermore, I cannot imagine what company she has kept, during her hours

*of leisure, where such brutality can occur and go
unremarked!*

*I write to you, ma'am, as I know you have taken a
deep and most creditable interest in the girl's welfare.
If there is any moral force you can bring to bear that
may persuade her to name her assailant — for I fear
there can be no other explanation — then I would urge
you to do so. I do not doubt there is a man — rather, a
brute! — at the root of this unhappy incident; and if
Miss Hungerford continues to mix with such persons,
there can be little doubt as to the future course of her
life.*

I remain, your servant,

Mrs. G. Prendergast

'It is quite awful,' said D.

(Pity, not condemnation! How good is my wife's
heart, even when she is at her worst!)

'If she will not say who has struck her —'

(The sentence unfinished; for my own thoughts
turned to my efforts on Ellen Hungerford's behalf —
all utterly wasted!)

'She must be afraid to speak. Can nothing more
be done?'

'I suppose I might talk to her,' I replied.

'You ought, my dear.'

I might talk to her, of course. But then — what
more am I to do?

Friday, 25ᵗʰ April

I went to the receiving-house, but nothing from EH. I had a fancy that she might write to explain herself.

In any case, I have thought long and hard on the matter. The wound can only be the work of the boot-maker, Halifax. Did he chance upon her in Regent Street or Soho? I should suppose she is still afraid to name him before a magistrate.

If he has renewed his 'attentions', however, then there is great danger, not least if EH herself is to be cast out onto the street.

I will not see that vile brute triumph.

With Dora's consent (although, of course, I have said nothing of the boot-maker &c.) I have written to Mrs. Prendergast that she is to find modest but respectable accommodation for EH for the next fortnight (for which we shall find the rent); and to tell her that I shall write to her, once such lodgings are found.

If only she might be persuaded to bring a charge against the boot-maker!

Saturday, 26ᵗʰ April

EH has removed to lodgings in Mortimer Street; a relative of Mrs. Prendergast.

I have made arrangements to visit her to-morrow.

Sunday, 27ᵗʰ April

Went to church alone – D. too low – then walked to Mortimer Street.

I found the lodging-house located in a small, well-kept terrace of the last century. I was met by its presiding spirit, Mrs. Bracebridge, a stout elderly woman, dressed in a neat and homely fashion, who ushered me into the modest front parlour. It was a most respectable little room – but one in which any conversation, though conducted in private, might easily be overheard. Thus, when EH came downstairs, I casually remarked on the virtues of exercise &c. and suggested a walk in the direction of Regent's Park. There was, however, the question of *the wound*. EH had made no effort to conceal it and it was quite plain that she had been the victim of a heavy blow; one that had drawn blood and left much of her cheek dark and bruised. Thus I was obliged to wait a few minutes longer, until, at my suggestion, a veil was acquired from the landlady's wardrobe.

We exchanged only a few brief words of greeting then walked to the park in silence. There, I finally spoke out: saying that I had some idea of who might have struck the blow; that I understood why she had kept her own counsel; that I would do all in my power to help her; and that – if she could only summon the courage – the boot-maker must be brought up on a charge.

She did not speak for some time. When, at last, she spoke, her voice was quiet and nervous.

'I thought I shouldn't see you again, sir, after –'

She turned her head shyly to one side. I replied that I would rather that the events at the Polytechnic – an unfortunate misunderstanding – were forgotten. I said that it was her injury – and its consequences – which had given me gravest cause for concern; and that she must tell me everything that had occurred.

'But you might not like to hear the whole story, sir. Nor who did it, neither.'

I replied forcibly that, given such an evasive answer, she was morally obliged to reveal the truth that instant.

She hesitated, then spoke in a whisper – like that of a child confessing its own wrong-doing.

'It were your father.'

I cannot say what disturbed me the more. The explanation or the manner in which she gave it, as if she herself were the guilty party. I urged her to tell me the entire history; reluctantly, she complied.

'I had my evening's leisure, sir, and I didn't want to sit with Mrs. P. all the while – and I ain't got so many friends in London – and the other girls is older and didn't want me – so I got out and thought I might surprise your pa. I knew he'd get his cab at the Cross Keys at eight o'clock – that's when the night-men begin – so I had a fancy to go and see him, before he started out.'

I remarked that it was unwise for a young woman, one who found herself in a respectable situation, to visit a public-house, unaccompanied.

'It *was*, sir,' she said, with heartfelt emphasis, 'but I thought I'd meet your pa, see? I weren't going inside.

And –' (I wonder, did she blush beneath the veil?) – 'I ain't never had a ride in a cab, neither.'

Thus a poor foolish girl was willing to risk all her prospects in life *for the sake a ride in hackney!* I said nothing, however, and begged her to continue with her account.

'Well, he weren't there; neither him nor his cab, see? So I asked the waterman if I'd missed him –' (Another pause) – 'and he said something I didn't quite understand, not at the time.'

I asked her to continue.

'He looked at me very queer – I didn't know *then* what he meant by it – and said that I *had* missed him, and he'd *reckoned he'd already got a girl, but I could wait inside the house, if I liked, and he supposed he might give me a turn later on, if she got tired of it.* Then he said something like, *where's your regular patch, anyhow?* Well, I didn't say nothing – I thought he was in his cups – except to say that I'd be going, and to tell your pa that I'd come and asked for him.'

'But then you met with my father?'

'It was my bad luck, sir. If I hadn't –'

Here she faltered and became somewhat tearful. I gave her my handkerchief and she went on.

'I was walking back and coming up to Tottenham Court Road. And I saw this woman standing on the corner, all by herself – a little way off, but I saw her under the gaslight. Well, I'm not so green I didn't know her for what she was – I could see she painted; and that she was on the look-out. Then a fellow comes up and they talks and she takes him off, down the road a little while. Then this cab comes up beside them. And I recognised the driver, see?'

'My father?'

'Just! Then the pair of 'em got in – bold as brass, with hardly a word – and he drove off.'

I remarked that he should have refused such custom.

'No, sir – not just *that* – you don't understand!' she protested. 'It was what the fellow at the Cross Keys had said, see? – I twigged it there and then – I felt it so strong – terrible wrong of him, too, after all you'd gone and done for him – and I know I shouldn't have done nothing but –'

Here, she grew almost impossible to comprehend. I urged her to calm herself. We walked more slowly until, at length, she recovered a little.

'So I went to the coffee-stall on Oxford Street – the big one, you must have seen it – and I had a cup there and I waited. I put up with all sorts of chaff, sir, from men and women too – none of *them* better than they ought to be, neither – but I waited.'

'For what?'

'Why, for your old man! And he did come back, not twenty minutes later. That same girl got out of the cab and went back to just the same spot and stood there – and he waited in the cab, too, until she'd got another fellow on her hook.'

It took me a moment to understand her meaning; the nature of the crime which she attributed to my father. She did not spell it out – thank God! – but, at last, it became plain to me: *that my father had reserved the cab for the exclusive use of such women and that he profited accordingly.*

'I ran up to him, sir. I couldn't stop myself. I told him it was wrong – so wrong, after everything you'd done – to repay you like that – that he'd end up in the jug for it – and you'd be had up for helping him get started. I don't know what else I said – only I expect I shouted and made a fuss – because the man went off and your pa said I'd lost him a shilling and I should shut up –'

'And then he struck you?'

'I don't think he *meant* to, only he was so angry –'

Enough. I will not record the rest. It is sufficient to note that, even in recalling this abuse, she did not hesitate to defend him.

I don't think he meant to!

Thus the boundless magnanimity of a woman's heart – its greatest strength – is also its greatest weakness!

I will not say I did not pity EH on hearing her account. My overweening emotion, however, was one of anger – bitter anger that my father should –

No, it is foolish to write more on that score.

It is sufficient to record that I then returned EH to her lodgings. I also gave Mrs. Bracebridge a brief description of my father (without explaining our relation!) and, having given her a shilling for her trouble, made it plain that he should not be admitted into the house.

For my own part, I would happily wring his neck.

One o'clock. The afternoon and evening spent lost in thought. It is fortunate that Dora has not been 'herself' – if "fortunate" can be the word – she has not noticed my abstraction and anxiety.

I will not confront my father; for what purpose would it serve? I have now experienced every possible kind of betrayal; I know that there is no depth to which he will not sink. There is nothing to be gained by sermonising or casting blame, no matter how well it is merited. Indeed, I fear that he takes a perverse satisfaction in inducing me to trust him – for it shows his power over me – and then relishes observing that trust dissolve.

I will not give him that pleasure.

I have thought of the police – but if he should tell a magistrate that I paid his 'surety' for the cab; then I might find myself before the bench; and everything would come out.

I shall, at least, write to the cabman, Dennis – an anonymous letter – and tell him what I have learnt. If he is an honest man, then my father will be dismissed; if he is not, then I will have given him warning that *someone* knows his involvement in this revolting trade – and, likely as not, fearing the police, he will dismiss him regardless.

As for Ellen Hungerford – despite my every effort – he has contrived to ruin her best chance in life.

Poor girl! What remains for her now?

Monday, 28th April

Have told Dora that EH was brutalised by *her father* but refuses to bring a charge (some such story was required); that we might give her a small sum of money, with which she might find her own lodgings &c., but can do no more.

D. herself still 'low'; and the business with EH seemingly only serves to make her more miserable. Can she not rouse herself?

Alas! There is little satisfaction in home and hearth at present; and little joy in my life!

Friday, 2nd May

I have not set pen to paper for three days – how like the Roman's prayer: *it has been three days since my last confession!* – and never has a man had a better reason for maintaining his silence.

Indeed, this very evening, I have contemplated – in all seriousness – abandoning my diary-taking altogether and making a bonfire of the last few months.

Yet I *would* confess! What breed of fool am I?

I should, at least, be grateful that there is no priest – no friend – no man or woman alive – to whom I might unburden myself – no better confidant than these humble pages.

It is, in any case, not a question of *three days*. Nothing of note has happened since Tuesday night – nothing has kept me from this desk, except that I have lived in a state of constant fear and unnatural excitement.

Is it possible that – in writing these words – I may come to understand my own heart – my own deeds –

Enough! I shall write only the facts of the case; and, if I am to be damned, I shall be damned in my own words.

It was Tuesday night – a little after nine o'clock (Dora had already retired) that a boy came to the house with a letter. I did not recognise the hand and opened it in the study. It came from Mrs. Bracebridge and reported that Ellen Hungerford had just left her lodgings, not an hour previously, *in the company of a man*. She wrote that she had not let him into the house – as per my instruction – but that EH *had gone willingly enough*. She admitted, however, that, *though it wasn't her place to keep the girl under lock and key*, she felt obliged to write to me directly, as *the man had been under the influence of strong liquor and handled the girl very roughly in the street*.

I will not record the curses I heaped on the old woman's head. The man could only be my father. How often, as a boy, had I seen him torment my mother in his drunken moods – punish her for his own failure as father and husband? If my letter to Dennis had resulted in him losing the night-cab business – if he had been made to suffer for his venality –

Would he hesitate to visit his anger on Ellen Hungerford?

I immediately left the house, without a word of explanation to Mary-Anne or my wife, and walked towards Goswell Street. In truth, my blood boiled. I do not believe I planned any definite course of action. My only thought was to effect Ellen Hungerford's immediate rescue.

I made swift progress to Pear Tree Court. There, I worked my way through the stinking alleys and hurried up the steps that led to his door. I was far from certain that I should find my father 'at home'. My doubts on that score were soon quashed – for I heard raised voices within.

I did not trouble to knock.

The scene that assailed my senses brought back countless unwelcome memories of my boyhood.

First the overweening pungent aroma of gin; then the sight of my father – red-faced, his clothes dishevelled, his every movement wild and unchecked – berating the poor girl who cowered meekly at his feet.

At his feet!

There was no doubt that he had struck her, though I could not see the marks. For, in his hand, dangled the leather strap of his belt, which he raised again above his head.

How long had she been lying there, at his mercy?

Incensed, I leaped forward and wrestled the belt from his grasp. In turn – did he even know who assailed him? – he pushed me to one side with great violence.

I tripped over my own feet, falling backwards. My head rebounded against the exposed brick of the nearest wall. I felt an agonising jolt but stumbled back to my feet.

He knew me then; but the sight of *his only son* did nothing to cool his temper.

'Don't you interfere, my boy!' he exclaimed, pointing his finger. 'Or you'll get what for! Mark me!'

'Interfere? I will not hesitate to strike you down. Leave the girl be!'

'Leave her be? She doesn't know when to keep her mouth shut, my boy – that's all – I'm only learning her.'

'I warn you –'

My words were cut short because, from his waistcoat, to my astonishment, he pulled out his pocket-knife. I had no answer to this – I had not thought that he would stoop to such barbarity.

'There!' he shouted, in drunken triumph. 'There now, my boy! Ellie's happy enough here with me – don't you fret – we're old pals – she'll tell you herself.'

His speech was slurred and incoherent; the hand which held the blade unsteady. With his free arm, he pulled at Ellen Hungerford's clothes – her face streaming with tears – tugging her to her feet. Precisely what he intended – for he still held the blade outstretched before him – was impossible to fathom. The result, however, was utterly unforeseen. For, in their struggle, the girl slipped on the uneven boards; and, as he held her arm tight, a counterbalance for his drunken bulk, the sudden shift of her weight pulled him down on top of her.

She screamed – I recall that all too well – pushing and squirming like a trapped animal, frantic – until she had wriggled free from underneath his body. At first, I could not comprehend why *he* did not lift himself up. Then my eyes alighted on the dark stain on the front of her dress; and the pool of blood forming beneath his stomach.

A dreadful low moan escaped from my father's lips; my own feet, meanwhile, turned to lead.

'He is dead – I've done for him.'

She said the words, not once, but thrice; a dreadful liturgy.

My father did not move.

I remained rooted to the spot – drained of all feeling – whilst EH began to pace back and forth, as if her limbs were beyond her control.

'They will take me to the gallows – I shall hang.'

And I shall hang too.

That is the only thought that I can recall from that moment – no pity for Ellen Hungerford; no sorrow, as I watched my father breathe his last.

I swear I felt the noose tighten around my neck; and all breath disappear from my body.

How long did I stand there? I might have remained there for all time – gripped by that terrible fear – had I not faced a more immediate danger. For EH, quite heedless of the world around her, collided with the rickety deal table that lay at the centre of the room. The two candles that had stood on the table tipped over and fell into the bundle of rags that served as my father's bed. Instantly, the bed was ablaze. There was nothing in the room to douse the flames. The tatty blankets, meanwhile, little more than scraps of old cloth, were a tinderbox. In mere seconds – I could hardly believe it – the room filled with smoke.

I roused myself, grabbed EH's arm and dragged her down the stairs.

Did we shout 'Fire!'? I truly cannot recall. The cry went up swiftly enough. Even as we descended the stairs, the dilapidated houses began to vomit all their wretched inhabitants into the court. A noisy panicking crowd of men and women, young and old, jostled for the alleys, not scrupling to push or pull at their neighbours. I myself joined the scrum – driven by the terror of being trampled down amidst the chaos; the fear that we all might so easily be burned alive.

It is something of a miracle that we escaped. We came out onto Goswell Street just as the brigade finally arrived – in time to observe the gawping passers-by who had gathered in a great mob, and thus obstructed the firemen's every effort.

EH was, at least, docile and compliant as I dragged her further down the street, away from the danger – away from the crowd – yet her mind seemingly wandered. I feared that she had lost her wits.

'I shall hang.'

I whispered to her to keep silent. At length, I took her down an alley, between two manufactories, that led towards the City Road and the canal. The sound of the blaze could still be heard; the roaring flames and crackling of the fire; and then a dull booming explosion. I was at a loss, until I recalled the small gas-works that overlooked the court.

I do not believe EH herself gave any thought to the fire – or her part in it – for she merely repeated the same three words.

I implored her to listen to me; to recover her senses. I told her that she was not to blame for anything that had happened – that it was my father's doing – but that she must hold her tongue. For already I could see the danger – that she would tell all, though she truly had done no wrong, and that a charge of murder – arson for good measure! – would be laid at *both* our feet.

I find it remarkable, now, that I could be so calculating at such a moment; that I could readily appraise the consequences of what had occurred and weigh up a course of action; yet, at the time, it seemed plain as day.

'But he is dead,' she insisted.

'An accident – he fell – you did not intend it – the blade was in his hand.'

'The police –'

'We cannot chance the police. You must trust me.'

She nodded. I assured her that it was so; that her future – my own – our very lives – relied on her silence.

'Yes, sir.'

I saw that she shivered and, without a thought, I held her arms to steady her, pulling her close to me.

I did not intend to kiss her; but, even in the darkness, I could sense that she did trust me; that she trusted me implicitly, and would do all I asked. My reason vanished as I bent down and my lips touched hers; all else was blotted from my mind.

I never thought I should make love to another woman after Dora; yet it was such a sweet release that – even now – I cannot think of it without –

Enough.

My father is dead. I have lived these three days in terror of the police; of a knock at the door. I have read the papers – a 'Terrible Fire and Explosion' – *the remains of an unknown man* – but no-one has come.

Is it possible that his identity may never be discovered?

The explosion of the gas – *the remains* – there may be no evidence for the police.

I have begun to believe that it *is* possible; that I will <u>not</u> suffer for my father's sins; that Ellen Hungerford, too, will be spared.

Am I an unnatural son? Undoubtedly; but he was a most unnatural parent.

My father is dead; and – if I am honest – I only feel relief that he will trouble me no more. It is providence at work.

As for Ellen Hungerford, I think no less of her; only less of myself. I have robbed her of such a prize; and I took such a terrible pleasure in it.

But what will become of us both?

CHAPTER EIGHT

Inspector Delby sat in the study and took the cup of tea offered by the young constable. He did not utter a word of thanks – he harboured a vague idea that it would be contrary to the maintenance of good discipline – but granted the young man a cursory nod.

'You've read all this, constable, haven't you?' said Delby, gesturing towards the papers on the desk.

It was a rhetorical question – for the constable was the self-same individual who had first placed the sheets in their proper order.

'Yes, sir. Well, some of it.'

'Enough to form an opinion of the man?'

'Of Jones, sir?'

'Of course. Tell me what you make of him.'

The constable hesitated, plainly surprised to have his opinion elicited.

'A queer sort, sir,' he said, at last.

Delby shook his head, disappointed. 'That means nothing, my boy. I am asking what do you make of his character?'

The constable paused for thought, mustering his courage.

'A bit full of himself, sir.'

'Arrogant, you mean?' said Delby. 'Yes, I'll give you that. Go on.'

'And very particular, I should suppose. I mean, writing everything down like he did.'

'Quite right – a methodical man; given to introspection; quite thorough – a typical clerk, one might say – and yet –'

'Sir?'

'This business is far too chaotic – his relations with the wretched girl – I do not like it – something is amiss –'

'I don't quite follow, sir.'

'No, constable, neither do I. What are we missing? There is something concealed in all this verbiage – I'm sure of it – I cannot put my finger on it.'

The constable, thinking silence the best option, said nothing. Delby, in turn, glanced back at him and, noticing his rather nervous expression, could not help but smile.

'Do not worry, constable, it's my job to find the fellow – not yours. Now, I take it there's nothing more of the doctor or his wife?'

'Shall I go and inquire again, sir?'

'Yes, you had better.'

Delby waited until the constable had left the room then rose from his seat, putting his drink to one side. His only motivation was a degree of restless energy; an unwillingness to be inactive. He paused, however, by the cabinet in which Jacob Jones had kept his bound diaries, and idly selected a volume from those which remained on the shelves. He flicked through its contents, finding nothing of interest. When he came to replace it, however, he noticed that two flimsy pieces of paper had been crushed behind the books.

They were, he discovered, two items cut from a newspaper.

TERRIBLE FIRE AND EXPLOSION. Last night a disastrous fire broke out in Pear-tree-court, Goswell-street. The district thereabouts contains many narrow alleys and passages and is considered by its neighbours to be a veritable 'rookery'. It is impossible to state the origin of the blaze with any certainty. Many old buildings of timber construction were consumed by the conflagration and the danger was increased by the proximity of the works of the London Gas and Coal Company. The alarm was conveyed to various stations of the Metropolitan Fire Brigade and eight steam and manual engines were conveyed to the spot, together with more than eighty men, under the command of Captain Shaw. It became plain that nothing could be done to preserve the houses, as a tremendous mass of fire reared and leapt high into the air, throwing out a terrific heat. The destruction also extended to one gasometer, which suffered a rupture. Gas then rushed out of the aperture and was ignited, causing a loud and fearful explosion which augmented the destructive force of the flames. The blaze itself could not be extinguished until the houses had 'burnt out'.

> *The conflagration was accompanied by a further tragedy: the remains of an unknown man were discovered amid the ruins. A coroner's inquest will be held to-morrow.*

Delby read the first article at speed; there was nothing in it that he did not know already. The second item, however, was a different matter.

> *ST. LUKE'S. Yesterday, the sitting magistrate, Mr. Urquhart, received £25 in accordance with the will of the late Rev. Samuel Pierce, to be placed in the poor-box of the court, for the relief of distressed and deserving objects; also £1 under the initial "J." for the Christian burial of the unknown victim of the Goswell-street fire, following the coroner's inquest of Tuesday.*

The policeman was still pondering its significance, when the constable came back to the study door.

'No sign of the doctor, sir. Nor his wife,' said the young man.

Delby, however, seemed to ignore the information and merely held up the piece of paper, as if exhibiting it in court.

'Sir?'

'An item from the Police column of the *Times*, constable, unless I'm much mistaken. I found it at the back of that cabinet. It rather suggests that Jones quietly paid for his father's burial. I think he couldn't decide whether to put it in the diary. There's no mention of it. Imagine! A man who will confess to adultery, to theft, to every conceivable wrong-doing, but he will not admit – not even to himself! – that he buried his own father. What sort of man is this fellow, eh? Here, you may read it if you like.'

The constable did as instructed.

'You think it was Jones who sent that money, then, sir?'

'I am sure of it, though it is of little help to us. I suppose it may betray a guilty conscience.'

'Guilty? You think Jones killed him, sir? Murdered his father and his missus?'

The inspector glanced at the papers on the desk. 'We have only his word to the contrary – although, I admit, it bothers me that there is nothing thus far to contradict him.'

The constable hesitated. 'Then it all comes down to finding the girl, don't it sir? If Jones is still alive, he'll stick to his story. It all depends what the girl has to say for herself.'

'Ellen Hungerford – yes, constable, you're quite right. I only hope the doctor or his wife may provide some vital clue. It all comes down to the girl – and I should like to find her –'

'Sir?'

'I have sent men to her former lodgings; with no result. She had no family – to the best of our knowledge. The girls at the drapers had no high opinion of her; but they have said nothing to Sergeant Preston that might help in our investigation. It seems, constable, that Miss Ellen

Hungerford has vanished; and I have no idea where to find her.'

DIARY

Sunday, 4th May

After church, we received Mama and Papa Willis for lunch.

The meal itself was excellent — Mrs. Galton's roast beef was admirable — but quite impossible to describe the vast gulf between the inanity of the conversation (Papa W. having just been to the Exhibition in Kensington) and the contents of my own mind. For the death of my father has cast a long shadow. It has left me with a lingering dread of retribution: an irrational fear that, even if not at the hands of the police (and, surely, something may yet come from that quarter?) I will nonetheless pay some unforeseen price for what has occurred. I remind myself constantly that *it was not my doing*; but it does little good. Thoughts, too, of Ellen Hungerford crowd in upon me — her part in it all — the capital I made of her confusion — that dreadful stain on my conscience. I have not exchanged one word with her since it happened. It is unmixed moral cowardice on my part: I cannot bear the prospect that she will look upon me with blame in her eyes — that she will silently condemn me as her seducer. For she has *fallen* — the very fate that I would have spared her — and *I am to blame*.

Poor girl!

Mama W., meanwhile, has proposed that she take D. to the Kensington Exhibition next week; little enthusiasm from D. herself. I am far from certain that her mother will persuade her. Dr. Antrobus's assertion that 'time will heal' &c. has certainly not been borne out – not yet. If anything, I believe that Dora is worse. The lethargy prevails; she remains trapped in the house; her only mental exertion is of the most trivial nature: fussing over an article of dress, or Mary-Anne's arrangement of the dinner table. Moreover, these rare instances of activity are more a source of anxiety than satisfaction. She worries over trifles; returning to the cause of her frustration again and again, becoming increasingly irritable and unhappy. She approaches the question of EH – 'the welfare of that poor needlewoman' – in the same spirit. She came back to the subject this very morning; I encouraged her not to dwell upon the matter.

What am I to do amidst all this chaos? I have written to the party in Broadstairs recommended by Mr. Hibbert. I have no other recourse available to me; I must pin my hopes on that.

I will mention it to Dora to-morrow.

Tuesday, 6th May

Some improvement in our affairs. I told Dora yesterday of my proposal to holiday in Kent. She seems to have reconciled herself to the idea; even to have taken it up. For, as I left for the office, she talked of needing a new summer dress and asked whether I thought Mrs. Antrobus might go with her to the milliner's. I remarked that I felt sure any such proposal would be most welcome.

(Indeed, I would welcome it – whatever the hat may cost! – just to see her leave the house on her own account.)

There was nothing of consequence at Moorgate – or, at least, nothing that required much of my attention. Thus, my mind turned to other matters – yet again, the question of EH. The situation must be addressed. The matter of her lodgings is a pressing one: we assuredly cannot 'keep' her in Mortimer Street; nor is that any doubt that she must find herself some new form of employment. It is plain to me, too, that I must 'break' with her – for the sake of us both.

How is it to be managed?

It would be simple enough, except that the recollection of our terrible intimacy still plagues me.

I do not believe it would have occurred if all were right between D. and myself.

Wednesday, 7th May

It seems that attempt I have made to help my wife – to improve her condition – is fated to meet with disaster. This evening has proved no exception.

It began well enough. On my return from Moorgate, I learnt that D. *had* been to the milliner's with Mrs. A. (a success!) and purchased *yet another* straw bonnet (how many of such articles can a woman require?). In retrospect, she did not exhibit the same degree of feminine pride which normally accompanies such a *coup*. Nonetheless, the fact that she *had* made the effort gave me courage and prompted me to act.

Can I confess in these pages what happened next? It is not a agreeable thing to write; and yet, if I do not record it –

No! I shall use plain words. Indeed – why should I not be utterly frank? For who shall read this but my future self; and he will only look back with disdain, if he encounters half-truths and veiled meanings.

After D. had retired, I entered her room and attempted to renew our marital relation. For it seemed to me that, if *that* might be accomplished, it would do much to right things between us. She did not object and the business was soon complete.

How wrong, however, was my hypothesis!

No tenderness, nor affection was there in our joyless union! It was the mere performance of the act itself – the marriage bed turned to stone – an altar on which D. played the part of sacrifice. I do not dispute that, on occasion, it is natural and necessary for a wife to submit to a husband out of love – one might even call it duty – for I am quite sure that a woman rarely feels that same burning passion that is natural to the male. But how terrible when the unlucky man finds his wife has <u>no life in her</u> – when his love does not stir the slightest smile – the merest loving touch!

This evening has been a revelation to me. I have known for some weeks that my wife is in the grip of a debilitating mental disorder, which has sapped all her strength – her will – completely. Yet I now realise that what I have seen in fleeting glimpses –

the occasional show of spirit or vital energy – is mere play-acting; a charade for my benefit – and one which she cannot maintain when the veil is lifted.

When all was done in the bedroom, I looked at her – and she looked back at me – we might have been utter strangers.

How did this terrible state of affairs come about?

Friday, 9ᵗʰ May

I have spoken to Dora about EH; for it is necessary to come to some conclusion regarding the lodging-house, rent &c. The solution is this: I shall give EH sufficient money to remain there another fortnight – or wherever else she might choose – during which she must seek new employment. Willis's will not take her back and it is unlikely that we may find her another opportunity. The girl must, therefore, obtain whatever work she can find.

I have sent a letter to Mrs. Bracebridge to say that I will visit her to-morrow and settle our account. Whilst I am there, I will seize my courage and speak to EH myself. I will make it clear, too, that I intend to sever our acquaintance.

D., meanwhile, is very gloomy. I wonder if I should have kept the entire business quiet. For 'the fate of that poor needlewoman' has become a morbid pre-occupation.

I have also had word from Broadstairs; they cannot accommodate us until the 4ᵗʰ of June! The delay is a nuisance but I have replied to say that we shall take the cottage for a week; for, in any case, the weather at present is unseasonable; and inferior accommodation would only serve to try D.'s nerves.

Saturday, 10ᵗʰ May

Went to Mortimer Street. Paid Mrs. Bracebridge her due (rather *too much* gratitude from the woman – did she think we might baulk her?) and took EH to the park a second time. On this occasion, she wore a simple veil, without any prompting.

(I happened to glimpse her face at the house; the wound itself, in fact, much healed.)

We exchanged only a handful of words as we walked, both of us, I suspect, afflicted by shame and embarrassment. I bad her to sit down on a bench, in a secluded spot. After a long interval of silence – for want of anything better! – I asked her if she was well.

'I suppose,' she said quietly. 'I have not slept so well –'

She could not bring herself to say the words; but I understood – *since that night.*

'Tell me, have you spoken to anyone, concerning what happened – I mean to say, my father?'

'No. Not a soul. I daren't. Who would I tell?'

'You must remember what I said. We have done nothing wrong. But we cannot presume that a policeman – a jury – a judge – might reach the best conclusion.'

She tilted her head, hesitated, then pulled back the net of her veil.

'*Nothing* wrong?'

Did I blush? Again, I took her meaning well enough and – Lord! how weak is the flesh! – merely looking at her face – the very same temptation of the senses came over me – just as it had that night.

'That was very much my doing,' I hurriedly replied, 'a terrible aberration. I am deeply sorry for it.'

'An aberration?' she said, stumbling over the word.

'A foolish mistake.'

A look of confusion passed over her features; she turned her head and drew the veil back down.

I was mystified. Did she expect some other answer?

I persevered and told her of the money; that she might do with it as she wished, that she must find work on her own account; that we should not meet again. She fell silent; then, finally, replied in a whisper.

'I don't want it, sir. I don't want no money from you.'

This seemed to me a perverse reply. I asked her if she had already found work; she shook her head.

'Then you have every need of it.'

'I'll find my own way. Now, I had best be getting back.'

I told her this was foolish pride; that she was in want of the money; that she need feel no embarrassment –

My words fell on deaf ears. She rose from her seat and began walking back along the path. She neither eschewed my companionship, nor acknowledged my presence during the entire walk through the back-streets – except to bid me good-bye at the door of the old woman's house.

Thus ended both my interview with Ellen Hungerford – and what must be our last meeting – in the most peremptory and unsatisfactory fashion!

I shall not see her again. I have done all I can; let her live off her pride!

Midnight. I cannot sleep. Thoughts of EH. If the manner of our parting has somehow offended her – then she has it in her power –

No, she will not go to the police; I am sure of it.

One o'clock. These are night terrors; they will dissolve in the light of day. She will not risk her own neck – she understands the danger – she is naïve, but not a fool.

I will take some brandy.

Sunday, 11th May

My nocturnal fears have, indeed, diminished in the daylight; but they have been replaced by another. For I informed Dora yesterday of Ellen Hungerford's refusal of the money. Now I wonder if I ought to have concealed it. The consequence? My wife's anxiety as to the girl's welfare – an interest which I once foolishly instigated and encouraged – has produced a new dilemma.

In brief, Mrs. Antrobus called this afternoon. She arrived at three o'clock and Dora managed to receive her in the drawing-room. An hour later, I heard a knock at my study door. To my surprise, it was not Mary-Anne but our neighbour.

I inquired how she had found my wife.

'My dear Mr. Jones' — everyone is *dear* to Mrs. Antrobus's heart; most likely even the dustman! — 'I fear your sweet wife is sorely afflicted by her nerves. I find her really quite agitated. She has been telling me all about the poor needlewoman, the girl whom you recently befriended.'

I replied that Dora was still kind-hearted, for all her troubles, but liable to fret over nothing.

'Nothing? But, my dear sir, am I right in thinking that this poor young woman, because of her father's brutality, has been robbed of her employment and thrown back upon her own meagre resources?'

I said that, like countless other young women in our great metropolis, she would have to shift for herself.

'Yet she is a young girl of good character?' — (Did she observe me flinch?) — 'Your wife certainly praised her manners; and I believe you know something of her family and history?'

I could not make head nor tail of such questioning; its purpose was quite opaque to me. I said that I knew a little; that I had no reason to doubt she possessed good morals (was there ever a greater hypocrite?) and came from a good family.

What else could I have said?

'Then she might suit going into service?'

My surprise was plainly writ large on my features, for she continued:

'My dear Mr. Jones — don't look so astonished — my present girl is merely on trial and I am determined to be rid of her. I have tried three tiresome females since

I dismissed Martha – who, may God have mercy, now labours in the House of Correction – and all of them have proved quite unsuitable. Now, a young girl, a lively, clever little girl, who might be trained – who would be grateful for a place – that might suit me admirably. What do you think, Mr. Jones?'

What did I think? I confess that I felt a rising panic. For it seemed to me that to put Ellen Hungerford in such a position – in such proximity – could only lead to disaster. How might she keep our secret from a woman such as Mrs. Antrobus?

Yet I felt myself at a disadvantage. Having placed EH at Willis's – having lavished praise on her character – how could I say that she would be utterly unsuitable for such preferment by Mrs. Antrobus?

I dissembled. I suggested that I was not sure she possessed any experience suited to domestic service – 'I might teach her to do everything to my liking, my dear sir!' – that she had little education – 'Hardly an impediment, Mr. Jones' – that I was not even sure of her current address – 'But dear Dora would be so pleased, I am sure, if you were to make some inquiry –'

I am left with a great dilemma. For I *was* obliged to concede to Mrs. Antrobus, before she left the house (indeed, I wonder if she would otherwise have quit the premises!) that *I would make the inquiry.*

What am I to do?

Under any other circumstances, I would think it wrong to deprive the girl of such an opportunity. Moreover, if she has suffered these last few weeks –

at the hands of my father – *at my hands* – then who else should make it right?

Yet I cannot discount the risk to myself – that every secret should be revealed –

No, I shall do nothing. I *must* do nothing.

Tuesday, 13th May

I have passed two nights beset by doubts; but, this morning, I finally thought I was reconciled to the awkward necessity of inaction.

However, a letter arrived this very afternoon from Ellen Hungerford herself.

> *Dear Sir,*
>
> *I will not give the address, as I am sure you don't want it, but you will be pleased to hear that I have found new lodgings.*
>
> *I write to tell you that I am sorry for how I was with you at the park and how things was between us. I know as well that what happened before was wrong and that you are not fond of me no more than any other. I had my own silly fancies but they were nothing and I hope you will forgive me for acting like I did. I know you did not mean no insult by giving me money; and I am not so proud as you must imagine.*
>
> *I am still your servant with humble best wishes,*
>
> *EH*
>
> *p.s. I have found a job of work with Mr Halifax in Greek Street and when I have earned enough*

> *money, I will pay for my lodgings and all I owe you and your wife.*

What am I to make of this?

The girlish talk of 'silly fancies' – was that the was the nature of her confusion and disappointment in the park? Did she expect me to declare my undying love? A romantic liaison?

Then, the postscript: *with Mr. Halifax of Greek Street.*

The boot-maker!

Does she now consider herself so worthless that she prostrates herself at *his* feet?

And yet, have I not done – by soft words and good intentions – however unplanned and unwitting – the very thing which he would have accomplished by brute force?

Why has she written to me in this fashion?

Is it to lay the ruin of her life at my door; to show me the full consequence of what I did on that night; how low she must now abase herself?

What price will she pay – has she paid already – to work for Halifax? Have I reduced her to *that?*

Does she seek to punish herself by adopting this course?

It is all done to a purpose: to show me that I am to blame for what she will become; the common fate of any girl who has been ruined by a heartless man.

And that is the worst of it; the fault *is* mine.

Wednesday, 14ᵗʰ May

Thoughts of Ellen Hungerford – still! – interrupted. This afternoon, a letter received: a reply from Mr. Filks – with his comments upon my MS.!

It is three long months since I placed my work in his hands; three months in which, beset by so many battles of life, I have utterly retreated from literary ambition. And yet, amidst all my difficulties, how welcome was this distraction – the letter placed on my desk by Mary-Anne – and with what trepidation and excitement did I open the envelope!

Upon reading the note, however, I had half a mind to burn it on the spot.

It is a truly dismal missive; there is little to savour. Indeed, it is only in the spirit of self-reproof – or is there some distant hope that I may yet rise above even this rebuff? – that I shall include it herein:

> *The Gentleman's Remembrancer*
> *8, Crane-court*
> *Fleet-street*
> *14ᵗʰ May*
>
> *Dear Sir,*
>
> *I write with regard to your tale 'An Unfortunate Progress', which you kindly submitted to our esteemed journal, with a view to its presentation before the general public.*
>
> *I must write to inform you that the public will have to be disappointed in this particular instance. I do not say that your work entirely lacks merit. It is lively and interesting in parts, with several dramatic*

convolutions, of the sort that are pleasing to the reader.

There are, however, many infelicities in the writing itself. For example, can an item of furniture truly be said to 'repose itself'? How would one 'catalogue' a man's face? These are but two egregious examples amongst many. We hope that you will not consider us ill-mannered in humbly drawing them to your attention. Our intention is simply to provide a light to guide you, so that your future endeavours, when exposed to the critical sun, will be marked by fewer blemishes of this nature.

The principal difficulty, however, lies with what one might term the 'mechanical parts' of your creation. In particular, we did not feel that the death of old Mr. Avery was sufficient cause for his daughter's ruin; nor that the legal difficulties entailed by the inheritance were comprehensible to the reader. This served to greatly reduce our interest in learning the denouement of the tale.

With regret, we are obliged to conclude that, though your work demonstrates some literary ability, it is not suitable for the Remembrancer at the present time.

We do, however, wish you every success with your future endeavours.

Yours sincerely,

G.W.Filks, Esq.

p.s. We shall return your manuscript within the week.

This, then, is the fruit of three months' patience! It is, perhaps, a trivial disappointment, when I think of all that has happened. Yet, it has left me thoroughly dispirited. For, although I am one of nature's pessimists, I had allowed myself, in this instance, *to hope*.

I informed D. of the contents of the letter; she merely remarked that I should 'send it to another gentleman'. I cannot describe how much this angered me (although it now seems ridiculous that I should write of 'anger'). It was not the words themselves, however, but *the disinterested manner in which they were spoken*. I daily repeat to myself – and I am sure it is true – that such things are a symptom of the malady which afflicts her. Nonetheless, yet again, I increasingly feel myself to be married to a female incarnation of the chess-playing Turk; an *automaton* that merely plays the part of my wife.

Midnight. Amidst my own disappointments, I find myself returning to Ellen Hungerford.

What are these 'silly fancies' that she has put aside? I fear that, through my own ignorance of the female heart – and, then, the foolish – nay, criminal – spending of my passion – I have encouraged her to think of me in terms of affection – perhaps even love – and that *her* disappointment has driven her into the arms of a villain; a man no better than my father. She has taken the blame unto herself and – how like my poor mother – colluded in her own punishment.

I do have it in my power to interfere –

But have I not learnt my lesson?

Thursday, 15th May

Dora's brother will be in London to-morrow afternoon, an unexpected visit, before sailing again on the evening tide.

Mama W. has made arrangements, therefore, to convey D. to Chelsea in the morning – so that she might see him for an hour or two – and return her home on *Saturday* evening, to permit a night's rest 'with the family'. Moreover, if D. is in good spirits, they may also 'do' the Exhibition on Saturday morning.

D. herself has agreed to the proceedings; but the proof of the pudding &c.

I fear, however, it will take more than Chelsea – though I will concede the air is a good deal better than Islington – to leaven my wife's moods.

One o'clock. Ellen Hungerford haunts me still! Worse, she has now become a spectre of my imagination! I have had such a dream –

Brandy.

Friday 16th May

It is peculiar how following the dictates of conscience – or, at least, that acute mental anguish that results from consciousness of one's own wrongdoing – is the often most dangerous course. Yet, tonight, I have risked my own future happiness – or, at least, security – to rescue Ellen Hungerford from a vicious course which, without a doubt, would have led to her doom. It is, perhaps, a form of madness to stake so much on the fate of one girl. Yet, I am left with the conviction that *I have done the right thing.*

It was, I suspect, Dora's absence that spurred me to action. Despite her languid moods, the house tonight seemed strangely empty without her; and I was thrown back upon my own thoughts without any possibility of distraction. In my solitude, I finally came to the conclusion which I have fought against these last few days: namely, that I was morally obliged to seek out EH and put Mrs. Antrobus's offer before her. Indeed, to shun my responsibility for her future – taking all that has happened into account – would be the greatest moral cowardice.

The first difficulty, of course, was to find her. There seemed but one place where I might seek her out. Thus, I quit Amwell Street after dinner, telling Mary-Anne that I was going to visit an old acquaintance (!) and took a cab to Greek Street. The boot-maker's commercial premises were already closed, just as I had expected. There was, however, a side-door, behind which, through a soot-crusted fan-light, the glow of gas was just visible. I gave it a sharp knock and a narrow grating opened. I knew, in an instant, that this was the entry to the boot-maker's gaming-house – the self-same establishment in which my father had lost his three pounds – for, as a young man, on more than one occasion, I had dragged him from just such a fortified den.

'Who are you?' said a voice from within.

'My name is Jones. I am looking for a girl.'

'Not here, my friend. Try the Haymarket.'

'A girl by the name of Ellen Hungerford,' – I took a shilling from my pocket and made sure it fell within the porter's sight – 'and it is worth a little something if I should find her. I believe she has just come into Mr. Halifax's employment. I have some news she might care to hear; something to her advantage.'

The unseen porter – whether softened by the sight of a coin, or his master's name – adopted a more conciliatory tone.

'Is she a little thing, with yellow hair?'

I replied in the affirmative.

'I know the one, I reckon.'

'Is she inside?'

'Here? No. Maybe later.'

'Where, then? Does she have lodgings nearby?'

The man fell silent; I took my cue and pressed the coin through the narrow slit. It disappeared from my fingers, as if eaten by a greedy animal.

'Try the Argyll. I heard he's taken her dancing.'

My stomach turned at this reply; not least, the word *dancing*, said with heavy irony. Nonetheless, I thanked the man and turned my steps westwards, through the narrow Soho streets.

The Argyll! The worst saloon in London. What man can hear those words without thoughts of profligacy and vice? Thus were all my fears – for EH's future and, indirectly, my own – played out before my mind's eye.

I reached Windmill Street, paid my shilling entrance, and walked down the steps into the building's infamous marbled hall – an initiate into a world I have always avoided.

My first impression, amidst the fug of tobacco smoke, was that the grand *salon* resembled any other place of public entertainment. The gilt and gas-light – the pendulous chandeliers and polished stone floor – might have suited any theatre or opera-house. Likewise, the music – a lively *schottische* played by an orchestra of forty or fifty. But the loose attitudes of those who stood around the floor, watching the couples dancing – the prevalence of champagne on every table – the secluded curtained alcoves, protected from the public gaze, at which a select few 'took supper' – told a different tale.

I had no idea where I might find EH. I began to wander about the place, ignoring several imprecations from certain females to 'stand us a glass of fizz' &c. (seemingly the common currency of the place amongst the womenfolk). As luck would have it, I stumbled upon my quarry within minutes. She sat in one of the alcoves on the opposite side of the hall (the curtains, thankfully, not drawn) beside the bullish form of Halifax, and facing two other men. They were gentlemen, by their appearance, both wearing evening clothes. I did not recognise her at first. The plain sensible dress which had been supplied by Willis's had been supplanted by a velvet gown (!); and her cheeks either brightened by rouge or, perhaps, merely the hot flush of champagne.

At first, I doubted my judgment; I wondered whether it would serve *any* good to approach her. For I had come to prevent her final moral ruin; yet *she* had placed herself in the boot-maker's power; *she* had come to the Argyll Rooms, let herself be dressed in a fashion which left no confusion as to her purpose. Then I saw one of the men stand, and attempt to take her hand – to lead her into the dance – and (blessed girl!) how she did struggle and protest!

Nothing could have given me more courage than this instinctive revulsion – the tremor of fear that passed over her face – whatever had brought her to the such a pass. I crossed the floor, to the annoyance of several of the whirling Bacchants, and interposed myself between the man and his reluctant partner.

'This young lady does not seem to want your company, sir.'

(Did I say this boldly – or did my voice quiver? I fear the latter!)

'The devil!' exclaimed the man; the tone of his voice well-bred, but slurred with drink. The boot-maker, meanwhile, stared at me; an appraising, menacing glance.

'Mr. Jones, ain't it? I never forget a face. Well, sir, whatever do you mean by this ridiculous interference? Are you drunk?'

'Far from it. I wish to speak with Miss Hungerford.'

The two men protested indignantly at the 'damned impertinent' interruption to their evening; but neither seemed inclined to do more. Ellen Hungerford, meanwhile, gazed up at me in astonishment. It was left to the boot-maker to reply. I had expected curses and argument, but, to my surprise, he spoke in a measured fashion, seemingly devoid of emotion.

'I fear there is some misunderstanding here. Perhaps we had better speak outside, sir. Away from all this noise and bustle.'

'I will not leave Miss Hungerford here, unaccompanied, except by men who are utter strangers to her.' – there was no denial of this charge – 'Besides it is she with whom I wish to speak – not you.'

'*Miss* Hungerford' – heavy sarcasm here – 'might accompany us, I should suppose.'

I reluctantly agreed. The boot-maker, in turn, made his apologies to his companions and led us back towards the entrance, then out onto the street.

Thus did the predator decoy his prey!

For, like a fool, I followed the man until we came to a quiet entry by the side of the building, Ellen Hungerford trailing behind us. There, he turned, and, before I could move a muscle, *grabbed me by throat and pushed me flat against the nearest wall.* The brute's strength was such that – try as I might – I could do little to free myself.

'I've no particular quarrel with you, sir,' he said, between gritted teeth, 'but if a fellow makes me look a fool, I'm damned if he won't pay for it.'

I protested that such was not my intention. Even as I spoke, however, the brute punched me in the stomach – without the slightest warning or provocation – and began to rain down blow after blow upon my body.

Is it necessary to describe the brutal attack to which I was subjected? My attempts to defend myself were in vain; and I could no more match the speed and power of his fists than I could have stopped a bullet fired from a gun.

(How I wished that I possessed some such article, which I might have used for my own protection!)

Ellen Hungerford screamed. Halifax, meanwhile, laid into me with such force that I thought I was in danger of my life.

It is a strange thing, however, how life may turn on a mere chance. For, at that very moment, I heard the sound of rapid feet on the cobbles.

My first thought, my mind addled by the bootmaker's dizzying assault, was of the police, alerted by the scream. It became plain, however, that the newcomers were a trio of young men. When Halifax refused to desist from the attack, they proceeded to set about him with the same rough violence he himself had meted out to his victim.

I cannot claim that this three-against-one, no matter Halifax's overweening bulk, was a gentlemanly contest. Yet how – even though in a stupor of confusion – I did inwardly rejoice!

To my amazement, as they exchanged blows, I recognised a familiar voice and a fourth man pulled me to my feet.

'Lord! It is you, guv'nor!' exclaimed Fortesque. 'I hardly believed it.'

Thus my junior clerk – quite by chance – was my salvation!

For it was none other than Fortesque and his 'pals' (about to enter the Argyll for their night's revel) who had happened to observe the boot-maker's attack. Indignant at the patently unequal contest –

with F. swearing to my good character – they had determined to intercede and pay Halifax back in kind.

Never again will I decry 'fast' young men and their 'high spirits'!

In truth, I cannot recall the next few minutes in any detail – my head swam – but a cab was found – Ellen Hungerford and myself placed inside. The last I recall is the cry of 'Watch out! Peelers!'

Then I slipped from consciousness.

I awoke in the cab to find Ellen Hungerford wiping my brow. The relief on her face was patent; she had plainly feared that I would not wake. I told her to desist and asked what had happened. I learnt that something resembling a riot in miniature had ensued. Several more young men – largely the worse for liquor – had come to the aid of both sides – until the sound of a sprung rattle heralded the arrival of the police. I had briefly fallen unconscious – my aching head a testimony to the cause – as the cab sped from the scene.

'Where are we going?'

'Your friend told him the Angel.'

My friend!

The memory of Fortesque – who had stayed outside the Argyll to defend his friends – *and what he had seen* – all came rushing back to my consciousness – even as my head ached all the more. For it was plain to me then that he *had* seen Ellen Hungerford; and that he could not have supposed she was my wife.

There were, however, more pressing matters to consider.

'Why did you come?' asked my companion, as I raised myself upright in the seat.

Even in my dazed condition, I sensed the danger in this question; that I might rekindle the same 'silly fancy' which had been her undoing. I replied, slowly, that she must understand I wished to undo the harm I had done her after the fire; that I did not wish to compound it. That I believed I had offended her with talk of money when we last spoke – but that to place herself in the hands of a man like Halifax was to abandon all hope of a future. That, in short, I had come solely to save her from herself; not for any other base purpose.

The mention of Halifax seemed to have a chastening effect.

'I didn't do nothing,' she replied, with lowered lids. 'He said I should meet some friends of his – have a glass of *sham* – that's all. Then I should watch 'em play cards later on.'

'Just that? Nothing else?'

She shrugged. In truth, I believe she *had* understood fully what the boot-maker had planned for her, and had become resigned to it.

'What does it matter now?'

I told her that I had seen her protest; that her very nature revolted against such behaviour.

'Maybe I ain't cut out for it,' she said, with deep sadness in her voice. 'But what am I to do, then?'

I steeled myself – for this was the moment – and said that I had come with a proposal from a friend; a proposal that involved a vacancy for a domestic servant.

'Who'd have me, sir, as I am?'

I could not help but allow myself a slight smile of satisfaction. I replied that I knew just such a person – a woman who, although perhaps a little opinionated and eccentric, might be relied upon as a good employer. That Mrs. Antrobus would give her a second chance of a decent life, if only she would turn away from the path she had set herself upon. That nothing more need be said – about her past . circumstances – about her current position.

'It's no use,' she protested. 'Mr. Halifax – he'll find me.'

I replied that I would protect her; find her new lodgings, without delay, until such time as I might speak with Mrs. Antrobus.

There was a moment's hesitation then –

The girl broke into tears and threw herself at my feet. Sobbing, she offered such earnest and heartfelt thanks, that I could not doubt my decision a moment longer.

It is done.

I shall tell Dora to-morrow and speak to Mrs. Antrobus on Sunday.

I have conjured up so many dangers and phantoms these last few days – yet, the girl only has to hold her tongue and work hard. She has shown herself capable of both. The past – my father – that night – must all be forgotten.

I *have* saved her.

CHAPTER NINE

Inspector Delby turned on the gas in the morning-room. It was growing dark outside and he knew the day would soon draw to a close – with no progress in his investigation. He returned to reading the diary, still scanning its pages for some clue to Jacob Jones's whereabouts. Then a hint of movement caught his eye. It was a cat, a sleek-coated black and white animal, that had crept into the room and tentatively begun to sniff around the fireplace and cabinets. The policeman feigned not to notice; the cat, in turn, came over and brushed against his legs.

'You haven't disappeared, then,' he muttered, glancing at the animal's fathomless eyes. 'Shame you can't give us a statement.'

'Sir?'

The human interruption to his thoughts startled him. It was a constable at the door – a man he didn't recognise.

'Well, what is it?'

'McAuley, sir. G Division. I've found this girl you were after.'

'The girl? Ellen Hungerford?'

The constable, frowning, shook his head. 'Sorry, sir. This one's called Mary-Anne Bright.'

Delby sighed.

'Ah, I see. Well, I suppose I should congratulate you, constable, all the same. Some good news, at least. Is the girl outside?'

'Brought her over in a cab, sir.'

'And did you tell her what has occurred here?'

'No, sir. I thought –'

'Never mind,' said Delby. 'You may tell her now; the bare bones of it, at least. Doubtless she will cry. If I know her kind, she will cry. Let her do so. Then, when she is able to talk sense, bring her to me.'

§

Red-faced, Mary-Anne Bright sat down in the arm-chair, facing the policeman, who held his notebook open before him, a pencil in hand. It was plain to Delby that sitting down in the study – on equal terms with the room about her, no longer a servant – was unsettling for the girl. She shifted uneasily; and seemed quite unable to rest in one spot.

'So, Miss Bright, I must ask you a few questions, in the hope it may assist our understanding of this awful tragedy. Where shall we begin, eh? Tell me, did you take to Mrs. Jones? Was she a good mistress?'

'Take to her? Bless her memory, sir,' said Mary-Anne, touching her eyes with a rather dirty grey handkerchief, 'I thought she was the finest young lady as ever was – and I mean a proper *lady* too. I can't believe she's gone, sir. Not like this.'

'Indeed. It is a terrible affair, my dear. Forgive my ignorance – how long were you in her employment?'

'Since she got wed, sir. February last year – her and her husband started out in Clapham, then we all came up this way at New Year.'

'Now, you mention Mr. Jones,' said Delby. 'I don't suppose you have any idea as to his whereabouts?'

'No, sir.'

'Do you know of any family or friends – anyone with whom he might have taken refuge?'

'Not likely, sir. He kept himself to himself; I never knew him even have a visitor; not on his own account.'

'Well then, what about you? Were you on good terms with him?'

Mary-Anne frowned. 'I wouldn't say that, sir, but we rubbed along well enough. But then he gave me the push – and now this –'

'This?'

'Well, he did for her, didn't he?'

'Is that your opinion, Miss Bright?' asked Delby.

'Well, that fellow outside, he told me –'

'Constable McAuley should learn when hold his tongue. Suffice to say that Mr. Jones is one of the principal *suspects* in our inquiry. Now, was Mr. Jones ever violent towards you?'

Mary-Anne paused for thought, as if scouring her memory for something worthy of the inspector's attention. At last, however, she conceded defeat.

'No, sir.'

'What about his wife? Did he ever strike her?'

'No, sir. Not that I know of. But he was an odd sort, sir, and it don't surprise me that he should have gone off his head. Why, some days he'd give me such looks – such queer looks – that I couldn't account for it.'

Inspector Delby smiled to himself.

'Miss Bright, I had better be frank about something. In fact, it may account for Mr. Jones's "looks". You know, perhaps, that your master kept a diary?'

'Know it! Don't I just, sir! Don't I know how he got ink on all his shirts! I'd almost say he were never out of this very room – who spends every night writing, I ask you! – unnatural –'

'One moment, allow me to continue. You see, in Mr. Jones's diary, there are some revealing and highly delicate passages. In one instance, for example, he recounts waking during the night, and following a certain young woman – I won't name her – into the grounds of the New River Company – just down the road here, I believe – where she met with a certain gentleman – a labourer of her acquaintance – need I go on?'

Delby paused. As he had anticipated, Mary-Anne Bright blushed. Before she could gather her thoughts, he continued.

'Now, I personally do not much care what that particular female was doing there; that is her own business. In fact, I wouldn't mention such an unseemly incident, were it not for a reason – to point out that such a young woman need not be too particular or shy, when I ask her a certain question. Do you understand me, Miss Bright?'

'What question?' said Mary-Anne, rather nervously.

'Did Mr. Jones ever make advances to you, my dear?'

'To me!' she exclaimed. 'No he didn't! And I shouldn't have let him, neither! And, anyhow, if you're saying what I think you're saying, then it's all a pack lies, from start to finish!'

'You needn't take offence, my dear,' said Delby. 'I merely wish to learn about Mr. Jones's character; not yours. If you and he were ever intimate –'

'Not me!'

'Well, was he friendly with any other females?'

'I wouldn't rightly know,' she replied, with a little hesitation. 'I'll tell you this, though, he had his little favourite, all right.'

'Who do you mean?'

'A little slip of thing him and the missus took pity on, name of Ellen Hungerford. They got her a place with the doctor's wife, skivvying. Not that she knew one end of a brush from another, from what I saw of her. The missus said it was charity but –'

'What?'

'I saw the master in the street one time – going past the doctor's house, when she was out doing the steps. Well, a woman can tell, sir. He had his eye on her *in that way*, if you know what I mean; and I don't reckon she was no better than she ought to have been, neither.'

'What makes you say that?' said Delby.

'She came round here once – her missus had sent her to get some receipt of Cook's – and I asked her how she got on. Well, I didn't say nothing disagreeable, except as how the master had been so good to find her a place. Well, sir, if I'd spat in her face, I don't reckon she could have been more nettled. You have never heard such language as I heard that day!'

'Disregarding the language, what was the substance of her reply?'

'Disregarding it? I should have liked to! Well, I suppose she said – all nonsense! – that I shouldn't interfere in her business; that I shouldn't speak ill of the master; that I shouldn't do this and that, and if I did, she'd set me straight! I never met such a coarse and common girl, sir. If she was fit for service, I'm fit to be hung. You should speak to her, and see where it gets you. I wish you luck!'

'Well, that is my intention,' said Delby, dourly, keeping his own counsel. 'But we have not spoken of how things stood between Mr. Jones and his wife. Mrs. Jones was never well, I gather, not since she lost her child?'

Mary-Anne frowned. 'No, sir. I don't reckon she ever got over it. She had the blue devils most of the time; never rallied. God rest her soul. At least, I suppose they're together again, her and her boy, God willing.'

'And Mr. Jones?' said Delby. 'How did he take the loss of the child?'

'I don't know about him, sir. But things weren't never right between him and the missus again.'

'You think they were on bad terms for some time?'

'I suppose that's putting it strong,' said Mary-Anne. 'But I can tell you when it really got worse.'

'When?' said the inspector.

'When they got back from the sea-side. She got worse; leastways. Terrible unhappy.'

'Indeed?'

'To tell the truth, sir, I'd half thought of leaving after that. I'd had a week away from the place, see? Well, when they came back, it struck me that things were right; not how you'd like.'

'Yet, in fact, I gather from his diary that it was Mr. Jones who finally dismissed you, only last week. On what grounds, pray?'

Mary-Anne looked down at her feet. 'He said it was immoral conduct. But I got morals, sir!' – Delby raised his eyebrows – 'well, I have too! and least I ain't a bleedin' murderer!'

'There is no fear anyone will accuse you of that, my dear,' said Delby. 'So you think, perhaps, something happened between Mrs. Jones and her husband at Broadstairs?'

'Just! I'd stake my life on it.'

Diary

Sunday, 1st June

Church; then Mrs. Antrobus took tea with D. in afternoon.

Nearly two weeks have passed since Ellen Hungerford commenced her employment in Claremont Square. We have heard nothing but reports of her industry and perseverance, although her ignorance of 'even the most simple chores' remains a source of great amusement to her mistress. In another household, a maid-of-all-work who was unfamiliar with black-leading a grate would be summarily dismissed. In Mrs. Antrobus's way of thinking, it is 'so very droll'. In fact, I believe that Mrs. A. considers – rightly – that EH is a worthy object of instruction and that the result will be a girl uniquely suited to her own domestic economy.

If any woman *can* effect this wondrous transformation, it is Mrs. Antrobus!

Monday, 2nd June

The office has become something of a trial. Although I provided Fortesque with the fullest explanation for my adventure at the Argyll Rooms, he insists on making *knowing* remarks, whenever we take lunch together. Today, an item of police news in the paper about the Holborn Casino – a case of pickpocketing by a gang of females – which prompted F. to remark that *'a fellow has to keep his eyes peeled for that sort of harpy, don't he, guv'nor?'*

Under normal circumstances, I would have risen majestically above such vulgarity – to be addressed as 'guv'nor' indeed! Moreover, *he* would not have dared utter such words. Yet my junior clerk now considers me intimate with all the night-haunts of the metropolis – or, rather, he affects this altered estimate of my character – and it affords him great amusement to see me squirm. The fact that *he* would happily visit such an establishment as the Argyll or the Casino, *without his wife*, needs no further comment; but that I should be tarred with the same brush – even in jest – is hard to bear.

What am I to do? To chide him for such ill-founded attempts at humour, considering what occurred that evening, seems too much like base ingratitude. If, however, he continues in the same vein on our return from Broadstairs, I will have to speak some strong words on the subject.

On my walk home, I saw EH – for the first time since she began her work – in Claremont Square. She was collecting some small parcel from the postman, and stood talking to him at the top of the area steps. She looked healthy and fresh-cheeked; and the modest uniform of apron and cap suited her features.

I wonder now if I have done the right thing by *her*, but the wrong thing by *myself*. For, seeing her there, at ease with herself and the world, I felt a tremor of the same sentiment – that far from disinterested sentiment – as I felt *that night*.

It is, of course, a mere echo; a delusion. I will put it to the back of my mind. In any case, there is no possibility, now, that I shall spend time in her company.

My earnest hope is that Broadstairs will not only elevate D.'s spirits, but that the sea-breeze will blow all such cobwebs away.

Tuesday, 3rd June

Broadstairs to-morrow!

Returned home to find Dora 'at sixes and sevens', mountains of clothes scattered here and there, and Mary-Anne preparing *four trunks for a week's holiday!* I remarked that this was an excessive number, likely to cause considerable trouble and inconvenience on the journey, and stipulated that it must be reduced to three. D. replied, accusatory, that I would 'take her away with nothing but the clothes on her back' – *said not in jest, but in dour earnest!*

I believe that she is, at best, *resigned* to this holiday; she certainly has shown no enthusiasm for it. She knows, at least, that I will brook no obstacle to the plan; and that we shall go to-morrow, whether she is in good humour or bad.

Mary-Anne has darkened my mood this evening. For, going down to the study, a little before eleven o'clock, I was certain that I heard a man's voice in the kitchen. I went downstairs, but found only Mary-Anne herself. She informed me, unable to deny the charge, that it was a passing tinker whom she had just 'shooed off'. I replied that she should not admit such characters, if they were unknown to her, and locked the door. In fact, I am sure it was the labourer.

She had a distinct blush to her cheeks; I cannot say whether it was guilt or the unnatural excitement occasioned by his presence.

It is terrible to think that, for the sake of expediency, I have allowed such conduct to go unnoticed these many weeks.

I am glad, at least, that Mary-Anne will _not_ come to Broadstairs, but goes to her cousin. If Dora improves in the slightest degree, I shall give her notice immediately on our return.

Wednesday, 4th June

We have arrived at Broadstairs!

At breakfast this morning, D. _did_ complain of 'a head' &c. but, nonetheless, we were at Tooley Street by twelve noon, and caught our train to Margate in good time (_three_ trunks!). From the station, we took a shandrydan pulled by an ancient, plodding, patient horse. Our journey was no more than three or four miles; the animal, however, was dreadfully slow, despite many curses, whip &c. from its master. At the end, I noticed the mare bore many long-standing marks of the lash, all about her hindquarters. When asked to 'remember the driver'; I remarked that I _would_ remember him, and, upon our return, pick a man more kindly to the beast which provided his livelihood.

I will not record the choice words I received back!

Despite this unfortunate introduction to the locality, the cottage itself proved to be a delightful little place, some five minutes' walk from the harbour.

I do believe Dora has fallen in love with it. She looks brighter and more cheerful than I have seen her in some weeks. We have attendance morning and evening from a respectable woman of middling years, the wife of a local boatman, who goes by the name of Mrs. Sherridan. For lunch, we shall 'dine out' at one of the hotels, or make up our own humble fare in the little kitchen.

D. says the little stone cottage reminds her of 'playing at house'. Indeed, it rather has proportions of a doll's house; the narrow little desk on which I write these words – more suited to a nursery – is proof enough.

I have seen too many false dawns with Dora, to become over-excited by this modest improvement in her mood.

Nonetheless, there is hope!

Thursday, 5th June

Today, we have explored the amusements of the town.

One has heard tell of a slim volume entitled 'Snakes in Ireland', which begins by informing the reader, *'Concerning snakes in Ireland, there are none'*. A similar joke might be made of amusements in Broadstairs; for, in short, there are none. Yet, that is the charm of the place in a nutshell. It has none of the 'Halls by the Sea' which we passed at Margate; no 'nigger minstrel' or his ilk on the sands; no sun-browned cheap-jack plying his wares in the narrow streets and lanes. It is, rather, a most salubrious and decent place, quiet and respectable, and does not pretend to be any different.

The 'sights', if such they may be termed, are a narrow arch known as the York Gate – which would be utterly unremarkable if found in the metropolis – that marks the end of one of the principal streets; and a wooden pier, with painted black with white rails, on which the 'staying company' take a stroll or sit to admire the restless sea. There are a dozen bathing-machines upon the beach, packed close together and closer still to the boats and other small craft which litter the harbour. This is, perhaps, not quite as it should be; and I have been informed, in scandalised tones, by Mrs. Sherridan that there is no gender distinction enforced by the operators, such that men, women and children must mix 'promiscus-like, sir,' if they care to enjoy the waters. I am not sure that I maintain a rigid objection to 'promiscus' (!) bathing of this nature; for the machines themselves do all that is necessary to preserve decorum. The only question for me is whether Dora might benefit from sea-water, as well as sea air. I shall reserve my judgment. At present, I fear her constitution is too weak for the proverbial 'dip'.

The weather today has been very fine but windy; I shall need to find some black ribbon for my hat.

Friday, 6th June

Intermittent rain today, which has somewhat interrupted our leisure.

In particular, I had taken two rush-bottomed chairs from the cottage to the beach; Dora was busying herself with the collection of shells. The heavens then opened and we were obliged to seek shelter at the Albion – the white-stuccoed hotel that overlooks the promenade. At least we now know that it has a fine coffee-room; and the best people frequent it. We shall now make it our daily 'watering-place'.

In the afternoon, we visited a little shop (if that is not too grand a name for a fisherman's front-parlour!) where D. purchased some pink coral and foreign shells. Much talk from D. of creating a 'cabinet of curiosities' at home.

It seems to me that the change of scene *has* been efficacious; she has been more lively and talkative; the lethargy, if not dispelled, is in retreat. I, too, feel better in myself.

This evening, I confess, I have been giving much thought to our marital relation. We are thrown together very close in the cottage. In such circumstances, there might be nothing more natural between man and wife than that joyous and holy union of the sexes.

In truth, I am afraid to attempt it, lest it yield the same unsettling result as before.

Saturday, 7th June

A fine day. In the morning, walked two or three miles through the cornfields hereabouts and then back along the coast. I instructed Dora – if she would make her 'cabinet' – to look for examples of petrifaction in the cliffs (none were found!).

We took lunch at the Albion then walked along the promenade. I had been considering the possibility of organising a 'boat trip' (for Mrs. Sherridan has informed me that most of the boatmen will happily 'take a gen'l'man sea-fishing' or 'row you down to Ramsgate or Pegwell Bay'). My thoughts, however, were interrupted by a familiar voice which hailed us.

'Mr. Jones! My dear Dora!'

To my surprise and astonishment, turning onto the promenade from the direction of the High Street, it was none other than Mrs. Antrobus. Quite unaccompanied, she walked briskly to meet us.

I have neither time nor inclination to record the (lengthy, as always!) female conversation that followed. In brief, it became clear that out that our meeting was not a complete coincidence. Mrs. A. knows Broadstairs of old and has family at Ramsgate (a cousin with whom she has corresponded for many years and long promised to visit). It seems that – when she heard of our proposed holiday – she decided to 'kill two birds with one stone' (such a vulgar expression!) by visiting the cousin and simultaneously surprising 'her dear friends'. She is to spend three nights at the Albion.

Dr. Antrobus – sensible man – has elected to remain in London!

She has also brought Ellen Hungerford. She is 'sure that the girl may learn a good deal by merely watching the maids at the Albion – why, even the waiters are such exemplary creatures, are they not? And how often may one say that with any confidence?'

Of course, arranging this great 'surprise' – solely for our benefit – is typical of the woman's character. The theatre, one feels, still runs deep in her veins!

If only she had not brought EH.

Sunday, 8th June

To the local church, in company with Mrs. A.

Mercifully, she had already given EH leave to go to 'a dissenting chapel half a mile down the road' at the invitation of the Albion's scullery maid.

'I'm told that the preacher is an absolute ranter,' she confided in me, 'but a young man, my dear Mr. Jones, and terribly handsome.'

After the service, we returned to the coffee-room at the Albion. Mrs. A. has visited Broadstairs on four previous occasions and is thoroughly knowledgeable regarding the district. She even recommended a boatman who might be relied upon for a fishing expedition (but the threat of rain too great at present).

To-morrow, should the weather permit, Mrs. A. plans a pic-nic on the cliffs, *at which EH would inevitably be present.*

To refuse is, of course, impossible; but I must find some means to excuse myself. I do not think that I could bring it off; and, worse, what if my presence should provoke some unguarded word or deed from Ellen Hungerford herself –

No, I shall not go.

Monday, 9th June

What have I done this day?

I am a dog – a wretched dog!

In truth, I am lower than any animal; for a beast possesses no conscience of his wrong-doing; no intellect which might contain his animal nature.

A wretched dog!

Tuesday, 10th June

I look back and find that I have recorded only sentiment – self-pitying sentiment at that – for all that happened yesterday afternoon. Some weeks ago, I determined to be a sterner, more honest historian of my own affairs; and perhaps I shall find, in years to come, that there is some hope of redemption in that. Therefore, I shall – I <u>must</u> – record *the facts* of all that occurred.

The weather yesterday proved fine; sufficiently bright and temperate to encourage Mrs. A. to write a note proposing that her cliff-top pic-nic should proceed, at noon. Dora was very enthusiastic but I protested that I had caught a stiff neck during the night, from the draughty casement which lies beside our bed. Thus, after much debate, it was agreed that I should walk D. to the Albion – whence the modest party of Dora, Mrs. A. and 'a couple of charming old gentlemen and their niece, with whom I fell into conversation at breakfast' (thus ran the note!) might proceed towards the cliffs – whilst I should recuperate at the cottage.

I performed my duty and bid the party good-bye at half past the hour. I said nothing to EH, who trailed shyly behind her mistress. Then I returned 'home'. It was almost an hour later when I heard a knock at the cottage door.

To my surprise, it was Ellen Hungerford herself, despatched as a messenger *by my own wife*. She informed me, very modestly, that 'the breeze had got up' and 'Mrs. Jones requires her red shawl, as she says is hanging up on the door and might I have it, please'.

I knew the article and retrieved it. If only I had kept to my original resolve – held my tongue – kept to the charade of propriety – then all danger might have been averted.

'I trust Mrs. Antrobus treats you well?' (Could any remark be more harmless?)

'Yes, sir. Very well, thank you. She's been very good to me, sir.'

'A stroke of luck, too, that you should enjoy such a pleasant change of scene, so soon in your employment.'

'Yes, sir,' she replied. 'Only –'

I could not understand her hesitation; but she blushed even before she spoke the words.

'Only, it weren't luck, sir.'

Foolishly, I asked what she meant.

'It was my doing, sir. I mean, when she told me about you coming here, I told her how I'd never even seen the sea; and how I thought I never should; and I suppose I said all sorts of nonsense. Anyhow, I put the idea in her head and that's the truth of it.'

'Well, Mrs. Antrobus is a very considerate woman to act on your suggestion – if a little impetuous – though I suppose a holiday suited her. I would not trespass on her good nature too much, all the same. A good maid should keep her opinions to herself.'

'It weren't the sea, though, sir.' she said. 'I mean, I don't give tuppence for the sea.'

'Really? They why say such things?'

She hesitated; her voice, when it came, was so bashful and quiet, it was almost a whisper.

'I wanted to be near you, sir.'

My heart pounded in my chest; for I suddenly realised that the 'silly fancy' had not been abandoned. Not one whit! Rather, she had nourished and nurtured it in secret; and would not relinquish it.

A 'silly fancy'? No. Let us be honest and call it 'love'. What else can possess a young woman's heart, such that she offers no complaint when a man – a *married* man – steps forward and kisses her and she warmly reciprocates his passion? What else, when a kiss swiftly becomes that most intimate intercourse, the most profound exchange possible, between a man and a woman? Indeed, she *did* speak of love, although I cannot recall whether it was during our love-making, or at its end. Certainly, nothing else, when all passion was spent, could account for the tender look she bestowed on me.

Yes, I must concede *that she loves me*; that much is straightforward and easy to comprehend.

Do I love her? No. Something so dreadfully wrong – to break vows made before God – no matter how one may rationalise it – cannot be *love*; that is not the word for it.

It was some ten or fifteen minutes after her arrival that I bid EH good-bye.

No more that five minutes later, <u>Dora herself returned!</u>

Did she notice my consternation? She informed me that she had found the breeze 'far too fierce' and had not been inclined to wait for the shawl, fearing she had already caught cold. Moreover, that *she thought the silly girl had dawdled terribly and had said as much when she met her in the road.*

My sole response – hypocrite! – was to chide her for walking back unaccompanied (although I should have been astonished if she *had* met with any insult or annoyance in such a place as Broadstairs). This, however, met with no response. She has been miserable and distracted all afternoon.

What more should I write? I am filled with a deep loathing of my own words and deeds.

If D. had come back but a few minutes earlier –

I have left the worst until last. I am loathe to write it; to make concrete something I should rather dissolve in the memory.

When Ellen Hungerford parted from me; when she took the shawl up in her arms, and stood once more at the cottage door, she spoke these words:

'Shall I see you again, sir?'

And I replied –

'Yes'.

It cannot be – it <u>must</u> not be – and yet –

If she were to stand before me again – at this very moment – would I say 'No'?

Wednesday, 11th June

Dora has, unaccountably, sunk back into that lethargic condition from which I had hoped to effect her rescue, much to my despair. Mrs. Antrobus, meanwhile, returned to London with EH early this morning (a great relief!). I left word at the Albion that D. was unwell and that we should not have the opportunity to bid her good-bye.

After breakfast – D. remaining in bed – I informed Mrs. Sherridan of my wife's indisposition and the good woman offered to remain in the house with her. I then took a walk to the harbour and sought out a man by the name of Mr. Gregory – recommended by Mrs. A. for his proficiency in the art of sea-fishing. For I could not bear the prospect of a day of inactivity and introspection (having spent much of the night fruitlessly examining my conscience) and thus I resolved to do *something*.

I agreed terms with the fisherman (1s.); the bait (whiting punt) and lines were soon assembled; and the man rowed with a will out to sea, towards 'Long Nose Spit' where 'the catch is uncommon good'. I cannot deny that assertion for – a mere novice – I caught half a dozen codlings within half an hour of weighing anchor.

Gregory himself would make a fine study of the 'old salt'; he bears the careworn, rugged features of his trade and liberally sprinkles every utterance with severe oaths, in the approved nautical fashion. He took the opportunity of 'captaining' the vessel to rail against Parliament, steam-tugs, the French nation, and the Ramsgate life-boat (!) – I learnt that the latter 'robs' the local boatmen of money they once earned from assisting ships in distress. When we returned to dry land, I gave him an additional sixpence; for *he* had provided a better distraction than the sport.

Yet it is impossible to distract one's mind forever. I constantly ask myself this: can anything more be done for Dora? Hers is a terrible affliction; one that seemingly defies all attempts at a cure. It is terrible for her – and worse still for her husband. I had not thought that I should be married to a virtual invalid *in her twenty-third year!* What is our future? It is surely a miserable one; there seems to be no escape from it.

As for Ellen Hungerford, she too is ever present. I can give no excuse; I have twice acted the part of her seducer. It is ridiculous to deny it.

It must not happen again.

Thursday, 12th June

Back to London!

I accomplished the packing myself (a higgledy-piggledy affair, I confess) and then took Dora, despite every objection, for a final walk over the cliffs. We watched several steam-packets go by (D. utterly disinterested and listless) then back to the carriage which Mrs. Sherridan had summoned on our behalf.

The journey back to London from Margate was a tiresome one – the train quite full – and spent in silence. I had a fanciful vision that, on our return to Amwell Street, I should find Ellen Hungerford on the doorstep; very gratified, if it can be believed, to find only Mary-Anne!

I have written to Dr. Antrobus. I should like him to come and examine Dora; there can be little doubt that sea air has proved only a temporary restorative.

Friday, 13th June

I cannot say whether a man's happiness depends on luck or some predetermined fate – but, in either case, my life has been so dogged by misfortune, these last few months, that I feel myself cursed. In my blackest moments, I feel it all resembles some unholy punishment – not least when disaster strikes from such an unlikely and unexpected quarter.

I returned to the office this morning – greeted warmly by Mr. Hibbert *et al.* – and found that Fortesque was waiting for me, wearing a peculiarly anxious expression. There was none of his familiar chaff; rather, he immediately requested a private interview, which I granted.

'You recall Gresham, I suppose?' he said, without any preamble.

I replied that I had not forgotten the broker.

'Well, I have heard news, sir.' (Not 'guv'nor'! He did not dare!)

'News?'

'I've heard from an acquaintance that the police have taken him at the York races; it'll be in the papers to-morrow.'

I remarked that this was excellent; that the man would be punished for his double-dealing. All the while, my junior clerk wrung his hands.

'No, it ain't, bless you, sir – because whatever he gets from the judge, if he decides to sing out, I'll get a piece of it, too.'

Mystified, I asked him to explain.

'I mean to say, *he'll tell them my part in it.*'

In the minutes that followed I learnt the whole sorry tale from Fortesque's own lips. Fortesque's previous confession had been a tissue of lies. F. himself had lost nothing to Gresham – purchased no shares – the story was a convenient invention, concocted when I had interrogated him. Rather, he had played a critical part in one of the broker's numerous duplicitous schemes: *viz.,* over a period of several weeks, he had feloniously removed a number of our shareholders' certificates of proprietorship – left in our safe-keeping – and given them to the broker. Gresham had then forged a transfer and sold the relevant shares, *to the value of more than one thousand pounds,* splitting the proceeds with his co-conspirator.

The true source of the Fortesque's 'inheritance' now became painfully clear to me – *all of it stolen from the Company!*

Yet, even as he made this new confession, I could not understand why he should decide to unburden himself to me; for my duty was plain.

'I've been foolish, sir,' he continued, 'but you can help me.'

I said that I thought it unlikely; that I could only call the police, and, if he had finished his tale, I thoroughly intended to do so.

'No, not that,' he pleaded, grabbing hold of me arm. 'Have pity! If we were only to change a couple of pages of the register – we could say *he* stole those certificates – why, he's been in the office here often enough –'

It took me a moment to understand his proposal. He explained that he had made corresponding entries in the register of transfers for each sale, in order to conceal the illegitimate transactions. Now that 'the game was up' they would form the principal evidence of his guilt.

'If it's to be done, it must be done quickly,' he said, breathless. 'Don't you understand? I wouldn't come to you otherwise. Will you have pity on me?'

I told him that it could not be done; that I would not be party to forgery.

'It can!' he insisted. 'Say I'd spilled ink on the book; that I'd had to do a second draft –'

I do not deny that it *was* pitiful to see him there – begging for this venal indulgence. The idea, however, that I could embroil myself in such a fraud – even if it was only to 'turn a blind eye' – was impossible to countenance. I removed his hand from my arm, and replied that I would report the matter directly to Mr. Hibbert and, much as it might pain me, I would be obliged to give him in charge; that his best chance was to make a full confession not to me, but to the police.

I had not expected what followed.

'Oh, I'll talk, sir, if you like. I'll tell all. I'll make sure everyone knows about the Argyll, too; and that little girl of yours. Young enough to be your daughter, I'd say. Now, how would you like that?'

Thus, having received Fortesque's confession, in short order, I was now the subject of blackmail!

It was plain that he had come prepared, ready to apply this dreadful leverage; for he did not exhibit any compunction. I had, however, already told him my story of Ellen Hungerford's origins – her servant mother &c. – and I re-iterated it. I said that I had done nothing of which I might be ashamed.

'That's not what it sounded like,' he replied. 'Not when we carried you into that cab. I'd say she was very fond of you, sir. "Oh, my love," "Oh, my dear" –'

I fear my hesitation in replying told more than any words. I said the girl must have been drunk.

'If you say so, sir.'

It is too demeaning to record the remainder of our conversation. Suffice to say that it took the form of a business-like negotiation, with my own future and reputation balanced on one side of scales, and Fortesque's life and liberty on the other. Offers and counter-offers were traded, until an accommodation was reached.

The only consolation in this wretched business is that, at length, I gained the advantage. For I ultimately persuaded him that any revelation concerning Ellen Hungerford (no matter how damning!) would be preferable to gaol – and incarceration would be the inevitable consequence, if any counterfeit on my part was uncovered. Moreover, no matter what steps might be taken, if a bogus sale of the company's shares was to become known, it was plain that he must come under suspicion – his acquaintance with Gresham was common knowledge.

Thus we came to the following arrangement, *viz.* that he should flee London forthwith, with whatever money remains to him and fifty pounds from my own funds (Dora's money!); that I should say nothing to Mr. Hibbert or the police, but make some excuse for his sudden departure; that the register, however, should remain unaltered. He must take his chance and hope that Gresham holds his tongue. If so, it may be weeks – even months or years – before the fraud is uncovered in the general run of business. Where he goes or what he does next is his own affair. I advised him to book passage to the Continent.

If he is caught, he has sworn that he shall not reveal my part in the bargain.

What confidence, however, may I place in that?

We can ill afford the fifty pounds! Indeed, I wonder now if he seriously intended to attempt to conceal his crime, or merely hoped to make some capital of my embarrassment, by whatever means necessary.

In any case, to save myself, I have betrayed the trust which has been placed in me these last eight years. For I *should* have gone to the police, regardless of the consequences.

Of course, if the fraud *is* uncovered, even if I am supposed <u>not</u> to have connived in it, I can hardly expect to retain my position in the company.

Where should I go then? To Papa Willis's drapery, doubtless; an eternal object of pity and scorn.

I should blame Ellen Hungerford. She has laid me open to this dreadful extortion; yet I do not have the heart for it. It is *my* weakness that Fortesque understood so well – not hers – and now I am being punished for it.

How can I have been so blind?

Saturday, 14ᵗʰ June

Gresham *has* been arrested in York.

I cannot write; for I cannot contemplate my future; it seems too black.

Sunday, 15ᵗʰ June

Dr. Antrobus called this evening; no light, only darkness.

He has examined Dora and concludes that 'there is no serious organic disease but she is a martyr to her nerves, Mr. Jones, like so many of her sex.'

He can recommend no tonic, no method of treatment, which is likely to be more effectual than the 'change of air' which has already proved a failure.

There is no end to it; misery is heaped on misery.

Wednesday, 18ᵗʰ June

Nothing regarding Gresham, Fortesque &c.

Does Dora notice *my* despair? I do not believe so; she has shrunken within herself once more; she notices nothing of importance.

I have half a mind to abandon this journal; it is not worth the candle.

Monday, 23ʳᵈ June

When I last set pen to paper, I concluded with a silent covenant with the page that lay before me. I resolved that I should not recommence to despoil it with ink, unless I had good cause; that I should not dwell upon my own thoughts and fears (no matter how justified!) to the exclusion of all else.

Indeed, if truth be told, I half imagined that, perforce, that next page could only be written in a prison cell – or a madhouse!

(No, I should not write of *that* so lightly. And if it is madness that possesses me at present, it is a brilliant madness – a spark that illuminates all around it.)

In any case, I begin again because I have *good cause*. I have reached a turning-point; and I must record what has happened this day.

I quit my work a little after five o'clock – still, *dei gratia*, no reckoning regarding Fortesque – and walked back home along the City Road.

I saw Ellen Hungerford – for the first time since Broadstairs – on the corner of Claremont Square.

It was no mere chance; she had waited there for me. I quickly warned her that she would lose her place, if she absented herself from the house with no excuse. .

'I have an excuse, sir,' she replied. 'No-one ever had a better excuse, I suppose.'

'Whatever do you mean?' I asked.

'Please don't be angry. I could not bear it if you were angry with me – not now.'

I insisted that she tell me what she meant; but already I was filled with a grim foreboding. She studiously avoided my gaze, staring at the ground beneath her feet.

'I reckon I'm carrying, sir. I mean, I've missed my turn twice now, and that's a sure sign, ain't it? It's your little baby, inside me.'

I could not conceal my astonishment. She glanced up at me, fearful of what I might say or do, yet – there is no other word – proud of herself.

I had but one thought: *Dora had once looked at me with the very same eyes.*

'What shall I do?' she asked, nervously. 'You'll tell me, won't you? What shall I do?'

I could tell her nothing. I stood there, quite mute.

'I don't want to go to the big house, sir, not if I can help it. But I don't know where I *shall* go, I suppose –'

The workhouse! She talked incoherently, rambling, as if determined to fill the silence which I had left. At last, I collected myself.

'I need to decide what is for the best. We cannot talk here.'

'You ain't angry, though?' she said.

'No.'

Nothing more passed between us.

Thus, this very evening, I learnt for the second time that I should be a father.

It is useless to write of my agonies of self-recrimination; I have suffered enough torment. But a man must play the hand he is dealt, after all; it is no use wishing for anything else. Indeed, I have started this diary anew for a purpose: so that I may document my <u>decision</u> and know that it is the right conclusion.

I will <u>not</u> ask her to do away with it; for such things are difficult and hazardous – and criminal.

I will <u>not</u> deny it is mine; for that would be a vile calumny on the girl's character; and she does not deserve *that*.

What then?

The answer – the only answer I can find – is a revelation. I had thought that this news was the death knell of any hope of future happiness – until I realised the truth of how things stand. My *true* situation depends on the answer to a question which I have not asked myself these last weeks; yet, it ought to have been asked.

What, in my current life, am I striving to preserve?

My wife is a mere shadow of herself; she has been the same these last few months; I cannot make her happy or content. There is no prospect of improvement. There are no friends for whom I maintain any great attachment. If Gresham should impeach Fortesque, even my solitary means of earning a living – my very standing in society – is forfeit.

Therefore, what does this life of mine matter?

A man of more morbid sensibilities, faced with this conclusion, might think of ending his existence; but I am not yet persuaded of that.

Here, then, is what I have decided.

Let there be an end; but also a new beginning. I have done it once, when I slewed off my father's baneful influence; it may be done a second time.

I shall leave London *and take the mother of my child with me;* <u>that</u> is the promise of a new life; the only hope of joy to come. And just as she has laboured long and hard for Mrs. Antrobus, to learn the trade of servant, Ellen Hungerford may yet learn to be my wife. After all, she is young and impressionable; I have every proof of her love and affection; and what greater bond could there be between a man and woman, than the child which she will present to me?

Dora – poor Dora! – will return to the bosom of her family; and she will receive their love and care; they will give it more willingly than I ever could. It is only by committing this crime – I do not delude myself that the sacrifice of our marriage is anything else – I can ultimately do her the greatest good.

There! For the first time, I have the clarity of vision which has so long escaped me.

A phoenix shall rise from these ashes!

Tuesday, 24th June

Have seen EH.

She has agreed; she is willing and will come when I tell her.

Thursday, 26th June

It is remarkable, if a man sets his mind to it, how easily he may free himself from the hum-drum trammels of his existence. If only he will accept some uncertainty, some degree of risk, it is done in a matter of hours.

Money is the first consideration – I must take some of Dora's money; there is no alternative. We shall travel to Liverpool and then take a steamer; I have yet to decide on our destination.

Newfoundland, perhaps; or New York!

In any case, it must be *New*.

What wild fancy drives me now! Yet, if this a form of lunacy, I feel more content – lighter in spirit – than I have for many weeks.

How many men, after all, would have the raw courage to begin their life again, without the props and supports they have amassed over so many years?

It is a grand liberation of the soul!

The only anxiety – I fear Dora has observed the change in me; that somehow it is bright enough to have permeated the fog. Does some female intuition tell her that something is amiss? For she has left her bed and taken to following me around the house; a silent spectre, encountered at every turn.

Poor D.!

I *will* go.

Sunday, 29th June

To church, with Dora; silent, passive.

She is not the woman I married. Nonetheless, it will not be easy to leave her, when the time comes. Indeed, the giddy elation I felt only two days ago has yielded to –

No, I will not say remorse; but perhaps regret for what might have been, if fate had only allowed it.

Surely it is best for us both?

Tuesday, 1st July

I have withdrawn two hundred from Dora's money and hidden it. Only a modest sum remains; but I cannot help that. I have the railway tickets.

It is far too late to turn back.

One stroke of good fortune in winding-up my affairs: Mrs. Galton has asked for two day's leave, to visit her sister in Leeds – apparently on her death bed. I have told her that she may take a week and given her a shilling; she leaves to-night.

Three days remain!

It pains me to have deceived Mr. Hibbert in the matter of F.; but it is better that I leave before it is discovered.

Everything is in readiness.

Thursday, 3rd July

I have dismissed Mary-Anne Bright; I will not pretend that I did not take some pleasure in it.

'On what grounds!' she demanded, with typical impudence.

'Immoral conduct,' I replied, calm as you like. 'It has been brought to my notice that you have been keeping company with a certain labourer; allowing him secretly into this house.'

'I never!' she exclaimed – but her red cheeks royally displayed her guilt.

She has already left the house; I have told her that her trunk will follow.

Dora in tears – *how will she find a new girl?* &c. – but I have assured her that, granted her ill-health, I will take responsibility for it (!). In the meantime, I have told her that it might be best if she visits her mother, until a replacement might be found. Thus the ground is prepared.

There is nothing more to be done; I must bide my time. I shall meet EH, to-morrow morning, at Euston station; thence to Liverpool.

What will Dora think of me, I wonder, when she learns what I have done?

Two o'clock. My god! I must be the world's greatest coward.

I have just returned from Dora's room; I had a fancy to watch her as she slept – to take one last tranquil memory from our last night under the same roof – and –

It has completely unmanned me.

For, as I entered the room, she stirred, disturbed by the dim light from the landing. She opened her eyes – half-waking – *smiled at me* then returned to her slumber.

What agonies of the soul has that smile induced! How can such a small thing turn everything on its head?

Impossible!

Yet I am not sure I have the will to leave her.

Half-past two. I begin to think that I have been living in a dream these last ten days; that the clarity of my vision was a chimaera.

I did not believe there was any bond left between us; but –

Damn it all! She *is* still my wife.

Friday, 4th July

I know what I must do to-day. I will meet Ellen Hungerford at the station; I will give her what money I can manage, from my purse for the child's sake, and promise to send her more when it is born. She may use the railway ticket, if she likes; there can be nothing for her in London.

Will she heap curses upon me – to have led her so far – or will she meekly submit?

I have made my choice.

I will do all I can for her and the child – if my situation permits – but – God help me! – I must stand by Dora.

CHAPTER TEN

'You still here, sir?' said the constable. 'I was going to turn off the gas; I'd thought you'd gone home.'

'It is still early,' replied Delby, though half an hour had passed since the clock on the mantelpiece struck eleven.

'Still reading?'

'The final entry,' said Delby, grimly. 'I thought I would read it again.'

DIARY

Friday, 4th July

If you should come to read these pages – as someone surely must – you will doubtless ask what madness has possessed me, here at the last.

That I should take up my pen when –

I cannot bring myself to write it. It does not matter; I do not have long for this world.

Perhaps I *have* been mad – these last few days – weeks – months – I do not know.

I write these words – my <u>final</u> words – because these pages will serve a good purpose – one which I had not foreseen – *they* will bear witness on my behalf; *they* will testify against the unnatural creature – the wretched siren – who has ruined me.

I met EH at the station; as we had arranged. I told her that I had erred; that I could not abandon my wife; that if it were not for Dora, I should keep my promise – that I would gladly remove D. from any calculation of my future happiness, if only it were possible – but I could not betray her.

She cried; she protested that I had led her on – I could hardly deny it – that she would do anything for me &c.

That she loved me!

I said that she must take the train to Liverpool; that she must write to me; and I would do all I could for her.

I gave her twenty pounds. She hesitated; then took the money. For my part, I did not wish to prolong our parting; I quit the station and caught the omnibus directly to Moorgate.

The day passed uneventfully. I returned home at the usual hour. I had expected the house to be empty – for Dora ought to have gone to Chelsea. Instead, as I opened the front door, I observed a figure sat upon the hall stairs, a carpet-bag laid at her feet.

Not Dora, but Ellen Hungerford!

She rose and ran to embrace me. Astounded, I stepped back from her outstretched arms. I demanded to know why she had intruded in such a fashion.

'I could not leave you,' she said, reaching out to clasp my hand. 'It is *your* child. You will come to love it. I know it!'

I pitied her – what a prize fool am I! – I sat her back down upon the step, clasped her hands in mine, and explained myself a the second time: that the marriage vows I had sworn could not be broken; that to leave Dora would cause her infinite pain –

All the while, she stared back at me, a smile of triumphant self-satisfaction gradually forming on her lips.

'My love, that is all behind us now.'

My love!

I asked what she meant.

'I have done it for you. All that need not trouble you again.'

Then – although I had held her hands in mine all the while – I looked down and saw the stains on her sleeves; countless specks of dark carmine.

God help me, I went up the stairs and saw her. My poor wife! I wish now that I had not; but I had to know the truth of it.

I cannot say how long I stood there; I cannot recall.

When I finally came back down, Ellen Hungerford stood waiting – her eyes filled with hope – eager to see me – like some panting bitch, awaiting its master.

If only I had taken a poker and attempted to beat the life out of her or grabbed her by the throat and choked the last breath from her lungs! Those would be the actions of a man; I was but a child. For I sat down on the stairs, and wept bitter, uncontrollable tears, pathetic and impotent.

She tried to console me – can it be believed! – and spoke gaily of taking the train to Liverpool – our child – *our future* –

I pushed her away; still weeping, I cursed her with every foul epithet I have ever heard. It was only then a hint of sanity returned. For I believe she then understood – even if her deluded mind could not encompass the evil she had wrought – that I would never be *hers*.

Only an hour has passed, but I can only recall the rest of what happened imperfectly. She has fled – I do not know whither – and, to my shame, I did not follow. I had no strength in my limbs; no heart for the chase.

The rest of the money has gone – she has taken it.

Dora –

CHAPTER ELEVEN

'Sorry, sir, I'm interrupting again, ain't I?' said Constable McAuley.

'No,' said Delby, returning the sheet of paper to the desk. 'What is it?'

'Just had word, sir. Mrs. Antrobus – the doctor's wife – she's just got home. Been visiting a relative in Hertfordshire –'

The constable hesitated.

'Well, out with it!'

'Begs your pardon, but she's very fatigued and can she speak to you in the morning –'

'I don't care if she's walked to the Isle of Wight barefoot and had tea with the Queen,' said Delby. 'You go over there right now, constable, and tell her there'll be a police inspector on her door-step in two minutes.'

'Sir, you told the boys to keep it quiet and so I don't think she knows it's a case of murder –'

'Then, constable,' said the inspector, 'I'll be sure to mention it.'

§

Mrs. Delia Antrobus took the proffered glass of brandy and sipped it. Her cheeks were red and streaked with tears; her hand unsteady.

'I would rather your husband were here as well, ma'am,' said Delby. 'I do not suppose you know when to expect him?'

'He is with a very sick gentleman in Mayfair, sir. I know nothing more. He may be out all night.'

'Very well, ma'am, then I hope you'll forgive me if I ask you some questions here and now – you may know something that is crucial to my investigation; something that cannot be left until the morning.'

'Of course. Forgive me, Inspector – if I had known –'

'Of course, ma'am. Do not trouble yourself. Now, having talked to her neighbours, I believe you may be the last person who saw Mrs. Jones when she alive.'

'Good lord,' said Mrs. Antrobus. 'Well, I last saw her on Friday.'

'Precisely. Tell me your movements on that day. You paid a call on Mrs. Jones?'

'I did. I was in the habit of calling on her, most days. She had been rather poorly – dreadfully low in spirits – and I do think it is one's duty to one's neighbours, you know –'

'Quite, ma'am,' said Delby. 'At what hour was this visit of yours?'

'Well, I should say it was about two o'clock. We talked a good deal – poor Dora – she so enjoyed our conversation – I cannot believe that she is gone – poor sweet girl! – really, Inspector, it must be the work of a lunatic!'

'How long were you there, ma'am?'

'Well,' said Mrs. Antrobus, 'I should say, half an hour or so. Can you believe – her husband had taken umbrage with their maid – not the best of her class, I'll grant you – given her notice and left his poor wife without any help! We did not talk for long, mind you. Dora was going to her mother at Chelsea, you see – fretting about a cab – she did fret so! I said that she might hail one in the square with the greatest of ease – I do wonder why she came back – it all seems so odd.'

'Came back?' said Delby, perplexed, struggling to follow his interviewee. 'You think she left the house? You saw her leave for Chelsea?'

'Well, not actually *see her leave* – must you be so particular, Inspector?'

'That is my job, ma'am. Why are you so sure she went to Chelsea, if you didn't see her go?'

'Well, since you ask, I have a delightful little mantle I just bought from Gregor's – a bargain! – cerise, quite the fashion – and I was showing to poor Dora. I left it behind. I am always doing it. You see, the weather was so mild –'

'Ma'am, I don't follow,' interrupted Delby.

'I went back, Inspector. I realised I had left it there – it cannot have been more than an hour or so after we said our goodbyes – and Mrs. Jones had already gone.'

The inspector sighed and rubbed his forehead.

'You went back and there was no answer? You are sure?'

'I rang the bell twice. Tell me, how is Mr. Jones? I cannot imagine his state of mind.'

'Nor I,' said Delby. 'He has gone missing.'

Mrs. Antrobus frowned. 'Inspector, you concern me. You take that tone – it sounds almost accusatory. You do not mean to imply that he has played any part in this tragedy?'

'If you had asked me that before our conversation, ma'am,' said Delby, wearily, 'I would have told you that it was a distinct possibility.'

'Sir?'

'I don't think Dora Jones ever set off for Chelsea, ma'am. I've no reason to suspect it. We've talked to every cabbie hereabouts and most of the servants; if she had, I'd have heard about it.'

'Then why did she not answer?'

'I fear because, by the time you went back for your mantle, she was already dead. The consequence of that, ma'am, if we make that assumption, is that Mr. Jones was at his office in Moorgate when she died.'

Mrs. Delia Antrobus's eyes widened considerably.

'She was already dead? When I stood outside the door?'

Delby ignored the question, and continued.

'Tell me, ma'am, I understand you have a new maid, just started yesterday?'

'I do, indeed, Inspector,' said Mrs. Antrobus, visibly relieved to change the subject. 'Why, the girls I have had! I have harboured a thief under this very roof – *she* is in gaol! The last girl – who I had thought a diamond in the rough – on whom I expended a good deal of energy – quit on Friday without a moment's notice. Poor Dora, bless her heart, championed the girl; and I was foolish enough to consent to taking her on. As I said to poor –'

'Thieves and murderers, ma'am,' interjected Delby, dryly.

'I beg your pardon?' said Mrs. Antrobus.

'I think it very likely that Ellen Hungerford –

'The very girl –'

'I think it very likely that Miss Ellen Hungerford killed your friend.'

Mrs. Antrobus fell quite silent.

'You do not, I suppose, happen to have any idea where Miss Hungerford might have gone?' continued Delby.

'Not in the slightest, Inspector – Lord! – whatever will my husband say! Ellen! She was a peculiar little thing, I admit but – my God! – it does not bear thinking about. Are you sure? Why, we might have been slaughtered in our own beds!'

'I think you were safe enough, ma'am. She did not have you in her sights.'

'But why on earth should she – I mean Dora! – the poor creature –'

'It's a long story, ma'am,' said Delby, wearily. 'I'm afraid I don't have time for it all now. I expect you'll hear it at the inquest. I'm afraid both you and your husband will be obliged to attend.'

§

'Any luck, sir?' said Constable McAuley, as the inspector descended the steps of Dr. Antrobus's house.

Delby shook his head.

'Not a damn thing of any use,' he said bitterly. 'And it looks like Mr. Jones is in the clear.'

'You don't seem happy about it, sir, begging your pardon?'

'Not one bit.'

FROM THE TIMES, 10TH JULY 1862

CORONER'S INQUEST. Yesterday afternoon, Dr. Lankester, the Coroner for Central Middlesex, and a jury of sixteen men of the parish of St. Mark, Clerkenwell, held an inquest over the body of Dora Jones, wife of Jacob Jones, which was found on the morning of the 7th inst. in her own residence, Amwell-street, Islington, under circumstances leading to one conclusion – namely that a murder of the most horrible description had been committed. The investigation was conducted at the Clerkenwell Sessions House and during its continuance the limited space which had been allocated to the public was filled to capacity.

Detective Inspector Delby had charge of the case and, in the course of the day, read from a diary kept by the deceased woman's husband, which excited considerable interest and astonishment and cast some illumination on the circumstances leading to her death. It was adduced, from Jones's own words, that he had instigated a liaison with Ellen Hungerford, a young maidservant. Having caused her to become pregnant, he had given the girl every encouragement regarding the prospect of an illicit elopement. He had, however, disappointed her. The terrible resolution to their amour was that the girl stole into his home and assaulted Mrs. Jones in a fit of ungovernable jealousy, a brutal attack which resulted in her death.

Inspector Delby indicated that all the resources of Scotland Yard were devoted to finding the girl and her lover, both of whom fled the scene of the tragedy.

Inspector Delby stated that Mr. Jones took a train to Margate the night of his wife's death, then proceeded to Broadstairs. Mr. Arthur Grauntley, a fisherman of that town, bore witness that he had seen a man meeting Jones's description swim out to sea in the early morning of Saturday 8th July; that he had lost sight of the swimmer whilst conducted his business and had not seen him again. Sergeant Preston, Detective department, deposed that a suit of clothes found on a beach at Broadstairs were proven to be the property of Mr. Jones. He remarked that it was his opinion that, unhinged by the discovery of his wife's corpse, Jones had ended his life by suicide, and that only a corpse remained to be found.

At four o'clock, at a time when several witnesses had yet to appear before the jury, Inspector Delby reported that new evidence had come to light during the course of the afternoon and a further inquiry had to be made.

The proceedings were then adjourned until Monday 14th inst.

CHAPTER TWELVE

'Coppermill Lane,' said Preston, striding down the dirt track. 'Walthamstow marshes. Middle of nowhere, ain't it, sir? Even the mill's derelict.'

'It is bleak, Sergeant,' said Delby, 'I'll give you that. Are you all right, doctor?'

'My boots do not suit this mud, Inspector, that is all,' said Dr. Antrobus, lagging behind the two policemen. 'And I do believe it has begun to rain. I trust it is not too far?'

'The local constable assures me he has planted a flag for us,' said Delby, offering the doctor his hand. 'It's good of you to come with us, sir, straight from the inquest. I know your time is valuable and it is much appreciated, rest assured. Watch your step – ah, yes, here we are.'

Delby pointed towards the side of the road, a tattered flag planted in the dirt. Next to it, a roll of greasy tarpaulin had been laid out over a narrow ditch. The doctor tutted, and bent down to pull back the canvas. He stared, grim-faced at what lay beneath it.

'She's been dead a few days,' said Delby.

'I am not an anatomist, sir,' muttered Dr. Antrobus, replacing the tarpaulin, 'but I am sure you are right. Several days.'

'Is it Ellen Hungerford?'

'Yes,' said the doctor. 'I do believe it is. Stabbed in the gut, unless I'm much mistaken. Most unpleasant. Now, I trust I have done my civic duty, twice over. May I leave this godforsaken place and go back to treating my patients?'

'You've been very helpful, sir,' said Delby. 'Most kind.'

§

'Explain it to me again,' said Preston, as the cab disappeared along the road, 'why that miserable old gentleman is snug inside an hansom, and we're still standing here in the rain.'

'Because, Sergeant, I intend to retrace the girl's steps, between here and civilisation –'

'Or Hackney Wick, whichever's soonest.'

'Very droll. The constable assured me there are two farms – we shall make enquiries there – and a public house by the canal, a mile down the track. She must have passed all of them. If she was noticed, we might, at least, find out precisely when she died.'

'It seems to me, sir, most likely she was off her head. Wandered out here that night – didn't know or care where she was going – she just wanted to keep walking – she had that money on her – met up with some villain on his way into London – I mean, I wouldn't be out here after dark –'

'That would account for it,' said Delby. 'Except I'm not sure I can believe in such poetic justice.'

Preston shook his head. The rain had begun to pelt down. He pulled his coat tight around his neck.

'What's your theory, then, sir?'

'I don't have one, as yet,' said Delby. 'Come on.'

'You think it could be Jones, don't you, sir? You think he followed her out here; took his revenge.'

'I intend to find out.'

§

It was some two hours later that the two policeman sat down in the snug of the Horseshoe public house, on the west bank of the River Lea. The rain had abated and both men had a pint of ale before them. Neither, however, seemed in good spirits.

'Two witnesses, sir,' said Preston. 'You can't get round that. It was the Friday – she came out here that night – ten o'clock or thereabouts.'

'I am not trying to get round anything, Sergeant,' said Delby, tetchily.

'We know when Jones turned up at Broadstairs. I've got a coachman and a hotel-keeper who can swear to it. If Ellen Hungerford wasn't on Walthamstow marshes until ten –'

'It could not have been Jones that killed her. I know it.'

Preston sighed.

'My opinion, sir, if I may hazard it –'

'If you must.'

352 •

'We know now what happened to Jones and the girl – as much as we ever will. That's an end to it.'

Excerpts taken from the Commonplace Book of Jacob Jones

354 •

Monday, 30ᵗʰ December

To my wretched father's new abode!

Pear Tree Court! The quaint name, of course, quite belied by the reality: a small plot of ground, littered with animal and vegetable refuse. It sits behind an old public house, upon the eastern side of Goswell-street, at the heart of a maze of alleys and passages, bordering upon the grey outbuildings of a small, foul-smelling gas-works.

In short, a dreadful rookery!

To my annoyance, I soon discovered that not one building was numbered or marked (not even the customary promise of 'dry lodgings') and I could not fathom which, if any, might contain my father. Knocked at several doors – to be met with blank incomprehension by a family of Irish; several rebuffs of 't'aint convenient, mister'; and, in one instance, the foulest abuse. At the last, contemplating abandoning the attempt altogether – despite a degree of curiosity – I heard a familiar voice.

'My boy! Come up, come up!'

I looked up, peering into the gloom. The only light was the dim glow of the lamps in the neighbouring works. Nonetheless, it was my father.

The room itself was wretched; bare boards and furnished with little more than a mattress. (How does he live in such squalor?) He greeted me with enthusiasm. I noted immediately, however, that he cradled his arm in a peculiar fashion and possessed a dreadful black eye.

I asked him if the injury was the boot-maker's doing.

'Don't speak his name, my boy! Tell me, though, have you brought his money?'

I informed him that I had not; that I would take it directly to his creditor.

'Don't you trust me, my boy?'

My answer was unequivocal. I reminded him of our bargain and he laughed heartily, remarking it was a good exchange; that, on this occasion, he had done me proud &c. &c.

He brought up the girl. She was a little thing with pouting lips and a transparent, white complexion – perhaps a little colourless – and languishing eyes. Most fetching and suitable. She was dressed in the plainest frock, perfectly neat, though the cream-coloured cloth was frayed about the wrists and betrayed various rents where it had been carefully sewn together. She cannot have been more than fifteen or sixteen and gave her name as Ellen. I signalled my approval. We walked to the usual house-of-accommodation in Bowling Green Lane – and I could not help but admire the graceful undulation of her rump – a voluptuous thrill merely to watch her walk!

She was a lively thing; not short of ways to please a fellow – a cut above some of the previous girls. She told me that she was very ambitious to 'improve herself' and 'mix with gentlemen'.

I expect I shall have her again.

§

Wednesday, 29ᵗʰ January

Awoke with very bad head. Too much champagne!

I should report, perhaps, that Mama Willis kept her promise and left last night. I do not regret taking a stand – anything else would have been unmanly. Dora herself very subdued. She said at breakfast that she hoped I could 'make it up' with her mother, for 'Mama is very dear to me, even if her manner can be a trifle abrupt and unsettling.' I replied that I would give the matter full consideration, but that I could not – would not – be gainsayed under my own roof; and that I had been made to look a fool. Moreover, that the proper place of a wife, at least one deserving of the name, is at her husband's side, and not clutching her mother's skirts.

D. went very pale and quiet; but obliged to agree.

In truth, I should not have been quite so fierce with my poor wife. For *my* evening, unchained from the ties of hearth and home, was sublime. How much more pleasurable is a night of *impromptu* dissipation! As for Ellen Hungerford, she is certainly a find. This was our third meeting and she proved most capable – happy to meet every demand I placed upon her person.

It is ironic that my father believes she thinks highly of him. In fact, she speaks of him with nothing but contempt; knows him as boastful and conceited; tells me that the drink makes him incapable *in every respect*.

He cannot even win the respect of his whores!

§

Sunday, 16ᵗʰ February

The police came this evening notify me that my father had been arrested outside the Wheatsheaf public-house, Goswell Road, for an assault on the person of one William Halifax (yet another quarrel with this man over a bad debt!). In custody, he prevailed upon the sergeant at Old Street station-house that a certain 'respectable gentleman' of Amwell Street, Islington, would vouch for his good character!

Did I, therefore, wish to attend the police-court in the morning, and say something in his favour?

I said not; denied all knowledge.

Nonetheless, I suppose I must pay the fine. It is the only way to ensure his silence.

He has gone too far; to have a policeman visit the house!

§

Monday, 17ᵗʰ February

Went to Old Street; paid the fine of forty shillings. I fear such misadventures are becoming all too frequent. It is the liquor; I can do nothing to stop it. How can I be rid of him?

I have, at least, experienced a rather pleasant revelation this very evening. I now know who sent me the valentine!

Thus, unless I am much mistaken, this day marks the beginning of a very diverting chapter in my life!

§

Thursday, 27ᵗʰ February

I am growing a little bored of EH – she chided me tonight that I had not seen her *in over a week!* It is time, I think, to 'cut her loose'. Besides, my valentine doth object; and my valentine is such a delightful, exhilarating (exacting?!) lovely and interesting article!

I am, however, still inclined to help EH with her grand project – to obtain a position in life that will one day let her 'marry some duke or count or some such toff' (such is her ignorant manner of speaking!).

My intention is to place her at Willis's – how amusing to have this little trollop – a skilful little whore, who happens to have some knowledge of the needle – in Papa Willis's employ! How I shall enjoy seeing her prim and proper behind his counters, whilst I count the number of ways –

No, I shall not be coarse.

I shall construct some plausible tale that will tug at Dora's heart-strings; EH herself merely requires a little coaching.

§

Friday, 28th February

Today I told my valentine of my plans for EH. She thinks it very droll.

§

Saturday 12th April

Dora awoke before dawn and could be heard pacing about her room. At breakfast, she confessed that, during the night, the visit to the Polytechnic had slowly assumed a rather fearful aspect in her imagination; that she had woken plagued by a host of anxieties (all quite trifling).

Ridiculous!

I returned home at two. Our cab had been ordered for half past the hour and arrived promptly. D. was a little dilatory in coming down – a question of *the right hat* (!) – but, at last, we set off.

EH was waiting for us outside the Polytechnic. She stood sentry upon the pavement, unaccompanied, a short distance from the functionary employed to take visitors' shillings.

What a queer sensation, to see her there, with Dora by my side!

'Is that the girl?' asked D. – I replied that it was. – 'She is rather pretty.'

I paid the cab, then hurried to make an introduction and pay for our tickets – for a large crowd was gathering for the lecture. EH herself played her part to perfection.

'I am pleased to meet you, Ellen.' – 'Thank you, ma'am.' – 'I understand your mother was with my husband's family?' – 'Yes, ma'am. She was, ma'am.' – 'For many years?' – (here, I confess, a pang of anxiety!) 'A dozen or more, ma'am.' – 'And then she married?' – 'Yes, ma'am.'

It was fortunate, nonetheless, that we had but a short time before the lecture began. Thus, with polite inquiries all but exhausted, I led the way up the steps, through the marbled hall, and into the theatre.

Mr. Plumptre proved to be an elderly gentleman, with a professorial mien, who did little to breathe life into his subject matter. The lecture itself dull and tedious; enlivened only by EH – who, under the cover of her shawl, contrived a little amusement that was both highly unsatisfactory and yet most diverting!

We quit the Polytechnic with D. in high spirits.

My poor sweet D.!

CHAPTER THIRTEEN

'My dear, I do not wish to discuss it at the dinner table. They took me to the marshes; I gave them my opinion.'

Mrs. Antrobus gave her husband an unabashed look of contempt.

'I merely asked what the Inspector had to say,' she said.

'You merely asked no such thing,' replied the doctor, with infinite calm. 'You asked me – if I recall – half a dozen questions – giving a fellow no time to answer any of them.'

'But you are sure it was Ellen?'

'Of course, I knew the girl's face – what was left of it – please, my dear, this is hardly fit conversation for the table, or anywhere else. I'm trying to read the damned paper.'

Mrs. Antrobus, however, did not let the matter rest.

'To think that we gave the girl our charity – our home! And – at first glance – such a quiet, inoffensive little creature!'

Dr. Antrobus huffed, taking a sip from the glass of port in his right hand . 'You are too naïve my dear. You can take these girls out of the back slums but the rot's already there. Tragic and all that, but the damned fool Jones should have left her where he found her.'

'Like you should have left me?'

'Hardly the same, my dear. Stage-door at the Adelphi Theatre's hardly the gutter, is it now? I could tell you were a lady; and I could have told you that Ellen Hungerford was – well, I shan't say it – and it's a mystery to me why Jones couldn't tell the difference. Poor fellow.'

'But you could?'

'Delia, why do you go on? The girl was "inoffensive," you say. First, the girl was plainly a lunatic. Second – I had not meant to tell you this, my dearest, but you oblige me – she had not been here a week before she gave me the eye.'

Mrs. Antrobus smiled.

'I imagine she could not resist you, Charles.'

'I'm damned sure you're right, my dear,' said Charles Antrobus, with a wink. 'Now may I read my blasted paper? They've set a date for this fellow Gresham's trial. Looks like he made fools of half the City of London.'

'Have they recovered much of the money?'

'I do not think so. My dear, please – if I may just read the damned thing?'

Mrs. Antrobus's silence was permission enough.

The doctor barely noticed his wife leave the table; nor the peculiar look she gave him.

CHAPTER FOURTEEN

Mr. Daniel Barton arrived in the village with little fanfare. It became known – via Emmy Harris, the girl who skivvied for him – that he had rented the old rectory for a period of twelve months; but that he would most likely stay until the following winter. He had made his money in the railways – perhaps in railway stocks, although Emmy Harris's understanding of such matters was rather imprecise – and he had come to Yorkshire to seek a more retired life. It was rumoured that he contemplated the purchase of a small-holding and fancied making himself a gentleman-farmer; but, on this score, no conclusive proof was ever offered.

His neighbours, on making his acquaintance, were relieved to find nothing objectionable in his character. If they happened to meet him, he remarked pleasantly on the view of the moors from his house – the bleak grandeur and infinite variety of the heavens – the clouds perpetually pregnant with rain – and praised the manners and customs of Yorkshire folk, talking disdainfully of the metropolitan life he had abandoned. Nonetheless, he proved somewhat reclusive and solitary. If invited to dinner, he pleaded an unfortunate digestion; if invited to take tea, he stayed only for as long as might be considered polite. Thus, after a week or two, his preference for his own company was noted and respected by all.

Six months after he had settled in the village, Mr. Barton was joined by his wife.

The story of the prior separation of Mr. and Mrs. Barton – which Emmy Harris had recounted to all her female acquaintances – was a most pitiful and romantic tale. In short, Mrs. Barton had gone to a foreign shore, in order to attend her mother on her death-bed *and herself contracted the very communicable disease which had ended her parent's life.* She had forbid her husband to travel to her side – fearing that he too would succumb – and it was only by the grace of God that she herself had survived.

Mrs. Barton arrived in a fly from the station, with only a single trunk to follow, having lost a good deal of her luggage during her journey from the mountains of Greece – or possibly Italy – few people in the village were quite clear on that point. Emmy Harris did remark, however, that Mrs. Barton was a fine-looking woman, despite her years, and that the pair indulged in a passionate embrace that 'fair made her blush to see it'.

Mrs. Barton herself (whose first act was to give Emmy Harris a day's leave) waited until the girl had walked all the way down the narrow lane before falling into her husband's arms, laughing uproariously.

'Did you see her face?'

Jacob Jones smiled.

'My dear, I have not seen my wife for six months; the girl can hardly complain if I should kiss her.'

'I think she will have to go. She is far too pretty.'

'I think not. You cannot pick and choose your servants up here; it is not London, my dear; they come with the property; they are positive fixtures.'

'Jacob —'

'Hush,' he said and kissed her a second time. 'Now, would you care to see the house?'

'I do not know. Must we really spend the winter in this dreary place?'

'I hardly think we should go back to London. We must bide our time here; the whole affair must be entirely forgotten. Then we may try somewhere more lively.'

'I should have preferred Paris,' she said, 'or somewhere on the Continent.'

'My dear — how would we manage, when neither of us speak the language? We should end up making ourselves conspicuous; and that is to be avoided. We agreed, did we not? Leave that little adventure to Fortesque.'

'You have not heard from him?'

'Heard from him? You do not imagine I have given him this address? Besides, if he chooses to spend his share of the money gallivanting around Paris — or Rome — or the North Pole — I do not wish to hear about it. No, my dear, we have parted company; that was our arrangement.'

'If he is caught —'

'Why should he be caught? Gresham kept silent; no-one has the slightest idea. Come, forget these foolish anxieties – let me show you every room.'

Mrs. Barton consented – accepting a brief kiss – and the couple began their tour. Mrs. Barton paused, however, in the little study at the rear of the house, having noticed several pages of handwritten script which lay on the leather-topped desk.

'I cannot believe you have kept up your diary.'

'I find it is a habit that it hard to break. It is a more tedious affair these days, of course.'

'So I should hope,' she said.

A scrapbook lay to one side of the loose sheets. She picked it up and flicked through the pages.

'This, too? All my letters – the newspapers – the diary pages – the original pages! – Jacob, you have kept them –'

'A commonplace book, nothing more. There is no need to sound quite so horrified.'

'If someone were to read it –'

'I keep it under lock and key. Besides, the girl cannot read.'

She shook her head.

'All the same, now we are together, you should burn it.'

'If affords me amusement, my dear. You had me counterfeit six months of my life; do I not have the right to reclaim them? Why, if I do not preserve these pages, in time, even I may forget what actually happened! How else shall I recall if dear Ellen was a saint, a slut or a lunatic?'

Mrs. Barton sighed. 'Do not be so facetious.'

Jacob Jones, however, warmed to his theme.

'Of course, the *Evening Chronicle* called her "a fiend in the body of a mere girl"! I confess, that is how I prefer to remember her. Or perhaps "a young woman capable of unfathomable evil" – you see, I recall all the reviews!'

'"Reviews"! I swear, Jacob, I would not be surprised if you were to give us up – just to see our names in the press.'

'No fear of that. I value my neck as much as any man. I merely like to think that I have "some literary ability" and here is my proof – for – is it not glorious, my dear? – I deserve a modicum of praise – they all believed it!'

Mrs. Barton could not help but smile. 'You are too cocksure. What about the policeman? He never believed the boatman's story.'

'That fellow played his part; it was enough to raise a doubt. As for Delby, he never had our scent, not for a moment – you persuaded him, my dear. You see, I am a great artist – you are a great actress – and we shall live happily together until the end of our days.'

Mrs. Barton gasped, as he suddenly grabbed her tight and danced a mock waltz about the room, knocking over several items of bric-a-brac in the process. She even laughed, as her lover tripped over his own feet, almost sending her tumbling to the floor. Yet, when he was done, she looked at him closely, utterly serious.

'You do not regret it – Dora?'

'Dora? It was a positive kindness. There was nothing left of her after she lost the child. You do not know, my dear, is what it is like to live with such an encumbrance

– a parasite. It crushes one's very soul! Besides, she saw us that day at Broadstairs, I'll swear. If she had told her father – or your husband – if she had told the police – what chance for us?'

'My dear husband would have posed little danger. I doubt, even now, if he has noticed I have gone. I suppose it may strike him in a day or two –'

Mrs. Barton hesitated.

'Do you ever think of Ellen Hungerford?' she continued, quietly. 'I expect that you have missed her company?'

'Her company? My dear, there was only one part of that creature that ever gave me pleasure; and it lay between her legs.'

'Jacob!'

'I merely speak the truth. Besides, the girl was an infernal nuisance. To lose her place at Willis's – some ridiculous scrap with a cabman who would not pay up – then to threaten me!'

Mrs. Barton bit her lip. 'She saw you in Pear Tree Court; she knew you set the fire. That was careless. One word and she could have had you hung. If she had confided in a friend –'

Jacob Jones shrugged.

'Friends? She had no friends; she was a money-grabbing whore; and she knew the value of her silence. You should have seen her face when I told her that I would yield to her blackmail and find her another place! You have never seen such self-conceit!'

'I still think you were fond of her,' said Mrs. Barton, although her voice adopted a rather teasing tone.

'She was nothing, my dear. A problem to which you suggested a most elegant solution. And you must admit the journal was a sensation! We gave the police their little murderess; the public found it intoxicating. I hope you do not think I should show remorse? I have none.'

'Perhaps,' she said, raising her hand to gently stroke his cheek, 'that is what worries me. After all, I do believe Ellen thought you were madly in love with her; she was quite prepared to run away with you that night.'

'It does not matter what she thought. She came to the house, and then waited at the marshes, just as we planned.'

'Waited for you.'

'Are you jealous of a dead woman? We both played our parts to perfection, my dear. Nothing could bind us closer. Now, please, won't you come upstairs?'

Mrs. Barton allowed herself a wry smile.

'Mr. Barton – whatever for?'

'You know the answer.'

'If you promise me you shall burn the book.'

'Very well – you have your way, as always. No-one else shall ever read a word of it.'

CHAPTER THE LAST

Mrs. Delia Antrobus lies half-asleep, half-awake on the bed.

She has a recurring dream – it is the house where she performs an elaborate mime.

She rings the bell; lets herself in; greets her friend.

There is no-one there.

She places a cerise mantle on a coat-hook by the front door.

She climbs the steps to the bedroom.

The woman's body lies stretched upon the floor, her head split open, already dead. She must stay there for half an hour or so; they must have a conversation. She could spend her time in another room entirely, of course; but she rather feels the poor little woman deserves her company.

What a marvel! To kill her and then calmly go to work! But that was their arrangement – an equal part in everything.

The dream shifts – a strange sudden progress – to a lonely road. A young girl is there, wrapped in her dirty shawl; the confusion on her face is quite plain.

It says, 'This is not who I expected – not at all.'

Mrs. Antrobus buries the knife in her and twists the blade.

§

Delia Antrobus wakes up. She turns and sees Jacob Jones asleep on the bed.

She has a recurring dream.

It does not trouble her a great deal.

Lee Jackson's website 'The Dictionary of Victorian London' (www.victorianlondon.org) contains several thousand pages of fascinating Victoriana, including 19th century maps, diaries, journal articles, cartoons and much more.

He also has a blog (catsmeatshop. blogspot.com) and twitter account (www.twitter.com/victorianlondon) on which he lavishes far too much time.